No Room in Paradise

LAWSON BROOKS

A MONROE GRAY MYSTERY

(Adult/Young Adult)

(Mystery)

All characters and events in this novel—even those who seem strangely familiar or remind you of your third cousin—are entirely fictional. Any resemblance to real persons, living or otherwise, is purely coincidental, a figment of your imagination or a rare case of déjà vu. (No, really—we checked.).

Type of Work: Fiction

Photos by Alex Hussein and Mitchell Luo/Pexels

Front Cover Design: Dash Parham

Back Cover Design: Hania Ali

Book Trailer: Rabia Habib

Special Thanks

Michael I. J. Bennett

Peter Jay Fernandez

Donna Gatling

Marva Goldsmith

Colleen Heeter

Flo Purnell

William "Butch" Radford

Gwen Russell

Dwight Smith

Vikki Scott

Saralee Todd

PROLOGUE

IS HEART WAS RACING, AND THE FEELINGS OF anxiety that had been aroused by his predicament steadily escalated in intensity. Focus was deserting him, allowing dysfunction to gain the advantage. His 1993 silver Honda Accord was pressing its limits as he bolted down 16th Street in Northwest DC. Aggressive driving was once his forte.

In Vietnam, Monroe had gotten plenty of practice. He had served on the personal staff of a three-star general, but he was his driver and, as he saw it, his at-will flunky. It bothered Monroe at first, particularly since the Black Power movement was coming of age. But the job kept him from roaming the jungle as a grunt toting an M16 and engaging an enemy that he had no beef with.

But on this day, the perception of danger unleashed skills that had laid dormant, which were now deployed at exactly the right time. The thoughts that occupied his mind were an assembly of contradictions. In the wake of the past few days, a cascade of events unfolded before him, surpassing even his wildest imagination. The prospect of a favorable resolution to his circumstances seemed distant at best and perilous at worst.

Matters had gotten complicated quickly, and within just a few days a chilling pattern had emerged. People linked to him were coming up dead, placing him under the scrutiny of police. Much to his misfortune, he had once again stumbled upon a grim discovery. Taken aback by his most recent encounter, Monroe navigated his vehicle on the path ahead with deliberate focus. Yet, he couldn't escape the image of the body he had found sprawled across the pristine cherry hardwood of the dining room floor. His mind drifted back to the moment of his discovery.

As the initial shock subsided, he knelt beside the motionless figure, fingers trembling as he searched in vain for a pulse. The harsh reality soon set in. Any attempt to restore consciousness would be an exercise in futility. The subject's eyes, unnervingly wide and open, remained fixed on the ceiling, signaling the departure of life. The entry wound, a small but gruesome hole in the center of the forehead, told a tale of brutal violence. Dark, crimson blood slowly oozed from the wound, forming a foreboding, thin stream that meandered down the victim's face, staining the skin.

The exit wound at the back of the skull was far more catastrophic. While he couldn't inspect it directly, Monroe observed the blood surrounding the victim's head, forming a dark, spreading puddle on the floor with brain matter and bone fragments within, creeping outward in an irregular pattern. The wooden floorboards absorbed the syrupy liquid, deepening its ominous hue.

The full extent of the damage highlighted the brutal effectiveness of the shot. An open robe, once a protective cover, now lay draped over the body that was partially clad, a silent witness to the actions of an uninvited and sinister presence. Monroe, accustomed to the solemnity of death, found this latest encounter disquieting. The scene and its haunting details were etched in his psyche. It was an enduring portrait destined to forever linger in his thoughts.

Monroe stood, momentarily paralyzed by the sight before him. His mind raced as he considered his options. The place had been ransacked. *The killer was definitely looking for something.* He noticed blood spatter on the adjacent wall, several pieces of furniture, and sections of the floor. Scanning the room for the ejected cartridge, he found none. This signaled that the assailant had either used a revolver or had picked it up on the way out.

As he considered his situation, logic urged him to call the police immediately, a step he regretted skipping during his last homicidal encounter. Yet, his recent ordeals had left him on edge, with anxiety and impulsiveness now clouding his better judgment.

Once again, his deep-rooted mistrust of law enforcement, fueled by his experiences as a Black man in a world where becoming a suspect was all too easy, reared its head. The thought of dealing with the Montgomery County Police Department, in particular, was undesirable. His mind echoed with recollections from the not-so-distant past, strengthening his resolve to vacate the premises. With an internal conflict waging as to whether he should stay or go, Monroe ultimately acquiesced to the whispers imploring retreat.

But before he could turn to go, three words popped into his mind: "Check the microwave." It was a directive that he had received earlier. Rushing to the kitchen, Monroe opened the black door that cloaked its contents. Inside was a coffee mug turned upside down. Raising it, he found a folded piece of paper and a key. Monroe carefully unfolded the note. It said: "Monroe, if you're reading this, it's not a good sign for me. This thing is more complicated than we could ever imagine. The box is at Riggs Bank. You're authorized. Be careful."

Monroe's heart pounded. He quickly stuffed the note and key into his jacket pocket. He decided that it was best to use the back door to leave. But before doing so, he retraced his steps and, with meticulous care, he attempted to wipe away all traces of his presence before disappearing into the late afternoon glow with a blend of fear and resolution.

Arriving at his car, which was fortunately positioned for a swift departure, Monroe made a beeline for the trunk. With a swift motion, he unlocked and opened it, grabbing a duffel bag and a worn plastic sack, then closed it promptly. Placing the duffel on the passenger's seat, he unzipped it and removed a pair of sneakers. Aware of the possibility of blood contamination on his shoes, he aimed to prevent any evidence from being traced to his car. He stashed the footwear he'd been wearing in the plastic bag that he would later discard far from the crime scene.

Monroe's objective was a quiet escape, but after driving a couple of blocks he realized that his plan had been thwarted. He was being followed. He turned left onto Georgia Avenue and immediately caught a red light. A Ford Crown Victoria that Monroe assumed was his shadow also turned left, but was several cars behind him.

He had caught a glimpse of the vehicle as he entered the homicide scene. It was occupied by two men and sat less than half a block from where he had parked, but he had paid little attention to them. As he waited for the light to change, a parade of Montgomery County police and rescue vehicles sped toward Bonifant Street, blanketing the area. Monroe had dodged a bullet. *Was I being set up again?*

The light turned green, and Monroe quickened his pace. But as he made his way back to the city, every attempt to lose the Crown Vic proved futile. The driver brazenly ran through several stop signs and traffic lights, clearly determined to keep him in sight. With each second, the nature of the pursuit heightened and became relentless. There was no doubt in Monroe's mind that the two men tailing him were highly motivated and harbored malicious intentions. But a deep dive into their motivations would have to wait. His immediate focus was the matter at hand: ditching his pursuers and locating a safe place to regroup.

It was obvious that Monroe couldn't go directly home and risk his two new friends finding out where he lived. *Maybe they already knew.* But not wanting to take that chance, he headed toward Rock Creek Park. The winding and mostly narrow parkway with its arterial side roads offered the perfect cloister that he hoped would help him evade his hunters. Monroe had gotten a peek at their license plate earlier, which indicated that the car they were driving was a rental. *Out-of-towners.* By using the park as a diversion, the vast woodland that bisected the District's Northwest quadrant and stretched to the Maryland border would play to his advantage.

Monroe darted past Colorado Avenue, and as he approached Blagden he made a quick right. He nervously took another look in his rearview mirror to see if the Crown Vic was still giving chase. Much to his relief, the sedan continued down 16th Street. Monroe heaved a huge sigh of relief. *What a rush!* The tension that his body jettisoned was intoxicating. But he couldn't relax; he had to maintain awareness.

Wanting to be certain, Monroe took one more look over his shoulder to make sure he was in the clear. *Damn!* Somehow his hunters had figured it out and were back on his trail. While they weren't on top of him, they were close enough to once again raise his level of discomfort. Making the situation worse was that he was being chased through Crestwood, an upscale, neatly adorned neighborhood adjacent to the park. It was the home to some of the city's most elite Black professional residents at that time. On most occasions, a fair number would be out walking around. But to everyone's good fortune, it wasn't the case on that evening. Monroe was engaged in a deadly game of cat and mouse, putting anyone nearby at serious risk. It wasn't a pleasant thought.

With *resoluteness* riding shotgun and *ingenuity* situated in back, he pressed on. Any other time a police car with a pair of officers and a radar gun would be parked along the street trying to make their ticket quota. *Cops. Never around when you need one.* Monroe neared the intersection at Rock Creek Parkway. He knew that he had four equally viable options for escape. He didn't hesitate. He made a quick right and accelerated up Beach Drive. He was sure that a quick decision would help him put a little time and distance between him and his trackers.

It was near the end of rush hour; the looming spring nightfall provided both cover and beauty. The brilliant rays from the sun streamed through the gaps of the countless trees that populated the park, producing a setting worthy of a master photographer's lens. He followed the roadway's bends and curves while hoping that the hoods who were chasing him had been successfully misdirected. As he approached Morrow Drive, the US Park Police District 3 Station suddenly appeared. It was like a rope thrown to a drowning man.

He had forgotten about its location. At no time in his life had he been happier to see a station house. It provided him with the perfect buffer, albeit temporary. He pulled into the very far right of the parking area among a cluster of trees, killed his lights, and sat. While Monroe waited in the shadows, he reflected on his plight and all that had transpired over the previous months and days. The question that he kept asking himself was: *How did I end up here?* It was one that was easier asked than answered.

1

Nine Days Earlier, St. Louis, Missouri

THE ATMOSPHERE AT THE UNION HALL on the city's north side was electric by any standard. Grand by its architectural design and authentic in its representation as a location for congregation, the purposely chosen venue was flawless as a setting for a campaign victory party. The haze of cigar smoke, the aroma of distilled spirits, and the echoes of intense debates were conspicuous inhabitants. Suspended from the lofty ceiling, a quintet of colossal chandeliers dignified the corners and center of the grand assembly room. Their muted radiance cast an aura of restrained energy. Etched into the two main walls were four perfectly sculpted busts of the organization's most prominent leaders of separate and bygone eras. Photos of others appropriately embellished appointed spaces.

From a glass-enclosed atrium adjacent to the union's executive offices, Monroe Gray and his newfound friend and business partner,

Gordon Blackwell, gazed down at the crowd of revelers filling the great hall. Standing a lean six feet tall with precisely styled black hair and a caramel-toned complexion, Monroe cut a striking figure in his pinstriped three-button suit, crisp white shirt, and red, blue, and silver paisley tie.

Beside him, Gordon, an imposing six-foot-three with a sturdy build from his college basketball days, displayed an equally polished look in a gray double-breasted Armani suit and a bold purple-and-black tie accented with splashes of gold. His light complexion, faint freckles, reddish-brown hair, and sleek horn-rimmed glasses lent him an air of distinctive, refined authority. Together, they appeared both commanding and confident—two men ready to seize the opportunities the night promised.

The riveting sounds of R&B and hip-hop music blared from an array of speakers dispersed throughout the venue. By mere presence, a tap of the toe, a movement of the body, or a bob of the head was instinctive and unavoidable. A celebration of epic proportions was on the verge of erupting. Darnell Mayfield would be the first elected Black mayor of St. Louis after surviving a brutal four-way primary race that included two popular White politicians who held state offices and the appointed incumbent mayor, Arthur Trimble.

A tall, angular man with an athletic frame, Darnell's hair was black and semi-straight with waves as its partner. His swarthy skin was polished and unwrinkled. The mustache he wore, while lush, was meticulously trimmed, and his generous smile's companion was a set of lustrous and orderly white teeth.

Darnell wore a sleek navy-blue suit that emphasized his build, paired with a bold satin tie woven in deep red, gold, and emerald green hues, and a matching pocket square in a puff fold. His look was completed with a pair of alligator loafers in deep, ebony black with a mirror-like finish that revealed the rich texture of the leather.

Catching a glimpse of Monroe and Gordon from the VIP area, Darnell raised his glass in acknowledgment. The pair responded accordingly. Grinning from ear to ear, Darnell bathed in the many backslaps and handshakes that were coming his way as he deftly engaged with each of his admirers. Although he'd seen him in action before, Monroe watched in awe as Darnell worked the room.

"Look at him, G," Monroe said, shaking his head. "The man's in his element. Makes me wonder if he was born in a crowd."

Gordon smiled knowingly, watching Darnell smoothly maneuver through his supporters. "He makes it look easy, doesn't he? Like a conductor with an orchestra. But don't be fooled—Darnell knows exactly who he needs in that room and why."

Monroe nodded. "Oh, I know. And I can guarantee you he's got half of them figured down to their bank accounts. Darnell isn't just playing for tonight; he's setting up his next five moves."

Gordon laughed and shook his head.

Monroe lifted his glass and took in the scene below. "This place is too live tonight. Makes you wonder if St. Louis has been waiting for a change like this for a while."

Gordon leaned against the glass, his eyes riveted on the scene below. "A new mayor, a new chapter," he replied with a slight grin. "If Darnell plays his cards right, he'll have all the support he needs. Folks down there look like they're ready for it."

Monroe chuckled, swirling the bourbon in his glass. "Trimble's not ready to hand over the keys just yet. Did you catch that interview last week? He talked like he still had a shot."

Gordon shook his head gesturing to the diverse crowd below, observing the faces alight with excitement and expectation. "He can keep talking all he wants. Everyone here knew who was going to win. Darnell's been fighting for this, and a lot of people are ready to fight with him."

"Maybe so," Monroe replied thoughtfully. "But he's gonna have to keep them on his side if he wants to make it last. Charm only takes you so far."

Gordon laughed. "Good thing he's got more than charm going for him. Look at them—they're not just here for the party. They believe in him, and that counts for something."

That couldn't be said for the political establishment and Darnell's three primary opponents. All had viewed him as an afterthought and his rivals trained their sights on one another throughout the campaign and in the televised debates. Why not? While having a sizable African American population, the ability for the community to rally around a single Black candidate had proved to be difficult in the past and this election was no exception.

With two African American candidates, Darnell and Trimble, running, it was thought that perception would once again become reality and the two would split the Black vote. Magnifying the uncertainty of the outcome was that all four candidates maintained a level of popularity among disparate constituencies. A closely contested outcome had been expected.

To the surprise of most observers, Darnell dominated within the city's Black community. However, it was his ability to garner votes in younger and more liberal White neighborhoods like the Central West End that propelled him to victory. With a majority of St. Louis voters registered as Democrats, Darnell's primary victory should have been tantamount to election.

But Trimble wasn't about to play nice. Instead of offering a gracious concession speech, he immediately declared that he would run in the general election, which occurred one month after the primary, as an Independent. Besides, he had gotten used to wielding the levers of power, so a quiet exit wasn't in the cards. Along with Trimble, a White Republican candidate had also entered the race.

Monroe took a slow sip, glancing over toward Gordon. "Trimble isn't going to make this easy. I think he likes the feel of that office a little too much to give it up without a fight."

Gordon offered a subtle smile. "He's stubborn, I'll give him that. But Darnell's got more than momentum; he's got these folks behind him. I'd say he's right where he needs to be."

"You might be right. But something tells me we're in for a show." Monroe tilted his glass in Gordon's direction. "This is St. Louis, after all. They won't just hand over the reins."

Trimble's doggedness was no surprise. He had run in the previous cycle against longtime mayor Sheldon Taylor and was beaten badly. When Taylor unexpectedly resigned five months before the end of his term to take a job with the new administration in Washington, it was Trimble who as the president of the Board of Aldermen succeeded him. He had planned to use the interim time as a springboard to the mayor's office when the primary election rolled around. While his primary defeat didn't deter him, it did leave him without adequate funding and support. Darnell had the Democratic machine at his disposal, and as the general election results rolled in, there was little doubt that Trimble would be a loser for the second time in a month. Darnell was winning handily.

With each update, Darnell's position as the second Black mayor of St. Louis and the first to be elected was assured. This was happening in the same city that had historically and effectively generated an organized pattern of racial segregation throughout its history. This, in the eyes of both residents and observers, was a "big deal."

Gordon exhaled, glancing at Monroe with a wry smile. "This could be the start of something big. Bigger than either of us imagined."

"For Darnell or for us?" Monroe asked, eyebrow raised.

Gordon grinned, lifting his glass in a silent toast. "Both, my friend. Here's to a new beginning—for all of us."

For Monroe, it was the beginning of an unpredictable adventure that exceeded the limits of his imagination and one that he couldn't have made up, even if he had tried.

NO ROOM IN PARADISE

2

IT WAS A CONVERGENCE OF CIRCUMSTANCES that put Monroe in the room that night. Those very conditions also placed him in a situation where the realization of life-changing wealth was within reach. He could never have envisioned the opportunity that was before him. After returning from Vietnam, Monroe graduated from Hampton University and Howard University School of Law. His sole intention was to stand up for the little guy in court. Rather than join a firm, Monroe set up his own shop and immediately began to troll courthouse halls for clients and received referrals from other attorneys who thought that certain cases weren't worth their time.

That's why hooking up with Gordon Blackwell, a reputable corporate lawyer, to pursue a multimillion-dollar opportunity was so inconceivable to him. While Monroe was comfortable in his lane and felt that he was making a difference, he found himself at a career crossroads and was considering options. Trying to grow his law practice or take an offer to join a small firm that he'd received were both on the table. He also had been toying with the idea of becoming a private investigator.

Over drinks one night, he shared this dilemma with Gordon, who listened intently. "You're telling me," Gordon said, leaning back, "that you're actually thinking about leaving the law to dig up dirt as a PI? Really?"

Monroe laughed, shaking his head. "I've just been feeling restless. Chasing cases day in and day out, defending clients no one else wants—it's satisfying, but it doesn't put much in the bank. I guess I'm just looking for... something more."

Gordon raised an eyebrow, swirling the ice in his glass thoughtfully. "Well, you certainly found 'something more' now, haven't you?" he asked, highlighting the idea of the casino venture that had been looming over their conversations. "This casino project could be it. We both know this isn't the kind of opportunity that knocks twice."

Monroe took a measured breath, nodding. It was true. At the time, he was, as he often put it, "financially embarrassed," and the idea of an ownership stake in a casino group had never crossed his mind. Why would it? There were no casinos in the DC area and he didn't care for Atlantic City. His only exposure had been a trip to Vegas for a conference. Besides, he'd always been too frugal to gamble his hard-earned money.

"Gordon, you really think there's a place for us in this industry?" Monroe asked, searching his partner's face. "I mean, this is uncharted territory. We're outsiders here."

Gordon's smile was wry, almost mischievous. "That's exactly why we should do it. You think anyone in that room expects two Black men to walk in and own a piece of the gaming industry? Hell no. And that's the advantage—they'll never see us coming."

It was that fire, that energy, that hooked Monroe. And it was all due to a chance meeting arranged by Darnell. The two had met during a business trip to St. Louis that Monroe had taken the previous year, and they'd quickly bonded as kindred spirits. When Darnell started making trips to DC to fundraise for his campaign, Monroe introduced him to his network, guiding him through social and political circles that offered invaluable exposure.

One night, after an event during the Congressional Black Caucus Legislative Weekend, Darnell had pulled Monroe aside. "Listen, I know you're focused on your practice, but I think you'd benefit from meeting Gordon Blackwell. He's got some big plans and could use a man with your grit."

"You're saying a corporate lawyer needs a guy like me?" Monroe joked.

"Not just any corporate lawyer," Darnell said, his tone serious. "This man knows casinos inside and out. He's about to open doors we've never even had a chance to knock on. You're gonna want to be on the other side when he does."

Monroe was more than intrigued. He knew that Darnell was on to something. Looking back, Monroe could see why Darnell and Gordon had such a strong connection. Both were former college basketball players and were equally ambitious in their own right. Part of Darnell's success could be credited to his ability to deftly navigate social classes. He was comfortable in any room.

Having attended undergrad school in upstate New York and received his legal education in New York City, Darnell possessed the ability to project an urbane persona. But make no mistake, the Northside of St. Louis represented his core being and comprised the cornerstone of his political ideology. That upbringing drove the strategic instincts that had served him so well. He was a formidable politician.

Gordon, on the other hand, was originally from Philadelphia. He had attended Drexel on a basketball scholarship and had long held NBA aspirations. But those were dashed when he sustained a serious knee injury during his junior year. It was that event that prompted him to pursue his other dream, a law degree. He obtained it at Temple University, and upon graduation Gordon was immediately extended an offer by a prestigious Philadelphia firm, Cummings, Wexler, and Platnick. His notable academic performance and his reputation as a local high school and collegiate hoops star helped propel him to become the practice's first African American associate.

As with any of his pursuits, Gordon excelled. He rose through the ranks and obtained partnership at the high-profile firm within five years. With offices in Philly, Newark, and Trenton, Gordon worked out of the latter location because of the firm's small but lucrative portfolio of casino clients. Over time, Gordon developed an interest and expertise in gaming operations and the legal issues associated with them. He quickly mastered the financing details and began to earn standing among operators in Atlantic City. He was a unicorn in an industry dominated by White males.

"Ever thought about how rare you are in this field, Gordon?" Monroe asked him one evening over dinner, genuinely curious.

Gordon laughed, but there was a hint of pride in his eyes. "Oh, believe me, I know. Some of them don't know whether to treat me like a threat or a novelty. But it's more than that—I'm a symbol. They let me in because I bring them value. But ownership?" He tapped his glass, smiling thoughtfully. "That's a different game. And I want a piece of it."

He was ultimately appointed by the managing partners to serve as counsel for one of the nation's largest casino operators and its most significant client, Voyager International. Gordon immediately recognized the potential entrepreneurial possibilities given that African Americans were shut out of the game. In the late summer of 1992, he resigned from his position at the firm, and with the encouragement and endorsement of his colleagues, he formed a minority-owned casino group to partner with Voyager on rapidly expanding domestic opportunities.

With that, Monroe could see it clearly: Gordon wasn't satisfied with just a seat at the table. He wanted to build the table, to own it. Without Gordon, the idea of having a stake in a casino wouldn't have even entered Monroe's mind. But after several detailed conversations with Gordon and a Voyager representative, he realized the potential.

"Monroe, think about it," Gordon had said, in a passionate yet rational tone. "You didn't come this far just to keep doing small cases, scraping by. You have the brains, the determination. This is a way to make a lasting impact—something real, something big."

Monroe leaned back, absorbing the impact of Gordon's words. "And here I was, thinking I'd end up as just another lawyer sticking it to the system, one case at a time."

Gordon smiled, his eyes flashing with excitement. "Well, why not stick it to them on a bigger scale?"

Gordon's words resonated with Monroe and together, they were about to step into a world where neither of them truly belonged, yet where both were determined to succeed. But little did Monroe realize the depth of the darkness ahead and the length of the leap.

3

W ITH THE SHAKE OF A HAND, MONROE BECAME Gordon's partner and confidant. From that day until the night that Darnell was officially elected, both men devoted themselves to the candidate's success, while launching their enterprise. Having financial skin in the game was necessary for everyone's credibility. But, the sparseness of funds populating Monroe's bank account in comparison with some of the other investors meant that much of his involvement would be in the form of sweat equity.

In Gordon's eyes that was a non-issue. Monroe brought a lot to the table given his broad range of contacts, fundraising prowess, and ability to negotiate intricate political environments. Monroe also acted as the group's unofficial crisis manager. Gordon's approach to conflicts was to stay above the fray. He derived satisfaction from the fact that Monroe was a war veteran known for his straightforwardness, which was perceived by some as blunt or ill-tempered. When he asked Monroe about it one night while having drinks, the former soldier offered a sly smile and muttered, "No one has ever said it to my face."

From the outset, the pairing proved to be effective. Within days of forming their alliance, the two had successfully negotiated an agreement with Voyager that turned out to be quite a coup. Word on the street was that minority participants in other competing groups were being offered limited partnerships. But as a result of Gordon's and Monroe's efforts, Gamers became a wholly owned subsidiary with 30 percent equity in the $200 million project. With the single stroke of a pen, Gamers transitioned into a company valued at $60 million on paper overnight.

As Gordon saw it, "financial paradise" awaited them. In just a few months he would be gracing the cover of *Black Enterprise* and celebrated as the nation's first Black casino owner. For his part, Monroe could give a damn about being famous. He just wanted to be well off to the point that money would be an afterthought. This unforeseen circumstance had the potential to make that dream a reality. The key was getting this deal across the finish line, and given all of the players involved it would be no walk in the park.

***

Gordon and Monroe found themselves immersed in the spirited energy of the raucous gathering. The crowd's excitement escalated as they eagerly anticipated Darnell's impending victory speech. Glancing over to their right, the men could see the presumptive mayor standing in a nearby conference room watching the returns on TV with union leaders and several other local and national politicians who had been early and ardent supporters. The group also included

Congressman Pressley Hancock, who had been ambiguous in granting his blessing to a particular candidate.

They both watched as a tuxedo-clad waiter breezed by, holding a tray of sparkling champagne flutes.

"Let's hope he remembers who was with him from the start. All these handshakes can make a man forget," Gordon remarked.

"I'd bet he won't," Monroe said, eyeing the scene. "But I wonder if the folks downstairs would say the same if they got a glimpse of all this."

Unlike the gigantic space downstairs that was exceptionally warm, the designated area for local luminaries maintained the atmosphere and trappings of an area behind the velvet rope at an exclusive nightclub. Formally attired servers roamed the floor offering champagne and wine from ornate silver trays. Uniformly dressed bartenders who dutifully staffed three small, dedicated stations dispensed top-shelf alcohol, while union executives and their well-connected patrons feasted on a lavish spread.

By contrast, the cuisine provided to Darnell's army of supporters and party crashers downstairs consisted of hot dogs, burgers, and other standard fare, with beer and wine serving as libation. Oblivious to the disparities, the celebrants' sole focus was enjoying the moment. This was a night for anyone who had a hand in Darnell's success to display their euphoria. A divided city found itself on the threshold of a seismic wave of political change.

Gordon shook his head. "It's always that way. They're celebrating the same man, but they live in different worlds. And once he's in office? Darnell's going to have to figure out how to straddle both. If he doesn't, those folks down there"—Gordon jerked his thumb toward the floor—"might not wait another four years to remind him of it."

"True enough," Monroe replied, taking a slow breath. "Let's go down and pay our respects. Besides, that's where the real stories are— at least the ones that matter."

Gordon and Monroe decided to escape the sedate surroundings of the executive area to go downstairs to hang out with the masses. In all honesty, that was their preference. The men exited the elevator and jockeyed their way through the crowd to greet several people. But it didn't take long for them to realize that they were incapable of dealing with the intensity of the crowd and the swelter that had been generated.

Like the droplets that occupy a leaf of emerald during a spring rain, beads of moisture settled on Monroe's face and forehead in ever-increasing numbers. The continued use of his now damp handkerchief proved futile. The meticulously dressed Gordon was visibly suffering as well, pulling his collar in an attempt to air out the back of his neck.

"It's hot as fuck in here and people are still trying to come in," he said with a look of distress on his face and anguish in his voice.

Monroe smiled, mopping his brow. "It's like a sauna bro and to be honest, I can't take this much longer."

With a silent exchange of despondent glances, Monroe and Gordon discreetly signaled their desire for the comfort of the campaign's VIP suite at the Marriott downtown, located by Busch Memorial Stadium. That was where Darnell's victory party was set to unfold. Stepping outside, the cool embrace of the early April evening brought a soothing relief from the crowd-induced warmth. They quickly hailed a taxi and were off in no time. In their escape from the madness, a sense of liberation washed over both men. New adventures awaited.

As they were being spirited down Market Street, a panoramic view of the St. Louis skyline materialized in the foreground with the

Gateway Arch overlooking it. Gordon tapped Monroe's arm, gesturing out the window.

"Take it all in, my friend," Gordon said with a grin. "That's his city now. And we're right in the middle of it."

Monroe laughed quietly, glancing at the picturesque sight as it shone against the night sky. "For tonight, anyway. Tomorrow, it's back to the grind. You think he's ready?"

Gordon shrugged, his gaze lingering on the skyline. "Doesn't matter. Ready or not, he's about to find out what this place is made of—and what he's made of, too."

Turning toward each other they both smiled in acknowledgment that, in a matter of minutes, Darnell would be the man in charge and for them all things were possible. It was going to be a good night. While the trip to the hotel would take just moments, Monroe had no idea that a longer, more dangerous journey was ahead.

4

WALKING THROUGH THE DOOR of the Penthouse Suite, the contrast with the frenzied activities that were transpiring at the Union Hall was stark. An atmosphere of quiet expectancy permeated the room. Monroe mentally prepared to pace himself. It was going to be a long night and he was looking forward to seeing how events would play out. He and Gordon strode directly to the bar to get drinks.

As usual, Monroe ordered a Jack Daniel's on the rocks. Ironically, he had never been a consumer of brown whiskey until the war. But after a particularly harrowing experience in which he almost met his end, he was introduced to "Jack" at a seedy bar in Saigon's "Soul Alley" where Black GIs hung out when on leave. They'd been sidekicks ever since.

"Back to the old standby, huh?" Gordon teased, requesting a gin and tonic. "Didn't figure you for the sentimental type, Monroe."

Monroe gave a half-smile, swirling the glass thoughtfully. "War has a way of making you form certain routines. 'Jack' here's been more faithful than half the folks I've met since I got back."

Gordon smiled broadly, but his gaze was keen. "Well, let's hope Jack sticks by you tonight. Something tells me you'll need it in a room like this." By contrast, Gordon was a social drinker. The cocktail that was sitting on the bar in front of him would be nursed for most of the evening.

The suite was composed of three sizable rooms, two bedrooms, and three baths. The décor was an understated ruby red and white and while not modern, the furniture was more than an appropriate fit. Inhabiting the quarters were a small cadre of Darnell's supporters and benefactors with more venturing in with each passing minute.

One thing Monroe liked about St. Louis and the Midwest in general was the tactfully embellished fashion in which people dressed—unlike the staid blues and grays that the self-important strivers in DC or New York trotted out daily. The folks who were out on this night sported colors that added vibrancy to the environment. For some men, hats were an implied requisite. Fedoras, bowlers, stingy brims, and other headgear were the completion of many of the well-appointed ensembles.

As they soaked up the scene, a giant presence appeared from the side of a room shielded from their view. It was Carlton Dixon. It wasn't that he was a giant of a man, although he was somewhat ample in proportions. But he had an aura, along with a fat wallet that led those who knew him or his reputation to become sycophantic in his presence.

In organizing their venture, Gordon and Monroe realized that they needed to round up a cadre of local investors and business owners whose companies could provide the collection of services needed for such a large project. They also required a heavy hitter with investment and political capital. That turned out to be Mr. Dixon. That's also how both Gordon and Monroe addressed him. After all, he was in his sixties and had accomplished much. Respect was warranted and his ego demanded it.

Carlton Dixon was a self-made man in the truest sense. It's been said that he was a bright but rambunctious kid who didn't take any shit. He quit school at age seventeen, a year shy of his would-be graduation, enlisting in the Army and serving in combat during the Korean War. Upon returning to St. Louis, Dixon performed a variety of odd jobs while dabbling in several business pursuits. He was an organized and focused hustler who was determined to succeed one way or the other.

In the early 1960s, he was befriended by a Jewish businessman who helped get him started in the parking lot business. After years of hard work and utilizing his connections, Dixon became the "Parking Czar" of St. Louis and a very wealthy man. He also became the go-to donor for local, mostly Democratic political candidates and an array of charities. Despite his rough edges, Dixon was a shrewd and calculating businessman.

Dixon, a man of above-average height and notable stoutness, possessed a round, brown-hued face marked by penetrating black eyes. Always impeccably groomed, his consistently clean-shaven appearance complemented by short, slicked-back hair that was trimmed with precision, Dixon presented a genteel image that camouflaged his origins. Drawn to Gordon and his backstory, Dixon saw the casino endeavor as tailor-made for him and wasted no time in expressing his interest.

As military veterans with shared experiences, you'd think that he and Monroe would have easily gotten along. But that wasn't the case. They harbored a begrudging respect for each other, but their similarities created a peculiar tension. Dixon's persona, marked by a gruff exterior, surpassed even Monroe's. The intense gaze and perpetually grimaced face had the power to penetrate one's soul. His dismissive attitude toward others often created an atmosphere of unease and enemies.

Okay, here we go. Monroe straightened his posture.

Dixon's gaze searched the room, landing on them with a practiced intensity that made most men fidget. Over the years he had gained a sense of entitlement. The one-time street hustler had climbed the ranks and was now considered a member of the city's Black elite. He relished in a reputation that he had built and enhanced over time.

"Mr. Dixon," Gordon said, his voice deferential yet relaxed.

Dixon offered a warm handshake to Gordon, grinning in approval. "Good to see you, Gordon," he said. "Tonight's the night, huh? All those meetings, all those headaches—finally paying off."

Gordon offered a wide grin. "Feels like it's been years coming. I'd say tonight's the perfect reward, don't you think?"

Dixon nodded. "Nothing's over until the check clears." His gaze shifted to Monroe; as always, his words were few. He extended a limp hand with a slight nod, his gaze unreadable. "Gray."

"Mr. Dixon," Monroe replied evenly, meeting the older man's gaze without hesitation. If Dixon wanted reverence, he wouldn't be getting it from him.

Dixon's lips twitched, almost imperceptibly. "How's the drink, Gray? They serve it strong enough for you?"

Monroe raised an eyebrow at Dixon's attempt at small talk. "Same as always, Mr. Dixon. I rarely deviate from the normal."

Dixon's smile tightened, and Gordon smoothly intervened, changing the subject. "I hear you brought in a couple of new investors tonight, Mr. Dixon?"

Dixon's demeanor softened instantly. "I did. Men of some means, good connections. St. Louis businessmen, the kind who know how to get things done. You'll meet them soon enough." He placed a hand on Gordon's shoulder, guiding him away. "Come on, Gordon. There are a few folks who've been dying to meet you."

As he and Dixon walked away, Gordon shot Monroe an over-the-shoulder glance and shrugged, an unspoken apology in his eyes. Monroe waved him off. He was content to enjoy his drink and observe the room, which was quickly becoming more crowded.

A man next to him leaned over, tipping his drink in Monroe's direction. "Some night, huh? Nothing like a St. Louis party," he said with a grin.

Monroe nodded politely, noting the man's overly eager demeanor. "Yes, sir, nothing like it. Lots of old friends of Darnell's here, I'm sure."

"Oh yeah, and then some," the man said, laughing. "But a lot of new ones, too. After tonight, there'll be a line out his door, you know?"

"More than a line, I'd say," Monroe replied coolly. "The question is who'll still be around after the dust settles."

The man laughed again, oblivious to Monroe's tone. "True enough! But, tonight all good, right?"

Monroe flashed a thin smile, then turned his attention back to the room as the man drifted off. Among the faces dotting the crowd were people he had come to know in the months since Darnell kicked off his campaign. Many were locals whose bonds with Darnell and members of his family stretched across a lifetime and were present to commemorate the moment. Others were a mix of residents and outsiders with ambitions of conducting business with the city and viewed Darnell as their ticket. Monroe had encountered his fair share of these fortune seekers, sharing drinks at a bar, engaging in conversations at events, or, on occasion, partaking in a meal. He wasn't impressed with many.

Just then, Gordon returned, sliding up beside him with an exasperated look. "Well, I'd say that was an experience. Dixon loves his introductions as much as he loves hearing himself talk."

Monroe brandished a smug look. "Did he anoint you as the 'second coming' again, or is your aura starting to dim?"

"He tried, but I told him I left my divine powers at home," Gordon said, laughing. "Besides, they weren't the new investors he was referring to; although they did express an interest in participating. Dixon's probably just padding his portfolio as a way of cementing his rep as a mover and shaker."

Monroe took a thoughtful sip. "Let him play his game, Gordon. So long as he remembers that we're in this to build, not bow."

Gordon raised his glass in agreement. "Here's to that—and to a city that won't know what hit it."

They both clinked glasses, knowing that tonight marked a victory. But as they observed the comings and goings, they both knew that beneath the veneer of goodwill, an unspoken emotional distance prevailed, inhibiting any genuine connections from forming. Familiarity would be left at the door as the pursuit of financial gains took precedence.

The vast sums of money involved extended beyond the confines of the casino project, encompassing virtually every city procurement—previously inaccessible to Black businesses. Under Darnell's leadership, the landscape would hold boundless opportunities, leaving no space for friendships, only strategic alliances. And as events transpired, even those would be tested to a point that no one could have imagined.

5

IN SURVEYING THE ROOM, SEVERAL DISTINCT GROUPS stood out to Monroe. To his left were investment bankers Michael Hill, David Harris, and Shedrach Miller. Mike represented a mainstream Wall Street firm, where he had worked since coming out of college. David was one of his former coworkers who had struck out to form his own company. Shadrach represented a regional firm that was headquartered in St. Louis. He was viewed as a door opener for Mike and David. Like everyone else, they were discreet in their thoughts and actions, shrouding any plans that they were trying to put in place.

Suddenly the sound of raucous laughter erupted to Monroe's right. The voices were all too familiar to him. Without looking, the identity of the culprits who were creating the ruckus was evident, Garland Bentley and Ambrose Pinkston. Look up the word *colorful* in any dictionary and their photos would appear next to it. As it was most times, they had a pair of striking women by their sides.

"Those two love a grand entrance, don't they?" Gordon said, shaking his head with a large smile.

Monroe could never get the sense if the ladies were actually with them or if they served as enticements for the men they sought to influence. "What's your guess, Monroe inquired under his breath, glancing at the compact entourage. "Personal arm candy or sweeteners?"

Gordon snickered. "My money is on the latter. I was on the end of one of their 'offerings' a while back. It didn't go as planned for them. But that's another story for another time."

"I'm going to hold you to that," Monroe quickly retorted.

Both Garland and Ambrose lived in Prince George's County, Maryland, outside of DC. Monroe was mostly acquainted with them from afar, with their few interactions taking place in social environments in Washington. Over the years, Garland and Ambrose had developed a reputation not only for business ventures that ranged from the respectable to the dubious but also for showing up in style—like the rumored white stretch limo they'd allegedly ridden to a meeting at City Hall. Chatter on the local grapevine was that Garland and Ambrose had been throwing around a lot of money in St. Louis, but there was no obvious source of where it came from. He also couldn't tell their level of seriousness in the development project, because of their absences at major meetings associated with the enterprise.

"Thank God they're over there," Monroe murmured, observing as the women giggled at something Ambrose had said. I'm not nearly buzzed enough for their circus right now.

At that moment, Dixon appeared at the entrance to the next room and signaled for Gordon to join him once again. "Well this is timely," he said laughing. Placing his hand on Monroe's shoulder, "You're on your own, bruh."

Without hesitation, Monroe sarcastically replied, "Fuck you too."

Monroe continued to scour his surroundings. Taking a glimpse toward the suite's entrance, he observed a familiar and foreboding-looking figure enter the room. Nimbus Bushrod stood just inside the doors. He had the look of self-importance as if he had just descended from Mount Sinai. All he needed was a staff to complete the portrait. As always, just behind him was his crew of mistrust, Alderman Demetrius Steptoe and Chauncy Prigmore, a local character of dubious repute who operated on the fringes of local politics and society as a whole.

Steptoe was a stout figure at five-foot-eight, with a penchant for loud suits that seemed to outshine his ever-shifting convictions. He had the air of a man who checked the wind before speaking and his flashy attire served as a distraction from the unpredictability of his loyalties. On his best day, Prigmore, or Prig, as he was known by all, was an acquired taste as a man. Tall, light-skinned with a freckled face, and a solid sturdy build, he was influential among the city's old guard. Individually, the unlikely threesome emitted an unsavory vibe, but together the essence of corruption was intense.

Monroe made it a point to avoid them when possible. Make no mistake, his aversion wasn't out of fear, but he had the good sense to know that Gamers' objectives and ethics clashed with theirs and he wanted to avoid any hint of impropriety. Monroe knew that crossing paths with them was like wading into a murky swamp—one step too deep, and you'd be pulled into something you couldn't easily escape.

Nimbus stood just below six feet tall and donned a distinctive appearance, which featured a thick, black, walrus-like mustache, sable skin, and a neat, short hairstyle that was well-groomed. His large, deep-set, dark brown eyes, inflamed and intense, could be rather intimidating. He wore a double-breasted blue suit, the color of which resided somewhere between royal and navy with wider-than-normal pinstripes, and a white shirt with a strikingly vivid red bow tie that was delicately speckled with understated bluish dots. His cufflinks featured some kind of sculpted design that could be generously described as garish.

Nimbus was born and raised in St. Louis and educated in Ohio. He and Monroe were acquainted from his time in DC where he briefly worked for one of the city's larger law firms. While he and Monroe happened upon each other occasionally around town, few words other than perfunctory greetings and the smallest of talk ever took place. However, Monroe's flourishing friendship with Darnell had made him a little more tolerable in Nimbus' eyes.

He hadn't noticed Monroe as he and his crew moved toward one of the back rooms, instead encountering Garland, Ambrose, and their companions as they strolled past. The two groups of men seemed to exchange ill-natured expressions that held conspicuous and violent undertones. The women who just seconds earlier had been laughing joyfully became stoic and unsettled. Even as a bystander, Monroe was left somewhat disconcerted. It was almost as if they were waiting for the first punch to be thrown.

One of the ladies inserted herself between the two groups and diffused the situation with a soft smile and a few quiet words. Spotting Monroe, Nimbus began to make his way over. Not one to let things go without making a statement, he lingered for a moment casting a dark, menacing stare back at Garland and Ambrose before turning back and walking toward Monroe. Steptoe and Prigmore slowly withdrew to the back of the suite.

"Gray," Nimbus said, nodding slightly as he came to a stop in front of Monroe.

To Monroe's surprise, Nimbus's tone was almost cordial, a rare shift from his typical brusqueness.

"What's up, Nimbus?" Monroe asked in a guardedly pleasant manner.

"Helluva evening, huh?"

"It is pretty cool. Seems everyone's come out of the woodwork to celebrate tonight."

Nimbus's mouth twisted into a smile that he must have stolen from a fox. "A lot of people have a stake in Darnell's success, one way or the other."

"Including you, I'm sure," Monroe replied, keeping his tone neutral.

There was an elusive spark in his gaze that was hard to pin down. "Let's just say that I have an investment in seeing the city run smoothly," Nimbus declared in a matter-of-fact manner. "No room for outsiders or distractions." He cast a quick eye back toward Garland and Ambrose. "Some people never learn their place."

Monroe raised his glass in a mock toast. "To knowing your place." *What a dick.*

Nimbus gave a curt nod, then leaned in slightly, his voice lowering. "There's a lot of potential money to be made here. With this city in the right hands, it all starts tonight. Maybe it's time you and I had a real conversation back in DC."

Monroe's smile was restrained. "I'll keep it in mind."

With that Nimbus withdrew, shooting another sharp glance in the direction of Garland and Ambrose. Monroe took a long sip of his drink. He felt the threat in Nimbus's words and demeanor. He knew that an alliance with him and his crowd would be unpredictable and most likely precarious. Monroe had learned from their past interactions that any vague agreement to meet up was hollow. Although neither lent voice to it, both men shared a silent recognition that their relationship was superficial and anything beyond that was pure fantasy.

Monroe turned away from the direction where Nimbus was heading and, to his surprise, Ambrose had sidled up next to him, seemingly appearing from nowhere.

"Do you know that inky muthafucka?" he asked, nodding toward Nimbus.

Monroe exhaled and steadied himself for what he knew would be a conversation full of Ambrose's brand of bluntness. "Hello to you too," he answered dryly.

Ambrose grinned widely, clapping his hand on Monroe's shoulder. "My bad. What's up, my brother?" he asked as he shook Monroe's hand and embraced him with such vigor that he almost spilled his drink. He continued, "Nimbus and those two assholes that he hangs with are some shady muthafuckas. He thinks he's hot shit."

"Assholes and muthafuckas, all in one sentence," Monroe said, laughing in an attempt to add some humor to the situation. The irony of Ambrose's statement didn't go unnoticed by Monroe. "I have the feeling he'd say the same about you," he said chuckling.

Ambrose laughed, a bit too loudly, as he was clearly not one for subtlety. "Well, he'd be right. But I don't go around like I own any place that I happen to be in. That guy..." Ambrose shook his head.

Monroe took another sip. "Not many saints in this room, Ambrose. I don't see one halo."

"True dat," Ambrose responded, his tone suddenly turned to serious. "Look there's more going on with Nimbus than you'd guess, Monroe. You're tight with Darnell, right?"

Monroe eyed him, intrigued but cautious. "Closer than many. Why?"

Ambrose glanced around, lowering his voice. "Let's just say, Nimbus has been moving in circles that would make you think twice. But this isn't the place for it. When we're back in DC, I'll fill you in on what I know. Trust me, you'll want to hear it."

Monroe's eyes narrowed, interest piqued. "Just let me know when."

"It'll be sooner than later," Ambrose replied with a conspiratorial grin. "But until then, keep an eye on that one." He tipped his head toward Nimbus. "The brother's got a way of making problems disappear. He won't hesitate to do whatever it takes to get it done."

"Noted. Now you'd better get back over to those ladies before Nimbus comes over and slips away with one," Monroe said, laughing.

"Not on his best day," Ambrose said, smiling. "If I don't see you later tonight, I'll see you back in the city."

"Chill out and enjoy yourself. You can fight your battles another time."

Monroe tried to put a few thoughts together as he continued to enjoy his drink. Nimbus, he assumed, had made his way up to the suite early before Darnell arrived so he could try to get some face time. Nimbus, Steptoe, and Prigmore had been with Trimble's campaign from the outset. Many of the so-called heavy hitters with the other development groups had been as well. Yeah, they all spread their money around with the other candidates, including Darnell, but for most of those players, Trimble was their guy. He had been for sale.

With the writing on the wall, it was apparent that Nimbus realized that his gamble on Trimble had blown up in his face, and getting back into Darnell's good graces was a priority. He had tried to walk a fine line between Darnell and Trimble, but as Monroe understood it, Trimble had made him promises that Darnell wouldn't commit to. Yet Monroe and Gordon, for his part, were unsure how Darnell would handle any gesture of atonement by Nimbus; after all, they'd known each other for years. And as it's been said by many, there are no permanent friends or enemies, just interests. Monroe was determined to monitor the situation closely to see how it would play out.

Lost in thought, he returned to reality when someone in the back of the room shouted for the TV to be turned up. One of the local anchors was doing an update of the results. It was official. Darnell won the election with an overwhelming majority of votes. As for Trimble, he edged the GOP candidate by less than two percentage points. He had to be pissed. Darnell would be the city's next mayor. The room erupted with cheers as more and more well-wishers began to stream into the suite.

The anchor redirected the broadcast to a live shot at the union hall. The place was going crazy. The loud chants and cheers along with the music in the background virtually smothered the voice of the reporter on the scene. You could hear him say that congratulatory phone calls had been made and concession speeches given. Gordon, who was standing with Dixon and his group in one of the other rooms, looked over at Monroe. Both men raised their glasses and smiled, a sign of belief that they were on their way. But to where?

6

THE PENTHOUSE CELEBRATION WAS GAINING STEAM. Monroe had been passing the time talking with several people from Darnell's campaign. He'd just ordered another drink when applause and loud cheers broke out. As the crowd parted, Darnell and his wife, Kenya, emerged. Both were all smiles and were soaking up the adoration. Accompanying them was Darnell's chief of staff, Tamara Treadwell, with Congressman Hancock in tow.

Monroe's eyes lingered on Tammy as she was called by most. A statuesque, captivating woman, she moved with a self-assured ease that contrasted sharply with her reputation as a no-nonsense political operative. On this night, her sharp edges seemed softened, her radiant smile surrounded her with an aura of undeniable warmth. Her pecan-colored skin was flawlessly smooth, and her full, glistening lips conveyed a level of sensuousness that was difficult to ignore. Her hair was of a reddish tint and curly.

Monroe had been intrigued from the time he met her. But he knew better than to let his admiration from afar cloud his professional senses. Tammy was off-limits for obvious reasons. She was Darnell's main confidante, and if he started something that he couldn't finish, it could be very bad for business. Still, there was an undeniable magnetism about her—an energy that filled the space around her like static before a storm, making it nearly impossible for him to look away.

Monroe's thoughts were disrupted as Darnell approached. He offered the mayor-elect a warm handshake. "Well, if it isn't the man of the hour," he said, hoisting his glass in a subtle toast. "Congratulations, Darnell. You da man now."

"Appreciate it, my brother," Darnell replied with a grin. "A lot of folks didn't think we'd get here, but here we are, right?"

"Right where you're supposed to be," Monroe affirmed, glancing at Kenya, who was beaming at her husband. "And Kenya, you've been putting in work too. I know you're glad it's all over."

Kenya laughed, giving Darnell a playful nudge. "He might have the title, but you'd be surprised how many of the little things fall to me. But I don't mind at all—that's what I'm here for."

With a soft hand, Darnell tilted her face upward, drawing her eyes to his. "Couldn't have done it without her. Hey, my man, we'll catch up soon. Maybe we can finally get down to the brass tacks then, huh?"

"That sounds like a plan," Monroe replied, nodding with approval. He wanted to press for more details on Darnell's plans for the city's development projects but held back, knowing that tonight wasn't the time.

As Darnell turned to greet others, Tammy caught Monroe's eye, raising her glass in a casual salute. Monroe felt a slight rush of adrenaline as he walked over.

Monroe's previous interactions with Tammy had been few and were limited to campaign activities. Despite the romantic constraints, he felt compelled to forge a stronger professional connection with her. Both he and Gordon regarded Tammy as the pivotal figure in unraveling Darnell's mindset regarding the development project. The soon-to-be mayor had been effectively concealing his intentions.

"Ms. Treadwell," he greeted, nodding. "Seems like all the hard work paid off."

"Please, Monroe, don't make it sound like I'm the one pulling the strings," she said, smiling. Her eyes twinkled brightly with a hint of mischief. "I'm just here to keep things running smoothly."

"You know that's modesty talking," Monroe said, his voice light but probing. "We all know you're the one who keeps Darnell out of hot water."

Tammy playfully rolled her eyes. "That's my job—to make sure he stays out of it, whether he likes it or not."

Monroe leaned in slightly. "Well, I think we're overdue for a real conversation. I have a few ideas I'd love to get your perspective on, especially with what Darnell's planning."

She raised an eyebrow. "Monroe, are you trying to squeeze secrets out of me already?"

He grinned. "Not tonight, just... someday soon. But let me know when you're ready to talk shop."

"We'll see," she replied with a tinge of intrigue in her words.

"That sounds a little vague, Tammy."

"Now Monroe, you know nothing comes easy," she said in a manner that left him wondering what she was actually referring to.

"I'm a patient man," he responded with a smile.

"Like I said. We'll see." Touching Monroe's free hand softly, she turned to engage other supporters who were waiting to greet her.

Darnell had seen a lot of politicians fuck up and put themselves in legal jeopardy and some cases prison for bullshit reasons. That made him overly cautious. He was determined to avoid any potential appearance that he had conflicts of interest, which is why Gordon and Monroe viewed a close relationship with Tammy as essential to their efforts. But Monroe knew it wasn't the time or place for such conversations. Giving her the hard press could be viewed as intrusive. So Monroe tempered any enthusiasm and continued to rub shoulders.

After about an hour or so, activity in the suite had subsided as people gravitated downstairs to the hotel's ballroom for the main event. Monroe did get the chance to spend a few additional moments with Darnell. Much of the conversation was general, but he once again promised to allocate some quality time to catch up during the upcoming American Conference of Black Mayors meeting. Monroe also joined Gordon, Dixon, and the potential investors for a private discussion in a corner of the suite that had been secured for the meeting. As usual, Dixon was driving the conversation. Monroe took mental notes.

With the suite virtually empty, the group decided to go down to the hotel restaurant, which was still open, to have a late dinner. Both Gordon and Monroe begged off. As always, Gordon said good night to Monroe and headed toward the elevators to go up to his room to call his wife, Nadine, and turn in. Given that it was his last night in St. Louis, Monroe wanted to have a little fun. Since he would be working from DC mostly going forward, he figured that he might as well hang out a little longer and enjoy the festivities.

He entered the main ballroom and was confronted with the sight of hundreds of well-dressed partiers throwin' down. The music was pulsating, and the dance floor was packed. If exuberance was a drug, there would have been a deluge of overdoses. Monroe scanned the room and was pleasantly spellbound by the scene. He had met so many people while traveling to the city, it almost felt like home. He then did what anyone in his position would do. He headed for the dance floor after being motioned over by a very attractive woman.

It seemed that time raced, and by 2 a.m. with the party still going strong, Monroe had grown restless. Hotel rules dictated that things would have to shut down by three. Several people were talking about after-parties. That was amazing to him since it was Wednesday morning. He had long ago lost the desire or ability to indulge in the antics reserved for night owls during the week.

On the verge of contemplating whether or not to call it a night, one of Darnell's people, Butch Ollie, approached him. Butch was over six feet tall, had the build of a linebacker, and walked with a swaggering stroll. He sported closely cropped hair, and his black mustache and goatee were precisely trimmed. His smile suggested an easygoing nature, a description that in reality was quite accurate.

"Monroe, my man," Butch exclaimed, embracing him and offering a few pats on his back. "You're looking like you're ready to call it quits, but I'm hoping to change your mind."

"Oh yeah?" Monroe asked, amused. "What's up?"

Butch flashed a grin. "You ever been to one of the East St. Louis casinos?"

The question drew Monroe's attention. "Can't say I have. Not really my scene, to be honest. I don't have the best luck with gambling."

"Luck, my ass," Butch scoffed. "It's about the thrill, my man. Look, I'm heading over there to try my hand at the slots, maybe some blackjack. Thought you might want to tag along, see what all the fuss is about."

Monroe hesitated. Though his inner voice urged him toward the comfort of his hotel bed, the invitation held his interest. "I don't know, Butch. Last time I gambled was in Nam, and let's just say I always seemed to leave with a lighter pocket than I came in with."

Butch laughed. "You're not in Vietnam anymore, Monroe. Plus, if you're gonna be working in gaming, shouldn't you know a thing or two about how the business works?"

Monroe grinned, realizing he had a point. "Touché. Alright, Butch, lead the way."

They headed out into the cool night, and Monroe felt a surge of excitement. As they climbed into Butch's car, he glanced over. "So what's your game, Butch? Blackjack?"

"Yeah, blackjack's my go-to," Butch replied, glancing at Monroe with a roguish smile. "But don't let me catch you counting cards. I've got a reputation to protect."

Monroe laughed. "I'm just along for the ride. I'll leave the gambling to you."

Butch grinned as he pulled onto the road. "That's okay, more money for me to win. Too bad though. Lady Luck could be waiting for you right across the river."

Monroe turned back to watch the St. Louis skyline recede as they crossed into East St. Louis. He wasn't sure what to expect, but he knew one thing—this journey would be anything but ordinary. Butch didn't know how right he was about what Lady Luck would have in store for Monroe. What waited was an immediate dividend and a future of uncertainty.

7

S PENDING SOME TIME WITH BUTCH OLLIE proved informative. He provided Monroe with harmless but useful insights into his relationship with Darnell. He also learned a little about his new companion in the process. Butch had dropped out of college to make some cash after he found out that he was going to be a father. He also did what he thought to be the right thing and got married. Both he and his lady were nineteen at the time. Unfortunately, the marriage didn't work out and over the years, he had worked a number of jobs that led nowhere.

As fortune would have it, Butch met Darnell just as the newly minted attorney's political career was taking off. From the outset, Darnell took a liking to him, eventually welcoming Butch into his inner circle. He eagerly executed any tasks assigned by Darnell, reaping the rewards of secure employment and a newfound stature. In exchange, Butch provided Darnell with an invaluable currency—loyalty.

As they stepped into the riverboat casino they were greeted by several rows of slot machines and video poker stations. The entire place was bustling. The sight of the hordes of people who were engaging in the various games was astounding to Monroe. He had been to properties in Vegas and Atlantic City, but this was the Midwest. Yet, to see such an energetic crowd taking the plunge in the wee hours of a weekday morning in East St. Louis, Illinois was a surprise.

After a brief period of idle observation, it became apparent that restlessness had taken hold of Butch. The beckoning tables were whispering his name, and his money was eager to escape his pocket. Monroe assured him that there was no need to worry and that he should go ahead and do his thing. After all, he was a big boy and would have no problem finding a source of entertainment. Bidding Monroe a hasty farewell, Butch Ollie promptly set off toward one of the cages to acquire some chips.

Now flying solo, Monroe strolled up to the bar and ordered his customary Jack on the Rocks. Leaning back with his right elbow on the bar, drink in hand, he closely observed the comings and goings of all who passed his way. Monroe couldn't let go of his fascination that the casino continued to attract a steady stream of patrons at that hour of the morning. The persistent sound of *ka-ching* echoed in his mind. Turning to the passing bartender, Monroe asked if crowds like this were typical given the time. The server not only confirmed it but added that another wave of players would be making their way in around five.

While driving over, Butch had told to him that crowds would be shuttling in and out all night, but Monroe dismissed it as hype. Yet there they were, customers of all stripes, many dressed to the nines, dispersed throughout the complex. Monroe was satisfied to just chill and check out the action. As he glanced across the room, he noticed an exceptionally attractive woman in a well-appointed sequined dress, a bejeweled band adorning her neck. She turned toward him and began to walk over. As she drew nearer their eyes locked. *Malaika Sinclair*.

From what Monroe knew about her, Malaika was a highly regarded lobbyist in Washington. The firm she worked for was extremely influential and boasted an A-list of clients, which included several heavyweights in the casino and entertainment industries. Monroe had first met her during a memorable limo ride in Detroit almost three years earlier.

He had commissioned a car and driver to retrieve a well-known mayor from a southeastern city who was speaking at a session that he was organizing for one of his clients. He later learned that Malaika and the official were seated next to each other on the same flight. Charmed by her many assets, he offered her a ride into town, which meant that Monroe was stuck with both. Not that he complained. Malaika was extremely easy on the eyes.

During the drive from the Detroit Metropolitan Airport to the Renaissance Center, which was where the conference was being held, Monroe kept trying to figure out her deal. The flirting going on between her and the very married, upstanding public servant was obvious. Monroe remembered thinking at the time, after giving her a twice-over, that if the mayor was trying to make a play, he was definitely punching up in class. But as it has been often said, power is the ultimate aphrodisiac. That charmer was later arrested on corruption charges. In Monroe's eyes, it served him right.

Since that time, Malaika and Monroe had seen each other at several political and social functions. Most recently it had been at an after-party at Club Desirée in the Four Seasons Hotel in Georgetown. However, their interactions had been consistently casual and unremarkable. Monroe intentionally chose not to inquire about the official in the limo. While he was more than interested in knowing what had transpired, he figured that it was none of his business. Besides, he didn't want to tarnish his elevated perception of Malaika, especially since all evidence of her being involved with that philandering scumbag was groundless speculation on his part. But the mere thought was unpleasant.

An imposing, yet graceful woman at five-foot-ten, Malaika possessed a curvaceous figure. Her luxuriant onyx-colored hair was slicked back and poker straight into an exceptionally long ponytail that draped her right shoulder. Her coffee-hued skin exhibited an appearance of lushness that gave credence to her name, which he later learned meant "angel" in Swahili. Monroe's eyes followed her every move as she approached him. This encounter was either serendipitous or by design, given the fact that they were in a casino hundreds of miles from their homes and well on the other side of three o'clock in the morning. Monroe's mind quickly returned to the moment. It wasn't the time to overthink the situation.

"Well, well, well. Ms. Sinclair, are you lost?" he amiably asked as she positioned herself directly in front of him. Monroe was genuinely surprised and also happy to see her. "I would never imagine seeing you in a place like this, let alone in this city."

"Now, Mr. Gray, you know that I'm a New York girl. Adventure is in my DNA," she said, flashing an intoxicating smile. "I got bored standing around the Marriott and the party was winding down," she continued. "One of our casino clients owns a group of properties and this is one of them."

"Really?" he said.

"It's also one of their most profitable establishments outside of Nevada. Since I was going to be in town for election night, it was suggested that I do a walk-through and get a glimpse for myself. Since I'm not flying home until tomorrow afternoon, the timing was right."

For the next hour or so, Monroe and Malaika delved into more meaningful conversation than ever before. Uncovering shared interests, it seemed they were on the brink of forming a deeper connection. While their exchanges spanned various topics, they subtly probed each other about their roles in the hotel/casino development project. It was apparent that this topic held significant interest for both. They each approached it with tact.

Around 4:30 a.m., Malaika proposed sharing a taxi back to St. Louis, an offer that Monroe promptly accepted. He excused himself briefly to locate Butch Ollie. In no time Monroe pinpointed him at one of the blackjack tables. He was laser-focused on his game and interactions with the dealer. With the intensity his eyes displayed, Monroe could tell that Butch Ollie was relieved when he told him that he was heading out. After a brief shake of hands, without missing a beat, he spun around and resumed his monetary pursuits while Monroe made his way to reconnect with Malaika.

With a line of taxis waiting to ferry patrons to their various destinations, one pulled up immediately and they quickly entered. The driver asked them where we were headed and almost simultaneously both responded, "The Marquette." Monroe and Malaika turned toward each other and immediately broke out in laughter. *Another coincidence?*

The return trip across the MacArthur Bridge to downtown St. Louis seemed quicker than the trip over. Maybe it was the company. Monroe and Malaika exited the taxi and went through the revolving doors and into the lobby. Given the time, it was no surprise that it was somewhat quiet. After all, it was almost 5 a.m. A smattering of celebrants from the events of the evening were settled in adjacent areas.

The frequent trips to St. Louis and their loyalty to the Marquette had allowed Monroe and Gordon to get upgraded more often than not. This was one of those times. Monroe had been awarded a sizable and well-appointed suite. Although he was tempted, Monroe wasn't going to be presumptuous with Malaika. While he was making headway, there was still a lot that he didn't know about her other than what she had shared that morning. But as they stood waiting for an elevator to arrive, she offered him a sultry gaze that accentuated her striking eyes. As the doors to the elevator opened she touched his arm and cooed, "Your room or mine?"

While he was taken aback, Monroe had never been one to overlook a moment of good fortune. The words "my place" rolled off his tongue without hesitation. She laughed. Monroe knew the look of surprise on his face was clearly visible. She thought it was cute. They walked down the hall arm-in-arm with her head leaning on his shoulder. After entering the room and placing their coats in the nearby closet, Malaika settled onto the sofa in the living area. Monroe retrieved a bottle of wine and a couple of glasses and returned to take a seat next to her. He began to insert the corkscrew into the bottle, and while doing so Malaika placed her hand on his knee. "Did you really invite me here for more drinks and conversation? Haven't you had enough of both for one night?" And with that question, all talking ceased.

8

FTER WHAT CAN ONLY BE DESCRIBED as a long and eventful night, Monroe scurried around to pack after Malaika left. He also ordered a late breakfast and a newspaper. As expected, impactful headlines and photos of Darnell dominated not only the front page but appeared in various parts of the news and local sections. He was the toast of the town. The entire experience since meeting him had been hectic, educational, and challenging. It had also been a lot of fun. While Monroe was looking forward to going home to recover and recharge, the respite from travel would be brief. He and Gordon would be heading to the Black Mayors meeting in New York the following week.

Monroe finished his meal about fifteen minutes before his 1:00 p.m. check-out time. Since both of their flights departed within minutes of each other, he and Gordon had arranged to meet in the lobby and share a taxi to the airport. Monroe rushed to the elevator, which was available almost immediately. When he emerged into the lobby, he found Gordon waiting patiently near the Concierge Desk, browsing a copy of the *St. Louis Post-Dispatch*. Looking up and spotting Monroe, Gordon neatly folded his paper, placed it under his arm, and grabbed his bag. They went straight to the hotel exit, where the doorman hailed a taxi.

Monroe gave Gordon the CliffsNotes version of the remainder of his evening as their ride headed toward the airport. When Monroe told him that he had run into Malaika, Gordon's level of interest turned up a notch. Gordon had met her at an industry event in Las Vegas prior to his meeting Monroe. She must have made an impression on him because Malaika was one of the people whom he asked if Monroe knew in their initial discussion. Monroe also got the sense that given his conservative social construct, that in a way, Gordon lived vicariously through him. He listened to Monroe's recounting with both interest and amusement.

While Gordon was similarly impressed with her smarts and somewhat fascinated by her looks, he was apprehensive about her motives and those of her firm. Monroe tried to allay any fears that he might have regarding Malaika, but Gordon was adamant that she be kept oblivious of their plans.

"Maybe you can afford to think with the wrong head. But I've got too much money wrapped up in this, so keep that in mind," he cautioned. Deep inside, Monroe knew that he was right.

Monroe and Gordon were both booked on TWA as usual, and their flights departed from the same terminal and gate area. Once through security, they searched for a couple of seats at a nearby restaurant to have a drink while reflecting on recent events. Gordon was happy with the progress made in such a short period but knew there were still plenty of obstacles. Both were confident in the local people who were involved and their ability to handle the day-to-day. Any trips back out to St. Louis for Monroe would be on an as-needed basis. That was fine by him. Gordon was going to also limit his visits as well, at least until the final proposal requirements hit the streets. Besides, other clients needed his attention.

The pair were deeply involved in their discussion when Monroe heard the final announcement for his flight. He quickly retrieved his things and made a mad dash across the concourse. With all of his recent travels to St. Louis and a few other cities as part of their efforts, Monroe had racked up quite a few frequent flyer miles and was able to upgrade to first class. At least he would be somewhat comfortable on the flight and maybe even get some sleep, which as a nervous flyer was rare for him. Since returning from Nam, anything that wasn't in his control caused him discomfort. It was probably the reason he hadn't married.

Monroe greeted and exchanged pleasantries with two very attractive flight attendants who stood in the galley facing the entry door. He turned to locate his seat in the first-class cabin. Much to his surprise, sitting in the bulkhead aisle seat was Malaika. *Another coincidence?* Monroe's paranoid inner man was telling him there was more to this than met the eye. But as quickly as that thought appeared, it vanished. After all, there were a limited number of flights between St. Louis and National Airport and they both had a long night, which made this one the most convenient since it would land in DC and allow them to get home at a reasonable hour. At least, that's what he told himself.

"Hi, stranger," she giggled playfully, flashing a rapturous smile.

"Well, another twist of fate or are you following me?" Monroe responded with a laugh.

"I could ask the same question," she quickly retorted.

"I wouldn't tell you, even if I was," he said as he eased past to find his aisle seat, which was three rows away.

Ambling back toward his seat, Monroe spied Congressman Hancock absorbed in an intense conversation with whom he assumed to be a staff person. Hancock looked up briefly and offered a nod of the head, but nothing more. Monroe could have cared less. After settling in and ordering a pre-flight beverage, he thought about orchestrating a move so he could sit next to Malaika. But since the passenger door was getting ready to close, it didn't make sense to disrupt her seatmate. Besides, Monroe wanted to get some much-needed rest and, from what he could tell, Malaika had work on her mind.

However, Monroe found the opportunity to have a brief conversation with Malaika midway through the flight as he passed her seat on his way back from the restroom. Her seatmate was asleep, head tilted awkwardly against the window, while she sipped a glass of sparkling water. Glancing up as Monroe approached, Malaika offered a smile. He paused, steadying himself with a hand braced against the overhead compartment.

"You certainly look at home in first class," Monroe said, his voice laced with amusement.

"I could say the same about you, Monroe. What's the occasion? Did you finally hit the jackpot, or are you just enjoying the perks of someone else's dime?" She replied laughing.

"Oh, so you got jokes," he said, feigning mock disgust. "Let's call it a little of both. Though truth be told, my luck's been all over the place lately."

"Well, I'd offer you a seat, but as you can see, it's already taken."

"Wouldn't dream of interrupting your seatmate's beauty rest. But since we have a moment, have you picked up anything interesting about Darnell's angle on the licenses?" he asked, his tone casual but his curiosity evident.

Malaika eyed him, her expression neutral but thoughtful. "He's staying out of the spotlight, letting Tammy handle the heavy lifting. She's been making all the noise lately, but I can't tell if that's deliberate or just her usual way of operating."

Monroe tilted his head slightly, considering her words. "Think she's overplaying it, or is it all part of her game?"

A faint smile flickered across Malaika's lips, though her tone remained low and measured. "She's too sharp to act irrationally. But Darnell on the other hand... he's impatient."

Monroe nodded, maintaining a calm facade as his thoughts churned. "Anything else you think I should know before we land?"

Malaika hesitated for a moment, then shook her head. "Nothing concrete, but keep your ears open. Darnell and Tammy don't trust anyone—not even each other."

The plane jolted slightly as they hit a pocket of turbulence. Monroe adjusted his grip on the overhead compartment and gave her a subtle smile. "We'll talk more when we're off this thing."

"It'll have to wait," she replied, her eyes meeting his briefly before drifting back to the in-flight magazine on her tray table. "I've got an appointment to rush to as soon as we land."

Monroe made his way back to his seat, his thoughts spinning. The more he learned, the more interesting things became—but if anyone could help guide him, it might be Malaika. One thing was certain, and he knew Gordon wouldn't be pleased. Malaika was growing on him.

After landing, they strolled through the terminal together, exchanging light conversation before parting ways—she headed for ground transportation to catch a taxi, while Monroe proceeded to the parking area for his car. It turned out that Malaika's appointment was a dinner meeting in Georgetown, and she was already running late. Monroe had offered her a ride, but she politely declined. They agreed to meet again soon, though Monroe had no idea that unforeseen complications were about to briefly intervene.

9

WITH ALL OF THE ACTIVITY DURING the previous week, not to mention his very long night with Malaika, Monroe was exhausted. He also had to play catch-up on work that paid the bills, so he was anxious to be home and unwind. Monroe walked through the door of his place around 7:30 p.m. Immediately his mind fixated on a hot shower, a glass of wine, and bed. He had cleared his calendar for the next day just so he could rest and recharge. No sooner than he had taken off his jacket and placed his bags down in the hallway, the phone rang. *Damn!* Monroe reluctantly answered.

"Hello."

"Hi. Is this Monroe?"

"Yes," he responded, with an undercurrent of curiosity. "How can I help you?"

"This is Yvonne Montgomery with Congressman Pressley Hancock's office. How are you? I hope that it's not too late." Her voice was warm, yet professional.

"What's up, Yvonne? It's been a long time. I didn't recognize your voice," he said, leaning back against the plush leather of his armchair. A hint of nostalgia accompanied his words.

"Yes, it has been," she said. She laughed softly, the sound weary yet pleasant, as if recalling a fond memory.

"Working late, aren't you?" Monroe asked, glancing at the clock on the wall.

"Comes with the territory," she said matter-of-factly, the faint sound of papers rustling on her end punctuating her words. "How was St. Louis?" she inquired, her tone brightening.

"I just walked in the door," he replied, feeling the drain of the long day still lingering in his bones. He was caught a little off guard by her question. "How did you know I'd been to St. Louis?"

"Word gets around," she said light-heartedly.

"By word, do you mean from your boss?" Monroe asked with muted sarcasm.

"Caught," she quickly responded. Her smile seemed to radiate through the phone, igniting a spark of familiarity between them.

"Well, now that you mention St. Louis, I'm surprised that I didn't run into you there," Monroe offered.

"My only connection to the city is through my work with the congressman. The local politics that don't directly influence the operations of this office are of little interest to me," she bluntly replied, her tone steady as if she were reciting a well-practiced line. "Besides, I had a lot to do here, and the boss didn't require my presence, which was fine by me." He could almost picture her shrugging lightly, sitting in the confines of her deserted Capitol Hill office.

"So, you're finally getting back to me?" Monroe asked facetiously to remind her of an earlier effort to reach out.

"Sorry for the delay," she said, frustration lacing her tone. "Someone in the office dropped the ball, but I gathered you were spending quite a bit of time in St. Louis, so I thought it best to hold off until after the election. I'll confess, even though you were on my call list, the congressman specifically asked me to reach out to you."

"That's a surprise," Monroe replied, raising an eyebrow. "When I saw him on the plane, he seemed pretty indifferent toward me."

"Ah, that's just his way," she said with a knowing chuckle, her voice lightening as she continued. "I wouldn't sweat it. If he ever comes across as overly friendly, you can bet he wants something.

"Good to know," he said, appreciating the insight into the congressman's enigmatic personality.

Gordon had been anxious for Monroe to meet with Hancock to get his assessment of the veteran lawmaker. Though pleased to finally hear from Yvonne, he couldn't shake a sense of suspicion regarding the timing. Having recently encountered her boss in St. Louis while in the company of Nimbus and his crew and just seeing him on the plane home, the outreach seemed oddly timed. Was there something that he missed, or was Monroe simply being overly suspicious? After all, she was the administrative assistant to an extremely powerful member of Congress, which was a demanding role, so it was understandable why it might have taken time for them to connect. But since Hancock had urged her to call, something must be up.

Monroe had seen Yvonne at several events on the Hill over the previous few years, exchanging nameless greetings on more than one occasion. While he didn't know her personally, he did by reputation. In many business environments, Yvonne's office title had clerical implications, but on Capitol Hill other than the members themselves, the persons holding that designation held the highest level of authority. The AA was in charge of the overall operations in the office, including the supervision of all staff, and more often than not, that person was the representative's closest confidant and usually had an unofficial hand in all things political, including campaigns and fundraising. That was one reason Monroe was surprised by her expressed disinterest in local politics, almost as much as he was when he learned that she had ended up in that position working for Hancock.

Unlike many overseers of congressional offices at the time, Yvonne wasn't from her boss's district. She wasn't even from Missouri. Despite this, she possessed a keen political acumen that earned her significant respect on the Hill. She had proven herself as a skilled operative, serving two highly regarded members for several years until circumstances forced her to seek new opportunities. With options both on the Hill and in the lobbying world on K Street, whatever carrot Congressman Hancock dangled in front of her must have been significant.

After exchanging opinions about the mayoral election and Monroe's impressions of St. Louis, Yvonne abruptly cut to the chase after several moments.

"I understand that your group is Voyager's primary partner, correct?" she asked.

"Yes," he said, not volunteering any more information than he was asked.

"Since this venture will have a major economic impact on the congressman's district, he asked me to set up a meeting with you as soon as possible."

"Care to shed a little more light?" Monroe responded.

"The congressman is meeting with all of the groups. Although he has no sway in who will win the contract, he does want to understand what each company is bringing to the table and the impact of each plan on his district," she said in an almost believable manner.

No sway, my ass. There's no way a powerful and arrogant prick like Hancock wouldn't try to influence any decision by putting his thumb on the scale. Monroe felt like Yvonne was trying to remove any apprehensions he might have before he could come out with them. In his few interactions with Hancock, Monroe's antennas were always up.

Though he had no tangible proof, a thick shroud of corruption hung over Hancock like morning smog blanketing the Los Angeles skyline, obscuring everything beneath it. To Monroe, any meeting would be more like a fishing expedition on Hancock's part, an attempt to reel any information he could use to his advantage. Monroe's initial goal had been to connect with Yvonne; the chance to engage Hancock for an extended period was an unexpected stroke of luck—an opportunity to gauge the man's character and intentions. He was also sure that Hancock had the same thought.

"Sounds good to me," Monroe said, his voice steady, masking the undercurrent of tension.

"Okay then," she replied in a manner in which her fatigue seeped through the phone. "Can you come in on Friday?"

"Friday?" Monroe echoed, momentarily taken aback by the urgency of her request. The week had passed in a blur, and the idea of fitting another meeting into his schedule felt a little overwhelming, yet he quickly adjusted. "Sure, I can carve out some time."

"Good," she responded, her tone now brisk and businesslike. "Does 2 p.m. work for you?"

"Sure," he said, intrigued by the thought of his impending encounter.

With arrangements made, the conversation came to a close. Monroe couldn't shake the feeling that he would be walking into a room filled with uncertainty and would most likely be at a disadvantage. He had encountered Hancock multiple times over the previous days, each interaction marked by the congressman's aloof indifference. Now, out of the blue, Hancock wanted to sit down and talk. Their chance sighting on the flight back to DC took on a new significance. His smug demeanor lingered in Monroe's mind like a neon sign in a dimly lit alley.

Adding to his unease was the knowledge that Yvonne possessed the ability to acquire any information at a moment's notice. He was certain Hancock's team had thoroughly scoured through every detail of his life. That realization hit Monroe hard. He knew that he would need to be as prepared as possible for his visit to the Hill, where the stakes were higher than he could afford to ignore. But further thoughts on the matter would have to wait; his bed was calling. Little did he know that circumstances beyond his wildest imagination were conspiring to overtake him.

10

HAVING GOTTEN A GOOD NIGHT'S SLEEP thanks to the glass of wine and a sleep aid, Monroe was reenergized. Rather than rest as he had planned, he decided to spend the day tackling his to-do list, which was sizable due to all of the travel related to the casino deal. He and Gordon weren't scheduled to meet again until the conference in New York, which would give him more than enough time to make some headway. Monroe also had various personal tasks that had gone neglected and needed to be addressed, so he made it a point to check off as many items as possible.

By day's end, having made substantial progress, Monroe felt he deserved a break. Anxious to see what he may have been missing out on in the DC social scene, he accepted the invitation from a member of his regular crew, Benny Harris. Benny and several other friends were meeting for drinks and he urged Monroe to join them. It was a gorgeous late April afternoon so Monroe decided it was the perfect time to get out and enjoy what was left of it. They were gathering at a popular spot called Hogate's, which was located on the Southwest

Waterfront. That sat well with Monroe because it was a five-minute walk from his apartment.

After showering and dressing, Monroe looked around to make sure he wasn't forgetting anything. Just as he walked toward the door to leave, the phone rang. For a moment he thought that he would let his answering machine deal with it. But an inner voice suggested that he pick up. To his surprise, the person on the other end was Carlton Dixon.

"Gray," he said in a gruff and amplified manner. As a former military man, he primarily used last names when addressing others, particularly Monroe. "We need to talk."

No hello? Just straight to the point. "We can talk now. I have a few minutes," Monroe responded.

"That doesn't work for me. Since I'm in town, we need to lay eyes on each other," he insisted.

Now his curiosity was piqued. Monroe didn't like Dixon's tone but was interested in knowing what he wanted. On most occasions, the man he considered a first-class asshole treated him with abrasive disregard. Suddenly, he wanted to talk.

"I've got a dinner engagement in an hour. Come by my hotel around nine. I should be back by then," Dixon said in more of the manner of a command than a request.

Inwardly, Monroe was steaming, but he didn't want to display any emotion. No matter how rich Dixon was, he wasn't going to put up with his attitude much longer. Monroe was done taking orders when he left the Army. But asking wasn't in Dixon's nature.

"I have prior arrangements myself, but I should be able to work you in," Monroe said, without trying to hide his growing irritation. "Where are you staying?"

"The Mayflower."

Monroe should have known. That was Darnell's favorite hotel. He talked it up so much that the management should have had him on the payroll. Most of his associates who visited town ended up there. "Okay, I'll see you then."

"I'm in 801. Buzz me from the lobby when you get here and come up," Dixon added.

"You want to meet in your room?"

"It's a suite," he said icily. "And yes, I do."

No sooner than Monroe could say, "Well I guess I'll see you then," a loud click penetrated his eardrums. *That muthafucka didn't even have the decency to say goodbye.* Monroe's temper was further spiked, but he knew that diplomacy was first and foremost in dealing with Dixon since he or at least his money meant so much to the project. But Monroe might do something rash if Dixon kept *fuckin'* with him. Giving an arrogant old man with an obnoxious attitude an *ass-whippin'* wasn't beyond him. He needed a drink.

The meetup with his friends was just what the doctor ordered. There was no talk of politics or business. Although it was Thursday, the bar was lively and the dance floor was crowded. It was good to be back and out in DC. But while he enjoyed socializing as much as anyone, Monroe had rid himself of the habit of hanging out at all times of the night. Since his tour in Nam, he'd enjoyed the peace that his home offered. It was like his tent during the war, a place of safety.

It was probably good that he was cutting his evening short, even though having to meet with Dixon was the primary reason. Monroe wasn't looking forward to it. So many people kissed the self-proclaimed tycoon's ass on the regular that it was expected when you were in his presence. He knew that his lack of deference was one of the barriers that separated him and Dixon. But despite any misgivings, Monroe was anxious to know what was on his mind. One thing was for sure, given their brief but subtly contemptuous relationship: the topic and results of any meeting were unpredictable.

As 8:30 approached, Monroe said his farewells and headed out. Since both the Mayflower and Hogate's were near Metro stations, he decided to take the subway. Jumping on a Yellow Line train for three stops, Monroe switched to the Red Line for two and was at his destination, Farragut North, in no time. Exiting to his right, he walked toward the escalators at the far north end of the station's platform, which led to Connecticut Avenue and L Street. The hotel was less than three hundred feet away.

A renowned property, the Mayflower was built in 1925. Throughout its history, the hotel had long been considered a DC institution. It welcomed dignitaries from around the world as guests and bustled with the comings and goings of visitors and local patrons. Monroe walked under the glass canopy that led to the three gold-plated double doors that were separated by two extended pillars. He approached the middle door, which was immediately opened by one of the several uniformed doormen who were scurrying about assisting guests. He walked directly over to a house phone that was stationed adjacent to the reception desk and called Dixon's room. No answer. *Ain't this a bitch. Maybe he isn't back from dinner.*

With time to kill, Monroe eyed the entry door to the Town & Country Lounge, which was walled off from the lobby. At least he could have a drink while he waited. The lighting in the lounge and dining area was understated; not bright or dim but somewhere in between. Since it was a Thursday evening, the bar and restaurant area were still alive with holdovers from the Happy Hour crowd that included a number of the city's power brokers. Monroe settled in one of the bar seats and surveyed the room as he waited to place his order.

Word had it that J. Edgar Hoover and his trusted deputy, later revealed as his partner Clyde Tolson, were regular patrons at the eatery for a good twenty years. Hoover gained a reputation for sticking to a consistent order on every visit—cottage cheese, grapefruit, and iceberg lettuce. It seems he wasn't a fan of the house dressing, always opting to bring his own. Ironically, the restaurant bears his name today.

The bartender approached Monroe and asked him for his order. Deciding to switch up for a change, he opted for Maker's Mark and, of course, it was on the rocks. "Kentucky Champaign" is what a business associate from Louisville once called it. Monroe liked both brands, but part of his preference for Jack Daniel's was that a slave named Nearest Green was said to have taught Daniel how to distill whisky. Monroe reasoned that was more than enough of a reason to stay loyal to his beverage of choice.

After about twenty minutes or so, he headed back out to the reception area to call again. No answer. It could have been that Dixon had fallen asleep and did so soundly, or maybe he had entertained a visitor who wasn't Mrs. Dixon. Monroe couldn't help but smile as he considered the latter thought. Although he was hesitant, he decided to go directly up to his room and find out. This may have been another one of the times that Monroe should have listened to his inner guide.

11

GETTING OFF OF THE ELEVATOR on the eighth floor, Monroe followed the arrow that pointed to the left for 801. He slowly walked down the long hall until ultimately arriving at a recessed area that contained two suites, 800 and 801. The latter was on his right. Before he could knock, Monroe noticed that the inner door latch was wedged open, leaving the door slightly ajar for anyone to enter. His initial reaction was to return to the lobby and call him again. However, a sense of unease gnawed at him, and the unusual situation only piqued his curiosity further.

He gradually opened the door and stepped into the suite's living area, calling Dixon's name in the process. The room was bathed in a muted, diffused silvery-white light that was cast by a full moon set against the backdrop of the clear nocturnal sky. This celestial glow seamlessly intertwined with the warm, orange radiance of the city lights on Connecticut Avenue, and an accompanying gentle breeze penetrated the swaying sheer curtains that adorned the two sizable and partially opened windows that were situated on the other side of the room.

While the illumination wasn't bright, it provided Monroe with just enough light to see the outlines of objects in the room. Unable to locate a light switch near the door, he hesitantly made his way across the room. Monroe noticed on his right a decorative fireplace and mantel, with objects atop the latter. A small table flanked by two chairs stood within reach. On his left was an entertainment stand on which a large TV was placed. He inched forward and came up on a chair and a desk.

A nearby lamp caught Monroe's attention. He reached to switch it on but an internal alarm warned him that something was amiss. He hesitated. Slowly, he pulled out a handkerchief from his right back pocket and used it to cover his fingers as he turned the switch. Glancing to his right, he saw an L-shaped sofa with two ornate pillows arranged in the middle. The longer section of the couch faced the windows, while the shorter part sat before a large recessed mirror. A tall metal floor lamp with a slender pole and a wide, circular shade of the same material was situated in between.

The scene disturbed Monroe. But instead of calling hotel security, he decided to check the bedroom alone. After all, there could be a very innocent explanation for Dixon's lack of response. He began the walk up the short hall, past the bathroom until he came to the bedroom door, which was closed. With a cloth in hand, he gently turned the doorknob—it was unlocked. Slowly, he stepped inside. In the dimly lit room, a figure lay sprawled in the middle of the bed, bound in a twisted arrangement that spoke of restraint and desperation. The air was heavy with the scent of anxiety, and it enveloped Monroe. This time he found the light switch and turned it on. *Holy shit!*

There he was, lying motionless on his side in the middle of the bed, naked as the day he was born. Dixon's face, contorted in a mixture of discomfort and fear, was the focal point of the ghastly scene. His wrists and feet were tightly bound, the rope biting into his flesh, rendering him immobile. The strained arch of his body formed a silent plea for release, accentuated by the rope coiled ominously around his neck. His rigid penis pointed directly toward the foot of the bed. Monroe had seen his share of death erections in Vietnam. The ones by hanging or strangulation were the result of swift and violent endings. Once again he weighed his options. Should he take flight and go downstairs and contact the police? He thought for a moment.

***

The bright lights of the stark interrogation room cast an atmosphere that felt like Monroe was being held captive under a scorching sun. Their brilliance and intensity left him distressed and disoriented. He sat mercilessly in the plain, hard-backed metal chair that was devoid of padding and armrests. Monroe's hands were uncomfortably cuffed behind him, forcing him to sit up straight, which made it difficult to move or alter his position. His situation was intentional. He had limited ability to adequately see and respond to the three White MPs who were putting him through the wringer.

This all came about because he'd crossed paths with his captors while off base. In their minds, the look he'd given a local White girl had been a little too long in length and accompanied by what they believed to be impure motives. In fact, the opposite was true. Her plainness led Monroe to wonder why so many White men viewed their women as the ultimate trophy for any Black man. The young lady in question would be hard-pressed to get the attention of most brothers, especially him. Monroe's gaze was borne more of concealed indifference. But the two White MPs who were on the scene didn't see it that way. Over his fervent complaints, they hauled Monroe away to an interrogation room in the disciplinary barracks on the base where a third MP waited. Monroe shouldn't have been surprised; after all, Fort Benning was in southern Georgia near the Alabama border and a few hours' drive from the "Redneck Riviera" of North Florida and the Gulf Shores.

As Monroe sat there helpless and constrained, he reflected on just how he had ended up in the Army. It certainly wasn't by design. While his father and grandfather had regaled him with stories about their adventures abroad in what was then a segregated military, Monroe wanted no part of it, particularly since the Viet Nam War was raging and the body count of soldiers from the Roanoke area had climbed. The armed forces wasn't a desirable alternative.

Monroe thought his plan was better. He would take a year after graduating high school and travel through Europe and Africa. He was curious that way. But before he could get out of town, the dreaded "Order to Report for Induction from the Selective Service System" came in the mail. Monroe thought about hightailing it to Canada, but the long-term implications for his life gave him pause. By not being enrolled in college and being in good health, all of the deferment preferences were off the table. He had little choice but to answer the call.

But now, as he experienced the verbal and physical brutality, Canada and the consequences of flight looked pretty good to Monroe in that moment. He had been alerted by family, including his father and grandfather, and friends who were veterans that despite some positive experiences, racism was rampant in the military. While he took those warnings to heart, he also thought that it couldn't be any worse than growing up in Virginia where Jim Crow and segregation had thrived during his childhood and adolescence. But if his first weeks in uniform were any indication, the reality exceeded Monroe's most unfavorable expectations.

And the harassment wasn't just from these MPs, who seemed to take pleasure in making the life of any Black soldier miserable. Black servicemen faced taunts and insults from White soldiers on an ongoing basis. That's why African American troops formed special bonds and friendships that exist to this day. They had to remain focused and continue to prove their worth and not let the power structure within the military think that their reckless disregard for the rights of Blacks, not only as soldiers but as men, had gone unnoticed.

In that instant, Monroe decided to match fire with fire. For every time he was called "nigger," he returned verbal fire with "cracker." Monroe talked about their mothers and the things he had done to them, which only incited them more. All of a sudden there was a loud knock on the door. One of the men opened it. Standing there with a look of disgust on his face was the sergeant for Monroe's unit, Dwayne Huckaby from Scotland Neck, North Carolina. Each morning when he roused them, his soldiers greeted him with dread. On that day, he was the most welcomed sight Monroe had seen in some time.

As their superior officer, Sergeant dressed down the MPs in vile language that was music to Monroe's ears. He told them that he'd be reporting them to their superiors and that if they ever came near another one of his soldiers that he would rip them a new asshole. Monroe's captors quickly uncuffed him and issued a weak-ass apology. He was just happy to get out of there. As they headed back to the barracks, Huckaby told him not to think he was special. It was his position and rank that had compelled him to do the right thing. Snapping back to his current surroundings, his quick trip down memory lane had resurrected old feelings. *Fuck the police.*

***

As Monroe inched his way closer to the bed, he tried to maintain the tenseness of the moment, but the shadow of a grin tugged at the corner of his lips in a fleeting expression of amusement. *Just who did Dixon piss off to get himself into this situation?* A cold shiver ran down his spine as Monroe took in the scene—a stark display of human vulnerability and suffering frozen in time. The dim light cast uneven shadows across the room, as if the walls themselves flinched at the grim scene, carving the image firmly into his memory.

On the nightstand adjacent to the bed were two glasses. One was partially filled with a cocktail that blended shades of pink and red, while the other held a drink with a brownish tint. The faint colors were the result of melting ice. But what caught Monroe's eye was a smudge on the glass of red liquid, which was clearly lipstick. *Was Dixon tippin' on that sexy young wife of his*? A tray on the dresser held two bottles of liquor. One was the parking czar's favorite, Glenfiddich, a single malt scotch that he would go on and on about as if he were a seasoned whiskey aficionado. The other was a high-end vodka, Stolichnaya—or Stoli as it was known—and positioned next to it was a bottle of cranberry juice and a bucket of melting ice. It was safe to assume that Dixon's paramour was drinking Cosmos.

Monroe glanced at a smaller table near a lounge chair. On it lay a magazine with lines of cocaine spread across the cover. In Monroe's mind, Dixon didn't seem like a drug user. He was far too old school for that. But then again, with a street upbringing and a young wife, who knew? Monroe felt the urge to snoop further, but it made more sense to get out of there. It was all too convenient. It seemed to Monroe that someone wanted him to find the body.

Was this an attempt to frame him? The door being open and around the time that he and Dixon were to meet was too much of a coincidence. Monroe surveyed both rooms as he made his way out. Just as he had entered, he tried to make sure that he left no trace of his presence. He locked the door to protect the body from unwanted discovery. As Monroe turned to begin his walk down the hall corridor, the chime of the elevator caught his attention. It signaled the arrival of someone whose identity was in question. With uncertainty looming, he quickened his pace.

Fortunately, he was passing the door to a stairwell. He entered immediately and began his descent as quickly and quietly as possible. Monroe was also lucky that when he emerged, he was at the 17th Street entrance, which was on the opposite side of the one on Connecticut Avenue. As he looked across the lobby, it was apparent that he had gone unnoticed. Wasting no time, he exited the door, turned right, and walked toward the Farragut West Metro Station. Monroe couldn't get home fast enough. He had a lot to process. He would later learn that he had missed the police by seconds. But they would find him soon enough.

12

MONROE CROSSED HIS THRESHOLD of his apartment around 10:30 p.m. and went straight to the small bar in the den. He was on edge, to say the least. Monroe had seen his share of dead bodies during the war, but catching sight of Dixon's the way it was staged was jarring. Part of him regretted not hanging around and calling the cops. But he didn't need the hassle, and his distrust of the law only hastened his decision.

For about thirty minutes, Monroe paced. As he reflected, he didn't have a clue who'd want to inflict that kind of pain and terror on Dixon. If it was just the coke that was in sight, it could be explained away as some type of cardiac event. But that wasn't the case. A lot of thoughts came into Monroe's mind. His focus continually returned to the mystery lady and her role. Or could she have been another victim?

The idea of a solitary woman overpowering Dixon and executing the elaborate setup seemed improbable to Monroe. Dixon's robust physique hinted at a strength that defied his age. The pieces didn't fit the puzzle. Just after 11 p.m., the tense silence was shattered by the ringing of his phone, reigniting his earlier paranoia and causing his already racing heart to make the climb to his throat. He let it ring four times before hesitantly walking over to answer it on the fifth. On the other end was Gordon.

"What's up?"

"Ain't nothin'. What's goin' on with you?" Monroe responded, hoping that his anxiety wasn't detectable.

"Same old, same old. Did Dixon get in touch with you?"

To lie or not to lie. Monroe opted for partial transparency. "Yeah," he responded. "He called me earlier today. "Said he wanted to meet up, but when I went by the hotel, he didn't answer when I called his room from the lobby. I decided to have a drink at the bar and wait. I called him again about fifteen minutes later and still no answer, so I headed home," he said, figuring that his explanation to Gordon sounded legit. It would also be the same story that he would give anyone else asking about his whereabouts, including the police.

"So you guys didn't get together at all?" Gordon asked in a somewhat pressing manner.

"No," Monroe responded curtly, somewhat irritated by the follow-up.

"Cool," replied Gordon. "Just asking. He was anxious to talk with you."

"Did he say why?"

"No, just that you and he had some business to discuss. He didn't go into it with me."

"Maybe he'll try to catch up with me tomorrow," Monroe said, knowing full well that wasn't going to happen.

Monroe and Gordon spoke for several more minutes before ending the call. During the conversation, Monroe mentioned his meeting with Hancock scheduled for the next day. Both were eager to see how it would turn out. Monroe had planned a productive day to make up for lost time spent in St. Louis. Now the meeting with Hancock and his predicament with Dixon being iced were complications he didn't want or need. After he hung up the phone, Monroe couldn't shake the nagging question of what Dixon wanted to discuss. He had no clue, but that didn't stop his imagination from wandering through a realm of possibilities.

To distract himself Monroe settled in for some TV time. After undressing and easing onto the sofa, he grabbed the remote. The familiar faces of Jim Vance and Doreen Gentzler, anchoring the eleven o'clock news on Channel 4, drew his attention. As various stories unfolded on the screen, there was no news of a body being found at the Mayflower, much to Monroe's relief. He was also reassured by the fact that there had also been no knock on his door. With the newscast over, Monroe convinced himself to try and get some sleep.

For most of the night, rest remained elusive. Monroe tossed and turned as visions of Dixon's lifeless body tormented him. The question of why Dixon had even been in town and how he met his demise continued to baffle Monroe. He finally drifted off sometime in the early hours. His last recollection of the time was 4:15 a.m. The TV in his bedroom had been watching him much of the time.

As usual, his alarm went off at 7:00 a.m. Rising, he swung his legs over the edge of the bed and let out a tired yawn. The scant hours of shut-eye promised that the day ahead would be taxing. The morning news was on, so he took a few moments to watch. After the sports guy finished his report, the camera's focus returned to the anchor, who did a rehash of what was the breaking news of the morning, the discovery of a body at the upscale Mayflower Hotel. He immediately tossed the story to the station's top crime reporter, Patrick Murphy, who was onsite. Standing under the Mayflower's

Connecticut Avenue entry portico, the bespectacled veteran correspondent somberly provided the details as he knew them surrounding the death of a prominent St. Louis businessman. *Oh, shit! Here we go.*

13

AFTER PROVIDING A FEW FACTS to open his report, Murphy disclosed that, although there had been no official announcement, his sources had confirmed that "the body had been identified as that of Carlton Dixon, a businessman from St. Louis, Missouri." As soon as those words were uttered, Monroe leaned forward to hang on to Murphy's every word. Dixon had been found by police officers just after 9:30 p.m. Someone had requested a welfare check, which could have meant that the caller probably knew that Monroe was supposed to meet with Dixon and laid a trap for him to be in his room when they arrived. Looking back, Monroe figured it was the police getting off the elevator as he made a mad dash down the eight-floor stairwell.

Details were few, but he was startled to hear Dixon's name come up. *It must have been a leak.* Murphy's source was likely a hotel staff member. Monroe was convinced that the detectives in charge would want to keep a tight lid on their findings and the investigation's status. The way Dixon's body was left and the cocaine that was out in the open would have caused a frenzy if known. "This is insane," Monroe muttered to himself. He wondered whether Gordon knew. As he pondered the question, the phone rang.

"Monroe, have you heard about Dixon?" Gordon asked excitedly.

"Yeah. It's all over the news here," he responded, trying to sound surprised. *I must have conjured him up with my thoughts.*

"I just got a call from a homicide detective. He found my business card in his room."

"Damn! What did they say to you?" Monroe queried.

"Not a lot," said Gordon. "He asked me about where I was last night and when did I last see or talk with him," he said, unable to mask his unusual lack of composure.

"I've got to be honest with you, G, I don't have to tell you this, but Dixon was an acquired taste for me. We didn't play well together.

"He could be somewhat of a dinosaur in his thinking for sure, but he and I got along pretty well."

That's a nice way of saying he was an asshole, but he had bank so I dealt with it. "According to the TV reports, the investigation is just getting started. After all, his body was found late last night," Monroe continued.

"Yeah, that's what I got from talking with the detective," Gordon quickly responded. "I'm sure they'll be in touch with you soon."

"Me? Why would they want to talk with me?" Monroe said in an attempt to sound believable. He knew he would be on the radar of the police, but he wanted to see if the detective Gordon spoke with had given up any info that he should be aware of.

"He found your business card in the room too. Besides, since you were part of our investment group, you should know that they would want to have a conversation."

Gordon was right, but Monroe already knew it.

"Monroe, I've got to run, but I'm coming down to Washington on Monday to take care of some business. I also have an appointment with the police, which I'm not looking forward to, so we can catch up in person then.

"That's fine. Having had my time with them, I can tell you it won't be a walk in the park."

"By the way, you should probably keep your schedule flexible next week, Gordon added. We're going to have to show up at Dixon's funeral, whenever it's scheduled. Word is just getting out about his murder, but I'm sure his wife will want to get the service over with as soon as possible.

I guess she will with the payday she's got coming. "No problem," Monroe responded. "I'll be around. Later."

Now Dixon's funeral became another mental obsession for Monroe. He hated funerals and tried to avoid them at all costs, particularly if he was close to the deceased. Fortunately, that wouldn't be the case with Dixon. Still, there was something undeniably sad about funerals, no matter how often they were billed as celebrations. Death is the final act on earth. But Monroe knew it would look bad if he didn't show up at the funeral. It could also raise suspicion with the police.

Not knowing Dixon's reasons for being in town continued to trouble Monroe. What ate at him most, however, was the deceased businessman's insistence on seeing him. Since the investigation was still in its early stages, Monroe was sure the medical examiner's office hadn't released an estimated time of death. Maybe the police knew, but if they did, they were keeping it quiet.

Yet the more Monroe thought about it, the more the mystery intrigued him. Did the motive behind Dixon's murder link to events happening here in Washington? If it was a local beef, why not resolve it in St. Louis? What really puzzled Monroe was the intended message from the assailant or assailants who had stripped Dixon's body and cruelly allowed him to strangle himself in his struggle for freedom. *And what was the deal with the drugs?*

What also piqued Monroe's interest was just what business Gordon was going to take care of in D.C. With Dixon dead, the only connection Monroe could come up with was Hancock. That made all the sense in the world, since Gordon, Hancock, and the others Yvonne had mentioned had secretly been planning an enterprise that didn't include him. Monroe knew he needed to find out more.

Dixon's death had thrown a wrench in the schedule Monroe had cleared to take care of personal tasks. With his focus squarely on Dixon, Monroe decided that he needed to come up with a consistent story about his activities on the previous evening. He once again questioned his decision not to report finding the body. But that was water under the bridge—he had to run with it now. In any case, he'd rather take his chances coming up with answers on his own than place his trust in the Metropolitan Police Department (MPD)—or any police agency, for that matter. Monroe was also lucky that at the time, few hotels had security cameras placed throughout the halls and stairwells. Even if they did, most were dummies or were prone to malfunction.

Kicking off his morning routine, Monroe headed toward his coffeemaker, which had completed its timed ritual. As he approached the machine, the enticing aroma of his morning elixir enveloped him. He prepared the first of what would be several cups of coffee that he hoped would serve as liquid energy after such a fitful night. Monroe sat at the table in the dining area, eagerly awaiting *The Post* to arrive. He was anxious to see if any of its local reporters had unearthed more facts. The paper finally landed at his door around eight, just as he had taken a sip from his third cup of coffee.

After scouring both the front page and Metro sections, he found only one article—a brief piece that lacked substantial details or context. Monroe fully expected that more expansive coverage would follow as the day progressed, especially since Murphy's disclosure of Dixon's name would send other reporters scrambling for more information about him. Like the TV news reports, the article did confirm Dixon as the victim, offering generic references to his business, philanthropy, and political connections, including support for Congressman Hancock.

Around 10 a.m. the phone rang, breaking Monroe's train of thought. It was Ambrose. *Thank God for caller ID.* Although he didn't relish the idea of engaging in Ambrose's verbal gymnastics so early in the day, Monroe found his curiosity piqued by the timing of his call. It could have been just a coincidence, but something about it created the urge to answer. One thing was certain, he was sure that Ambrose had heard about Dixon and wanted to feel him out, or maybe he knew something that Monroe didn't. With a hesitant hand, Monroe lifted the receiver.

"What's up, Ambrose?"

"Oh, so you got caller ID?"

"I do. I don't like to be caught off guard if I can help it."

"So, I made the cut?" he asked with a laugh.

"Barely," Monroe cooly replied. "All right, Ambrose, you've got my attention. Get to the point. Got no time for bullshit today," he said, trying not to sound as perturbed as he actually was.

"My bad man, my bad," Ambrose quickly responded. "I saw the thing about your man Dixon on the news. Awful! Just awful." After a brief pause, he continued, "Any more word on what went down?"

"Nah. I'm as much in the dark as you are."

"Man, that's some fucked-up shit."

"That's one way to put it," Monroe said.

"You know something? All those times we bumped into each other in St. Louis, I didn't realize that you were a part of one of the groups. I thought you worked for Darnell."

"I only told you almost every time I saw you," Monroe countered while rolling his eyes.

In hindsight, he could see why Ambrose may have gotten that impression given the situations in which they happened upon each other. As their conversation progressed, he suggested to Monroe that his relationship with Darnell would be valuable to him and Garland and that he should consider making the switch given Gamers' new reality. *Damn! Dixon's body isn't even cold and the Sharks are already circling.* Ambrose went on to say that he could have a Black Mercedes at the front door of Monroe's building the next day. *Uh-oh.*

With that, Monroe knew that this conversation with Ambrose was coming to a close. No telling who was listening on the other end. Rightfully suspicious, Monroe promptly threw a big bucket of cold water on the Mercedes idea. No way was he going to put himself in a position to have to explain to the IRS or a federal prosecutor how a luxury car that he had no record of paying for came into his possession.

As usual, Ambrose handled Monroe's rejection with humor by making a disparaging remark about his "Japanese piece of shit," referring to the Honda that Monroe drove. Ambrose also said that they would talk more at Garland's place the next day. With everything that had gone on over the previous twelve hours, Monroe had forgotten about the function. Before he hung up, Ambrose gave him the address and directions. The more Monroe thought about it, the more he felt the need to attend. While the time near the water would be a welcomed intervention given everything that was going on, he also might learn something in the process. And while his instincts would prove to be correct, his journey of discovery would begin sooner than expected.

14

AMBROSE'S CALL HAD GOTTEN MONROE back on schedule. He was glad that he hadn't ignored it. Staying on good terms with him could be useful. Ambrose and Garland operated on the fringes of all of the competing groups, and either one or both could prove to be a good source of information at some point. Despite giving Ambrose's offer a swift cold shoulder, Monroe was surprised to find himself contemplating it after hanging up.

While the prospect of a new car was tempting, the wise words of his grandfather resonated in his thoughts. "If somebody gives you something that you haven't earned, you'd better believe it ain't free. You just haven't got the bill yet." Besides, there was no way he could have gone into business with Ambrose and Garland. Sure, they were nice enough and pleasant in small doses, but dealing with them every day would drive him out of his mind.

Feeling the weight of events, Monroe realized he needed to relieve some stress. No sooner than he hung up with Ambrose, he reached out to Malaika. Surprisingly, she was in town and was free the next night. She sounded just as eager for a break as he was. They readily agreed to meet after Monroe returned from his trip to Highland Beach. With Malaika now occupying his thoughts on the regular, he considered skipping the gathering entirely, but his curiosity about Garland and Ambrose kept him from making a rash decision. Besides, as the saying goes, good things come to those who wait.

Although his exchange with Malaika was a much-needed distraction, Monroe's attention once again returned to the scene in Dixon's suite. He knew that a woman alone couldn't have been the perpetrator. There had to be more than one person involved. Untangling that puzzle would take time, and there was so much that was unknown. Monroe decided that his best bet was to maintain a low profile and steer clear of any unnecessary attention. His primary goal was to avoid becoming the scapegoat. But even a blind man could see that it was set up that way.

After catching up on other news and sports, Monroe headed toward the shower. But before he could get there the doorbell rang. *Who in the fuck is this?* The one thing that Monroe liked about living in his complex was the notification system that was in place whenever a tenant or owner had visitors. Tiber Island was a four-building cooperative complex in Southwest DC, with a telephone entry system at each access door. His apartment was in the main structure where the management office was located. It also featured a Concierge desk that was staffed 24/7. So how did whoever was at his door get past those hurdles without him knowing?

Monroe tied the belt to his robe and slowly and quietly ambled over to the door. He wanted to check out the stranger on the other side through the peephole before he committed to letting him or her in. To his surprise, two unfamiliar men of contrasting features came into view. One was short, somewhat stocky, and light-skinned; the other was taller, thinner, with a dark complexion. He had no idea who they were, but he knew *what* they were. Monroe slowly opened the door with the security chain engaged, limiting his exposure. Almost in unison, both men flashed their badges. *Shit!*

"Good morning. Are you Monroe Gray?" asked the thin one.

"Yes," he replied, hoping that the disquiet that he felt wasn't reflected on his face and in his demeanor. *These muthafuckas didn't waste any time in getting to me.*

"Do you have a few moments? We'd like to speak with you about a police matter," he said.

"Please come in," he said, trying to remain calm and even keeled.

As they were making their way into his unit, Monroe mentally hustled to come up with a game plan on the fly. Uncertain about the approach the police would take, he knew that his story would have to be tight. Monroe had dealt with all kinds of cops in his legal grind, given the type of low- to mid-level criminals he'd represented. The negative encounters he had experienced combined with his run-ins with the MPs during his time in the Army once again ignited his healthy and longstanding mistrust of law enforcement.

It also didn't help that he was very close to two people who had been murdered over the years. Neither case was ever solved. The police insisted that they had run out of leads; Monroe thought it was indifference. One of many lessons he learned from all of these interactions was that investigators carefully scrutinized all responses, emotions, and body language, looking for a tell. The good ones were laser-focused in trying to determine whether a person of interest or suspect was telling the truth. And there was no doubt that on this morning, he was in their crosshairs.

"Have a seat, Detectives."

"Don't mind if we do," responded the tall, thin one. "I'm Officer Otis Tyree of the Metro DC Homicide Unit, and this is my partner, Reginald Frazier."

"How are you?" Monroe replied, shaking hands with both and then pointing them to the table in the dining area. The men quietly seated themselves. Their stoic behavior added a feeling of gravity to the situation. Monroe's sense of unease ramped up a couple of notches as he considered the consequences that his words could hold. He took a place at the head of the black-finished wooden table facing both detectives, one to each side. *This is going to be interesting.*

Detective Tyree was wearing a gray, stingy brim fedora that he had neglected to remove upon entering. That was a pet peeve of Monroe's. He had always been taught that a man shouldn't wear a hat indoors. But he didn't raise the issue given the circumstances. There was no need to get off on the wrong foot. Tyree stood just shy of six feet tall. Though his frame was somewhat lean with a slight pouch, he carried himself with an air that hinted at a past life as an athlete. However, it was clear that those days were far behind him. His onyx skin was creased, yet slightly polished. His pencil-thin mustache was perfectly trimmed, and a compact patch of hair occupied the area between his lower lip and his chin. The coarseness in his voice signaled that he was a current or former smoker. Yet Tyree projected confidence that bordered on cockiness.

Frazier, on the other hand, fed into the stereotype of the donut-eating flatfoot. Like Tyree he was moderate in height, and his weight looked to be a little north of 220 pounds. His hair was short, somewhat wavy, and parted. His skin was the color of butterscotch and clear. His mustache, while broad, was neatly pared, and his manner was more relaxed. Of the two, Monroe sensed that Frazier was the more personable of the duo, but that had yet to be confirmed.

Both wore suits and white button-collared shirts that screamed Hecht's or Men's Warehouse, not that there was anything wrong with that. Besides, any cop who regularly dressed in designer clothes would probably garner more than a heightened level of suspicion, among his peers as well as the public. Blue was Tyree's color of choice, while Frazier opted for black. Colorful polyester ties with printed designs and pocket squares that matched served as accessories. Tyree wore his in a puffed style whereas Frazier donned points.

Immediately after Monroe took his seat, Tyree began to query him as Frazier took on a gaze that suggested he was sizing him up.

"Mr. Gray, I'm not one to beat around the bush. So, I'm going to ask you straight up: Where were you last night between the hours of 6 and 10 p.m.?"

"I was out with friends," Monroe responded succinctly. One thing he'd learned in past dealings with investigators was to keep your answers as short as possible. The more you add to your story, the more you have to remember.

"Out with friends?" Tyree parroted back, looking up skeptically with his right eyebrow arched. Taking the pad in front of him, he rotated it, placed a pen on top, and slid it toward Monroe. "We're going to need their names," he continued. "Can you write them down for me?"

"No problem," Monroe responded. That was the easy part. He still needed to account for the time between leaving Hogate's and arriving home, deciding to omit the detour to the Mayflower, knowing it would cause more problems than it would solve.

As his mind searched for an answer, he took the initiative. 'Let me ask you a question,' he said.

"Okay," said Tyree. "Go for it."

"Just how did Dixon die?"

A subtle exchange of looks between Frazier and Tyree caught Monroe's attention. The expressions on their faces suggested to Monroe that they were grappling with what to disclose or that he had taken them by surprise—possibly both. He sensed that the investigators were being guarded in divulging any information. Monroe's memory flashed back to Titus Armstrong, a former NYPD homicide detective and neighbor, who once mentioned that if a person of interest showed little to no curiosity about the cause of death during questioning, that was considered a red flag. *Point taken.*

Finally, Frazier leaned forward. "We can't go into any real detail, but for now it's been classified as a homicide."

"Really?" Monroe softly exclaimed while making every effort possible to react with a genuine sense of surprise.

"So what time did you leave your friends?" Frazier asked in a pressing manner.

"Between 8:30 and 9:00, I would guess," Monroe said, knowing that he had left precisely at 8:45. He didn't want them trying to create a specific timeline.

"And they will vouch for that?" he asked.

"No doubt."

Tyree methodically eyed Monroe, then the notebook with the names he'd jotted down. Redirecting his gaze back at Monroe, he asked, "Hogate's? That's near here, isn't it?"

"Yeah," Monroe answered, knowing that Tyree knew damn well where the popular establishment was located. From the looks of him, he probably spent more than his fair share of time at the Channel Inn, a nearby watering hole that was frequented by federal and District government employees.

Coming closer, he continued, "So if you left before 9:00 and you got home at 10:30, what did you do in between? he asked. "You only live a few blocks away."

Monroe had anticipated the question, knowing that the detectives were waiting for an inconsistent answer. "I've been traveling a lot and it was a nice evening," he replied. "I just walked around the neighborhood. I ended up on one of the benches near my complex just enjoying the scene by the water."

Tyree's response was a simple, "Hhhmmm,"

"What was your relationship with Carlton Dixon?" Frazier interjected to Monroe's relief.

"I'm sure you know he was an investor in a development project in St. Louis that our company is bidding on."

"We know that," said Frazier with somewhat of an edge in his tone as if he was assuming the role of bad cop. "But how did you two get along?"

"We got along well," Monroe said too quickly. He provided an impulsive response, and that wasn't his intention.

"Oh, yeah?" said Tyree. "That's not what we heard."

"So, what have you heard?" Monroe asked.

"That the two of you were like oil and water," Frazier quickly interjected.

"We weren't exactly the best of friends, but I didn't have a reason to harm him. He was our main financial backer," Monroe quickly retorted, curious about who they had spoken with to get insights about his relationship with Dixon so quickly.

"How much is this thing y'all workin' on worth?" Tyree asked, exposing his Georgia origins.

"Well, *this thing* is worth about $200 million in its entirety. Our company's stake is just north of $60 million," Monroe said in an intentionally nonchalant manner.

"Jeez!" Frazier exclaimed. "That's a lot of dough."

"The kind of money that can make people do some crazy things," Tyree chimed in.

"Let me be clear, I had a level of respect for Dixon. He was a self-made man and, like I said, he was our lead investor. But truth be told, I'd only known him for five or six months. I only dealt with him periodically, which was fine by me.

"How about your man Gordon?" Tyree asserted. "Were he and Dixon cool too?"

"Gordon had a much better relationship with him than I did. As far as I know, everyone in our group got along well enough. There was too much money on the table for conflict."

"What about any friction with members of other competing groups?" he continued.

"Any time you're going after business with high stakes, there is going to be some friction. Dixon could be a pain in the ass, but from everything I'd heard he garnered respect."

Tyree and Frazier once again exchanged looks that Monroe couldn't immediately interpret, but he had a strong sense that they weren't positive. Monroe pressed on, "Detectives, I will say this one more time. Carlton was a decent man, who I respected. We weren't boys, but I didn't have a reason to kill him."

After an uncomfortably long silence, both men stood up. An aura of skepticism surrounded them—though Monroe wondered if it might just be his paranoia distorting his perception. As they prepared to leave, each handed him a business card, though Tyree's offering was accompanied by an ample measure of stank-eye. Frazier assured

Monroe they weren't finished with him and promised to be in touch sooner rather than later.

Tyree emphasized the urgency, instructing Monroe to contact them immediately if he uncovered any pertinent information. As they exited his apartment, Tyree turned to Monroe and added, "We're going to find who did this and let the chips fall where they may." With that, they tread down the hall, en route to the elevator, leaving an air of uncertainty in their wake.

Closing the door, Monroe turned and leaned back against it. Feelings of relief and anxiety swept through his body. While he may have gotten past his first encounter with the police, he would have to be more prepared for the next one. He also would need a believable account, if it was discovered that he had visited the hotel. The worst-case scenario would be for him to fess up, if needed, and provide a plausible reason for lying.

One thing was certain, the meeting left Monroe with little idea as to what Tyree and Frazier knew. But he was also beginning to have questions about Gordon. He would have been the only person who had talked with the police who knew of his true relationship with Dixon. But any further conjecture would have to wait. He had to get ready to go into the lion's den and a meeting with Hancock. His initial brush with the law was in the rearview mirror, but as he saw it, he was just at the beginning of his quest for the truth. Little did Monroe know that his search would be more difficult than he'd imagined.

15

WITH THE APPEARANCE OF THE TWO DETECTIVES at his door, Monroe's day quickly spiraled out of his control. His initial plan had been to catch up on work and delve deeper into the backgrounds of Hancock and certain other characters as time permitted. With his meeting on the Hill scheduled for 2 p.m., Monroe fretted about the lack of time to look into the congressman and his closest associates. Despite a brief return to his routine, his thoughts were dominated by the chaos of the casino deal, making him question his ongoing involvement. With his trust in his partner beginning to erode and no satisfactory answers in sight, he began mentally preparing to walk away.

Monroe arose early that morning so that he could squeeze in a run. He also wanted some extra time to carefully review his "Hancock" notes, skim the newspaper, and take his time getting dressed. Hailing a taxi during rush hour was always dicey, particularly for Black men regardless of dress. Besides, with a Metro station right across the street from his complex and the Capital South Station located adjacent to the row of House Office Buildings just two stops away after a transfer, that appeared to be the better option.

The Army had taught Monroe that "on time" meant five minutes early. He arrived at the Rayburn House Office Building well ahead of schedule. Since its construction in 1965, Rayburn had always been viewed as the preferred structure among the three that lined Independence Avenue SE on the House side of the Hill. The other two, Longworth and Cannon, were built in 1933 and 1907, respectively. As the newest of the trio, Rayburn contained over two million square feet of space, and it housed the majority of members with seniority at the time.

The building was also the only one with a connecting underground train to the Capitol. Cannon and Longworth, which were closer, connected to the Capitol by walkable underground tunnels. Given Hancock's status and purported ego, having his offices located in Rayburn wasn't surprising. The fact that his committee and subcommittee rooms were located there also played into the process.

Monroe entered the security checkpoint through the Independence Avenue doorway and was scanned. He walked up the steps to the second floor and took the first available elevator to the third. The spacious corridors that featured walls of marble were swarming with mostly young staffers racing to complete their appointed tasks. Added to the mix were an array of lobbyists, visitors, and ancillary employees, each pursuing their separate agendas.

Monroe finally reached Hancock's office, which occupied a corner space. He opened the door and was immediately greeted by the receptionist, who sat behind a desk that was immaculately polished and highlighted by brass fixtures. Her nameplate read Rhodena White. She offered both a smile and the usual "May I help you?" A slender woman with unblemished coffee-colored skin and neatly styled hair that fell just above her shoulders, she was pleasant in both looks and demeanor. Using her name, Monroe introduced himself and informed her that he was there to meet with the congressman. She dialed an extension and alerted the person on the other end of his presence. Once she hung up the phone, she asked Monroe if he would like coffee. He gladly accepted.

By House standards, office space in Rayburn was quite generous, particularly those with corner locations. While offices in the other buildings contained large areas for the members, the rooms for staff could be tight. That wasn't the case in Hancock's office. It seemed that everyone could work in relative comfort. He noticed that the atmosphere was unusually calm, unlike the typically hectic environment in the offices of many House members. *Maybe just a slow day.*

Usually, his reason for arriving early was to have the opportunity to mentally review the information that he'd absorbed in preparing for a meeting and the questions that he wanted to ask. But having come up on the short end of getting the information he wanted, Monroe knew he would have to improvise and be ready for anything. With time to kill, he just decided to relax and collect himself before venturing into what he believed to be an encounter shrouded in uncertainty.

Finding the most comfortable seat in the receiving area, Monroe was enjoying the coffee that Rhodena had retrieved and was soaking in the atmosphere. He was perusing a copy of *Foreign Affairs Magazine* that he collected from a neighboring table when a familiar figure approached. It was Yvonne. Monroe's first thought as he watched her walk toward him was just how fine she was. He tried to block out his typical male response, but can you teach an old dog new tricks?

Their respective greetings were professional and exhibited no hint of familiarity. Yet, he found emotions of the good kind stirring within him. Their eyes were locked momentarily and each offered their best smile. After a brief exchange of pleasantries, Yvonne mentioned that she was busy working on a project and wouldn't be sitting in on the meeting. She also let him know that Hancock was running a few minutes late. *No surprise there.* He told her not to worry and that he had nothing else on his schedule until after two. He was good. As she walked away she casually suggested to Monroe that they catch up later. He smiled and nodded.

From his short tenure on the Hill, Monroe understood that those who occupy these positions are relentlessly overscheduled, swamped with priorities, and regularly in crisis management mode. Twenty minutes of relative calm had passed when Monroe heard a door open and abruptly close. At that moment, the pace of activity among the staff picked up. It didn't take a genius to know that Hancock was on site and had used his private entrance. After several more minutes, Communications Director Jerome Buford came out to greet Monroe and serve as his escort. Monroe stood up and the two men exchanged a brief handshake and greeting before turning to walk toward the congressman's office. *Let the games begin.*

16

LOOKING UP FROM THE DOCUMENTS that he was poring over, Hancock positioned his reading glasses above his forehead and rose to extend his hand as Monroe walked in. He exhibited a smile that bordered on cordiality. Monroe had never gotten this type of vibe before during his previous encounters with Hancock. He couldn't tell if it was genuine, but ultimately, it didn't matter. He decided just to go with the flow. Hancock invited Monroe to have a seat at a small conference table that was ten feet or so away from his desk. With his papers in tow, the longtime politician walked over and grabbed the seat at the head of the table. Monroe gravitated to a seat directly across from Hancock. He wanted to observe Hancock's eyes and mannerisms as they talked. Buford settled into one of the side chairs in between Monroe and the congressman.

Following a short period of casual conversation, which felt more like an information dig, the door opened, and in walked Cleo Hancock. Predictably, it was short for Cleopatra and, yes, from all accounts Monroe had heard, she was daddy's "little queen" and the favorite of his two kids. Not shy by any stretch of the imagination,

Cleo strode across the room toward Monroe and acknowledged him with a handshake. She walked around the table to an empty chair next to Buford and adjacent to Hancock. But before sitting she gave her father an affectionate peck on the cheek and several rubs of his back. *So much for professionalism.*

At first, the look on the congressman's face held a tinge of embarrassment. But when he broke out in a broad smile accompanied by a twinkle in his eyes, there was no doubt where Cleo stood with him. Monroe was sure that she used the influence she held over him to her advantage at every possible turn. Cleo was a woman of moderate height without heels and extremely attractive. Her skin exuded a warm and radiant amber shade, casting a vibrant and healthy glow, and her full, red-painted lips would be described by many a man as luscious. Cleo, opting for a more understated look, wore her chocolate brown hair wrapped in a bun. While she may have been a "daddy's girl," her features were a product of her equally appealing mother.

While Monroe didn't know her well, their paths had crossed on more than one occasion. Washington was small that way. What was interesting to him was that as much of a looker as she was, Cleo dropped more f-bombs and "muthafuckas" than the most profane men he knew. But she did it in a way that almost endeared her to you. She also didn't take any shit. Monroe had seen her dress down another attorney at a reception one evening for trying to enter what she viewed as a private event. The brother was so shell-shocked that his search for a comeback proved fruitless. Monroe also knew someone who had dated her. The guy told him that the sex was mind-blowing, but she wanted to control that. Those stories and others led Monroe to keep his distance. That was difficult because Cleo and Darnell's chief of staff, Tammy, were tight girls, so if he stayed engaged with the casino deal, he wouldn't be able to avoid her.

Cleo's entrance had sidetracked the meeting briefly, but Hancock abruptly got it back on course and cut to the chase by bringing up Dixon.

"I was so sorry to hear about Carlton," Hancock said, his words laced with a southern accent rooted in his Creole heritage. "He was a good man. Known him for years. He was one of my most loyal financial supporters from day one."

"I didn't know him as long as you did, Congressman, but for the brief time I did, I've heard nothing but good things about him," Monroe replied, hoping that his white lie didn't get him struck by lightning.

"In fact, he came by my office last week."

"Really?" Monroe said with more than an inkling of interest.

"Yeah," Hancock continued. "Carlton wasn't just a friend. We've had many business and social interactions over the years."

Monroe was surprised that Hancock had volunteered that information.

"Mr. Dixon and the congressman have always maintained a cordial relationship," Buford unexpectedly chimed in.

Having served the congressman for more than a decade, Buford was a bespectacled man of solid build and above-average height. A native of St. Louis, he played football at Morehouse College before achieving a law degree from the University of Missouri. Having worked his way into Hancock's inner circle, over time he emerged as a key figure, second in importance only to the congressman himself.

Peering over his reading glasses that had been returned to their original position, he went right to the chase. "I guess that since you were working with him on the development deal, you've been interviewed by the police."

"Yes, I have. It's only natural that I would be since we were in the same partnership group." Monroe waited for a reaction from Hancock, which was slow in coming. So before he could respond, Monroe queried, "Have you?" "He knew full well that Hancock wouldn't admit it, even if he had.

"Why should I? He was merely one of my supporters who came by to pay respects and catch up on things," he said with a dismissive wave of the hand.

So, this guy sees Carlton on the last day of his life and he doesn't think that Tyree and Frazier would be interested?

Monroe decided to see if he could get a rise out of Hancock by disclosing a few minor details of his grilling by the detectives investigating the case. Hancock perked up and his curiosity surfaced. He began to bombard Monroe with questions, from the cause of death to what the police knew and everything in between. But his answers were shorter and more vague than they were with Tyree and Frazier. He ended by suggesting Hancock might want to be prepared for a visit. The legislator threw cold water on the idea of meeting with the police.

At that point, Monroe felt that the subject of Carlton's death had been exhausted, so he pivoted to the development deal. Hancock dove right in. He was very curious about the positions within Gamers' partnership group. He also knew that with Dixon out of the way, the company was on the ledge from an investor standpoint. Monroe didn't tip his hand on whether or not there was a backup plan. Honestly, he didn't know. But Hancock was aware that Dixon's 35 percent would be difficult to secure in such a short time frame. The date to submit proposals was rapidly approaching.

From the time the subject had been raised, Hancock had been asking all of the questions for the most part, so Monroe attempted to turn the tables. He asked the congressman several questions not knowing how he would answer. Did he have a horse in the race? What were his ties to any of the players? And the biggie, did he or his family have any interests in the project? But Hancock didn't take the bait. He was cool. So much so that he effectively danced around all three.

"Now, Monroe—may I call you Monroe?" he asked in a manner that was both affable and condescending and without waiting for an answer. "Now you know that as a member of Congress, it would be both unethical and illegal for me to be involved in outside ventures of this nature. As far as my family being involved, it's a free country and they can do what they please, within limits." Cleo smiled.

In the blink of an eye, the thirty-minute meeting had run for forty-five. But one thing was certain, neither he nor Hancock had gained an advantage. At least, that was the way Monroe saw it. But Hancock's comment about his family piqued Monroe's interest, leaving him wanting to know more. His other takeaway was that while Hancock was smooth, he came off as slick as bacon grease. *He's up to something.*

Hancock stood up and walked past Buford to where Monroe was now standing. The two once again exchanged handshakes, but this time Hancock's smile carried a hint of smugness. That look contained a message that didn't sit well with Monroe. Cleo came over and shook his hand and gave him a hug that lacked enthusiasm, to say the least, while mirroring her father's expression. It was oddly chilling. Buford escorted Monroe to the door of the office. Just before leaving, Monroe spotted Yvonne near her desk. She smiled and signaled that he should expect a call later. As he walked down the hall Monroe was disappointed that he didn't uncover more. Hancock was far too cocky for his taste. He needed a jolt. Monroe knew that it would eventually have to come in the form of a strong-willed asshole of a detective.

17

GORDON HAD ASKED MONROE TO CALL as soon as the meeting was over. He knew that curiosity was a reason for the request, but Monroe also picked up on the discreet signs of anxiety that had infiltrated Gordon's thoughts. While the impact of Dixon's murder lingered, Monroe suspected that Gordon was losing his grip on a situation he had initially aimed to manage with finesse. Wanting to find someplace close by to make the call that would be quieter than Rayburn, he thought that the most immediate location would be the Ford House Office Building at Federal Center SW. It was a five-minute walk and in the direction of his apartment.

As he strolled down C Street SW, Monroe was consumed by the stew of crises that had been placed in front of him. Dreams of riches were descending further and further into the depths of his mind, and thoughts of murder, deceit, and corruption were commanding the spotlight. His meeting with Hancock raised more questions than answers. It also didn't help that the list of nefarious characters was expanding. Nimbus Bushrod, Alderman Steptoe, and Chauncy

Prigmore were now joined by Hancock and Cleo, with Gordon on deck to join them.

Adding to Monroe's uncertainty was the roles Ambrose and Garland were playing in all of this. There also could have been other explanations for someone having it in for Dixon. After all, his upbringing had been difficult. His life had started out on St. Louis' Northside and came of age on Chicago's Southside. To succeed, he had to have developed sharp elbows, which Monroe was sure had been used on more than one occasion. He could also have other enemies who, for whatever reason, wanted to see him dead. But that seemed unlikely.

Reaching the Ford HOB, Monroe entered through the 2nd Street entrance, which was between D Street and Virginia Avenue. Passing by the Wright Patman Credit Union, he proceeded to the elevators. Boarding one that was in wait, he pressed B and emerged in the basement near the cafeteria where a bank of payphones lined the wall. None were in use. Monroe sidled up to the one closest to him, pulled out a phone card from his wallet, and dialed. Gordon answered on the second ring. Stress occupied his voice.

"Monroe?" Gordon's voice was clipped, clearly preoccupied. Not waiting for a response, he went straight to the heart of matters. "What happened in there? Tell me exactly what went down with Hancock. Every detail."

Monroe paused for a beat, then gave him a version that wouldn't betray his growing suspicions. "It was mostly a feeling-out process. Nothing concrete. Hancock didn't say anything that tipped the scale one way or another, but I could tell he was testing the waters. Playing it close to the chest."

Gordon didn't seem surprised by this assessment. He was quiet for a moment, then responded, "I figured as much. He's always been like that."

Monroe pushed a little further, though he already knew what he'd get in return. "What's Hancock's role in all this? What do you think he's really involved in?"

Gordon hesitated, his tone shifting. "I wouldn't read too much into it. He's just... trying to stay in the mix, that's all. Focus on the next steps."

Monroe's suspicions deepened. The lack of clarity in Gordon's words, paired with the insights from Ambrose and Malaika, only added fuel to his growing distrust. "You're not giving me much to go on, Gordon," he pressed, his voice low but firm.

"Look," Gordon replied, his voice quieter now, "I'm just telling you what I know. We don't want to get ahead of ourselves. It's a mess, but I'll keep you in the loop. Just... trust me on this."

Monroe could hear the faint tremor in Gordon's voice, something he couldn't ignore. "Yeah, we need to stay in close contact. Let me know as soon as you hear anything important."

"I will," Gordon said quickly. "Just stay focused. This isn't over."

Monroe hung up, a sinking feeling settling in his chest. Something wasn't adding up, but for now, all he could do was wait for the next piece of the puzzle to fall into place.

After ending the call, Monroe dialed his assistant Monique to touch base and inquire about any urgent matters. She assured him that everything was calm. He informed her that he would be working from home for the rest of the day, which he knew would be fine by her.

It was almost noon, and hunger pangs and a growling stomach strongly urged that he get something to eat. Monroe rushed down to the deli at 3rd and C Street to pick up a fresh turkey sandwich and soup to take home. Just as he set his food on the table, the phone rang. It was Yvonne. She told Monroe that he had made quite the impression on her boss. Her tone obscured whether it was favorable or not.

Knowing she couldn't elaborate over the phone, Monroe proposed they meet for a drink after she finished work. She quickly agreed and proposed a downtown location. Given the social confines of working on the Hill, especially on weekdays, he was certain that part of her eagerness to meet at a location stemmed from a desire for a much-needed change of scenery.

Yvonne said that she would leave around 5:30 p.m., which would be early for her. Monroe decided that meeting at The Ritz would be perfect for his purposes. Hanging out there wouldn't be quiet or conspicuous, which was the point. Although he didn't know her well, he thought that taking her someplace where she could let her hair down a little might put her in a better mood to talk later. After getting off the phone, Monroe devoured his lunch and spent the rest of the day reexamining every significant event of the previous week and dissecting the motives of all of the characters as best he could. By the time he was leaving to meet Yvonne, he felt that he had a few pieces of the puzzle in place, but needed to know how they connected.

***

Monroe had spent less than five minutes standing outside the club when the taxi carting Yvonne pulled up. He waved to get her attention as she exited the vehicle. She walked to join him near the door. A long line of anxious partygoers had descended upon the club, with most coming straight from work. It was a point of pride with Monroe that he didn't do lines and had come up with a number of ways to avoid them.

Fortunately, he was acquainted with Rodney, one of several hulking young men who worked the door during happy hours. Monroe took Yvonne by the hand and strode toward him. He greeted Rodney with a handshake that contained a $20 bill. There was no need for him to examine what had been placed in his hand since he and Monroe had done this before. Looking around, Rodney briefly scanned the line of anxious partygoers and unhooked the velvet rope. No waiting.

The Ritz was a multistory building directly across the street from the rear of the FBI headquarters. The atmosphere was electric that evening. Smiles, laughter, and lustful gazes were being traded among the hunters and the hunted who filled the entry area that led to the main room. As they entered, the sound of Rick James' "You and I" was luring an army of patrons to the dance floor. Even those who occupied the spacious bar area with huge windows that faced E Street physically grooved to the pulsating and captivating music.

Although the Ritz had been open for about three years, it was Yvonne's first exposure. For the most part, she was an all-work, no-play kinda girl. But as she looked around the room, the look on her face conveyed pleasure. She seemed to marvel at both the size of the space and the level of activity. As the evening progressed, Monroe managed to persuade her to join him on the dance floor a few times. After a couple of hours, with the midweek crowd still pouring in, both felt it was time to go. Stepping out from what had become a sweltering indoor scene, they welcomed the cool evening breeze against the beads of perspiration on their faces and bodies.

Yvonne's home in the suburbs was in the final stages of a renovation project. Not wanting the renovation to interfere with her work life, she was staying with a friend near Union Station. They agreed to grab a bite at one of the restaurants there. Since it was her last night staying in the city, getting out to enjoy herself felt appropriate.

To separate themselves from the seemingly endless line of would-be riders, they walked half a block east to 9th and E Streets to signal for a taxi. One pulled up almost immediately. The conversation during the short trip was breezy and animated, with no talk of business. But during a rare moment of quiet, Monroe thought about how he should probe her for information that hopefully wouldn't cause her any issues at work. Little did he know that would be the least of his worries.

18

ARRIVING AT THE MASSIVE TRANSIT CENTER, Monroe and Yvonne exited their ride and stepped into the Main Hall, which was alive with travelers coming and going. No matter how many times he frequented the place, the station's architecture never ceased to impress Monroe, particularly since its renovation five years earlier. The high-reaching space boasted a ninety-six-foot-high gold-coffered ceiling and featured thirty-six Roman legionnaire statues that adorned ledges throughout its perimeter. They took a seat on one of the marble slab benches that were clustered around the main room to think over their options.

The Center Café, which sat in the middle of the hall, offered coffee, tea, and a light fare menu. The other three options were Uno's Pizzeria, sFuzzi, a high-end Italian restaurant, and America, a moderately priced eatery with a cool decor that held two levels. They chose the latter and strolled over to the host stand. The restaurant was busy, but not packed. Monroe asked the amiable young blonde who greeted them if a second-floor table overlooking the concourse was available. She replied that it was and directed them toward another host responsible for seating in that area.

Monroe's and Yvonne's evening together had been enjoyable and free of any talk of business to that point. But an air of expectancy lingered, oppressive and unspoken, like a shadow that refused to leave. Each had information that the other wanted, but neither knew where to start. Monroe hoped to find out more about Hancock, but he didn't want to offend or compromise Yvonne in the process. Monroe concluded it best to get through dinner and more wine before pressing matters. Not to mention that their waitress quickly arrived with menus, taking orders for drinks and appetizers. Yvonne opted for a Cosmo. Monroe briefly reflected upon the scene in Dixon's suite. *What is up with women and Cosmos?* He requested his usual Jack Daniel's.

The location couldn't have been better. After ordering their meals—sea scallops and Gulf shrimp for Yvonne, salmon for Monroe—and a bottle of Chardonnay to accompany them, the couple playfully observed and commented on the people scurrying below as they chatted. For the next hour, their conversation centered around getting more acquainted. Just as they completed dinner and awaited their desserts, Monroe steered the conversation in a more serious direction.

"Let me ask you something," Monroe said, swirling his wine glass before taking a sip. "Tell me about your boss."

"What is it you want to know?" Yvonne quickly responded.

"What's his involvement in this casino deal?"

"To be perfectly honest with you, I don't quite know," she replied in a manner that seemed to indicate sincerity. "Monroe, I'm the last person he would confide in," she added. "He views me as someone who operates by the numbers, a Girl Scout. The congressman knows that I operate like that. In other words, I'm not looking to cash in. The only reason I was hired by him was to keep the trains running on time so he could devote his energies elsewhere."

"Makes sense," Monroe acknowledged.

Yvonne continued, "He made it plain in my interview that my role was to make sure that his legislative, communications, and constituent casework teams performed at a high level and to make sure that there was no comingling of his office and campaign finances. The last thing he wants or needs is the Ethics Committee putting him under the microscope, particularly if he's actually up to something sketchy. My peers who work on his committees and subcommittees are under the same marching orders."

"So, Hancock honestly worries about ethics?"

"Make no mistake. I would bet that the brother's up to something," she said, before taking a sip of her wine. "But like most sane people, he doesn't want to go to jail." Placing her glass back on the table, Yvonne went on. "With that said, I might have been born yesterday but it wasn't last night," she added with a laugh, which drew a chuckle from Monroe. "There's some questionable shit going on. I'm just not clued in on it. But one thing is certain, it revolves around money."

It appeared to Monroe that he wasn't going to get anything substantial from Yvonne, although she all but confirmed his belief that Hancock was shady and needed to be watched. Besides, when he thought about it, there was no way he would confide in a smart, principled woman like Yvonne. Any nonsense he was up to would only be shared with people who had longstanding relationships with him. Their desserts arrived. They both had carrot cake.

He didn't know whether it was the wine or the flow of the conversation, but Yvonne began to open up a little more. "You know,

Monroe, the power of observation is a useful tool. I see who comes through the office regularly, and it's the ones who don't record their names in the log that trigger my interest."

"How so?"

"Well, for starters, Cleo and her brother Quincy. Since they're the congressman's children, they can come and go as they please."

"Quincy," Monroe repeated. "I'd forgotten all about him. What's his deal?"

"From what I hear, he and Cleo are in a competition to succeed Hancock when he decides to hang it up," Yvonne disclosed. "He's been out here trading off of his daddy's name trying to get rich for some time now. The congressman has been closemouthed about which one he's leaning toward, but their rivalry can get tense at times. It's also interesting that one or both of them turn up when certain people are in the office.

"Like who?" he asked while placing the fresh linen napkin in his lap.

"Nimbus Bushrod, Alderman Steptoe, and some character named Chauncy Prigmore are frequent visitors, with Nimbus showing up most often."

No surprise there.

"Carlton Dixon also came by whenever he was in town, which had been quite often lately. Sometimes he was with that group and sometimes not. But now...?" Her voice trailed off. "If you want to know the real deal about the casino project, those are people you'd have to talk with," she added.

"Fat chance of that happening," Monroe said.

Somewhat surprised, Yvonne responded, "You boys don't get along?"

"The short answer is no. I have zero trust in any of the people you mentioned."

"I've also seen a couple of guys who said they were from here but had business in St. Louis. They were real characters who couldn't shut up."

"Do you know their names?" Monroe asked out of curiosity but was sure he knew.

"One's was unusual. Hambone or Hambrose or something," she offered, grinning while trying to recall.

"Ambrose?" He said laughing.

"If you say so," she quickly answered. "I do remember the other one was named Garland something. They were a piece of work. The first time they came in, that Ambrose guy made so many passes I thought I was at a football game."

Monroe shouldn't have been surprised that they were cozying up to Hancock. Those two had been trying to make a way out of no way for months now.

"By the way, I probably should have told you this sooner, but I was sorry to hear about your partner Carlton Dixon," Yvonne said sympathetically.

"Appreciate it. He was a good man," Monroe said, continuing to hide his real feelings. "I'm anxious to see the cops get to the bottom of what happened."

"I'd met him on a few occasions. In fact, he came by with one of your partners, Gordon Blackwell, last week."

Last week? While Monroe tried to suppress any verbal reaction, he was sure a look of surprise had registered on his face. "Really? I didn't realize he was in town."

"Now that I know how deeply you're involved with them, I'm surprised that you weren't on the trip with them last month," she added.

"What trip?" he responded with a look of astonishment that he couldn't hide.

"You didn't know?"

"No, I didn't. Do you know the reason for the trip?"

"Not exactly, but I can tell you that they went to Botswana, Lesotho, and Swaziland. But I would guess that as always it was related to money."

Ain't this a bitch! "Anything else I should know?"

"I didn't realize that I was the bearer of bad news," she said in a tone that attempted to be comforting. "I guess I should tell you the rest."

"The rest?"

"The congressman had a long conference call shortly after you left today. The only person who I know was on it was Bushrod. I briefly heard his name mentioned. I had stepped into his office to place some materials on his desk. Dixon's name was mentioned just before he muted the call. I didn't hear anything else so I can't offer you any context. But based on the look he shot at me, I knew it was best to leave the room."

"Yvonne, I'll be honest with you, I was oblivious to all of this crap."

"I understand. If I hear anything else, I'll let you know. But my advice to you is to be careful. I have a feeling that these people are serious."

"The same goes for you. Now that your curiosity is aroused, don't stick your neck out for me. I got this."

They attempted to make the remainder of their time as pleasurable as possible. But the info Yvonne had dropped in Monroe's lap was impossible to unhear. It had become the elephant in the room that put a damper on the evening. At the first opportunity, Monroe paid the check and they made their way downstairs and left through the front entrance.

Yvonne was staying on F Street between 4th and 5th Streets NE, which was a short walk from Union Station. On any other evening, it would have been an enjoyable stroll on what was a pleasant, but somewhat cool, spring evening. But given the discussion that had taken place, the trek was a quiet one.

Monroe could tell that when they arrived at her doorstep Yvonne was tired and he was dispirited. It was probably for the best that the night ended there. Neither of them would have been good company even if they wanted to extend the evening. His mind was racing and he could feel the stress stirring throughout his body.

They briefly hugged and he thanked her again for the info. They agreed to get together again soon. She unlocked her door, and as she entered she turned and smiled. Monroe began the walk to Massachusetts Avenue to get a taxi home. He had to come up with a plan to get to the bottom of things, but executing it would have to wait until he returned from Highland Beach, where more dominos would fall.

19

ONROE'S DECISION TO PLACE GORDON on a
temporary need-to-know basis was solidified after his
conversation with Yvonne. The information she shared
was mind-boggling and underscored just how out of the loop he had
been. From that point forward, Monroe resolved to share only the
most basic facts. Since Gordon was now scheduled to be in town on
Monday for "business" and a meeting with Tyree and Frazier, he
thought it would be best to continue to gather more information and
confront him when they met. Monroe's previous attempts to get
Gordon to open about his dealings with Dixon had been unsuccessful.
What it did do was further trigger Monroe's suspicion.

To hear Gordon talk, his sole focus was finding new investors.
But although it appeared that he was working feverishly, there was no
doubt that Dixon's death was a major disruption. The fact that he was
wasted in an extremely violent manner had others in the group
planning their exit strategies and made recruiting replacements
extremely difficult. While the money involved was large, it didn't

mean much if you weren't going to be around to spend it. Monroe had the feeling that whoever killed Dixon wanted it that way.

Monroe awoke around 9 a.m. the next morning with another sleep-deprived fog engulfing his mind. He needed caffeine. After a quick visit to the bathroom, he slogged directly toward the coffeemaker to prepare his brew. He never used the timer on weekends. As he tidied up his place, the aroma prompted an awareness of his agenda for the day. He viewed one exploit with curiosity and the other with anticipation.

While Monroe had toyed with the idea of skipping the get-together in Highland Beach, his curiosity about Garland and Ambrose won out over his reluctance. With Dixon's murder making the rounds, it would be a good opportunity to see what others were thinking. His other appointment with Malaika that evening would be a welcome diversion from the madness. Besides, she might know something he didn't.

The weather that morning was bright and sunny, but a little crisp. After his infusion of brain juice and a quick scan of the newspaper, Monroe felt the need to go for a run. A kick-start to stimulate him mentally and physically was in order. Monroe had never been one for running, until basic training. He detested the early activity at first, but once he embraced it, the runs became a ritual after he was discharged. He enjoyed clearing his head in the mornings, no matter the weather. On that day he needed it.

Once on the street, Monroe headed down Maine Avenue, working his way in the direction of Haynes Point. Cherry blossoms adorned the many trees that lined the Ohio Avenue loop. He shouldn't have been surprised by the number of people who had made their way to the area. East Potomac Park was a great location for people trying to exercise, whether it be running, cycling, or walking. The area was also a great place just to hang out and picnic. The public golf course nested within the recreational area was exceptionally crowded due to the gorgeous spring weather.

Tourists also flocked to the area that time of year. Those who tried to drive the route found traffic at a near standstill. The smart ones took the Metro to either L'Enfant Plaza or Waterfront stations and leisurely walked the area. Whatever the intention, it was a great morning to be out and about. Monroe completed his usual 4.1-mile route and headed back to his apartment, stopping by the convenience store in Waterside Mall to pick up a bagel.

By the time he was ready to head out, it was 12:30 p.m. Ambrose had told him that he expected people to start showing up at noon. He also said that they would be winding down around six. Given the social norms of most of the people he knew, Monroe figured that the majority of folks wouldn't make the scene until two or three, which was fine by him. He wanted to have some private time with both Ambrose and Garland. He intended to get there early. It was 1:00 p.m. when he settled behind the wheel of his car to make the drive, which would take between forty-five minutes and an hour.

What should have been a serene drive to Highland Beach was marred by Monroe's racing thoughts. He knew that the police would have additional questions for him. From his interaction with Tyree and Frazier, he got the feeling that they thought he or Gordon, or both of them, could be involved in Dixon's murder. Given Dixon's significant financial investment, that theory made no sense. Despite Monroe's knowledge of his innocence, Gordon's recent behavior raised doubts. Yet, the idea of Gordon wanting Gamers' meal ticket dead seemed beyond reason. But if other motives existed, Monroe was determined to uncover them.

Exiting Route 50 in Annapolis, Monroe steered his vehicle onto Route 655, which led to Highland Beach. While familiar with the name, Monroe had never visited the small enclave that was situated along the Chesapeake Bay. It wasn't until a later chat with Garland that he gained some insight into its history.

Highland Beach was founded in 1893 by Charles and Laura Douglass. Charles was the son of nineteenth-century abolitionist Frederick Douglass. After being denied entrance to the restaurant in a nearby resort based on his race in 1892, Charles became determined to acquire adjacent land. This led to his involvement in the real estate business, the result of a chance encounter with a member of a local Black family, the Brashears, who owned forty-eight acres on the other side of a narrow channel from the resort.

In 1893 Charles Douglass and two of the estate's heirs, Daniel Brashears and Georgianna Lane, settled on the purchase of more than twenty-six acres of land that would become Highland Beach. Initially developed to be a summer retreat, Highland Beach was the oldest of the major resort towns in the US, comprised of Black residents. By 1915 Highland Beach was a year-round community, which was incorporated seven years later.

Throughout much of its existence, the town was the gathering place for an array of prominent Black influencers such as Paul Robeson, WEB DuBois, Langston Hughes, and Alex Haley. Also, many houses and properties were retained by descendants of the original owners. For a variety of reasons, the population of Highland Beach had changed over the years with the number of full-time residents and seasonal visitors much diminished.

Monroe turned onto Bay Highlands Drive, which would take him through another small development called Highlands Bay and ultimately into Highlands Beach. For whatever reason, there was no one at the guard's gate. As he had been instructed by Ambrose, Monroe made a left turn, which took him past the Town Hall, a small wooden building with a large circle-shaped gable window. He drove down Douglass Avenue to get a feel for the area.

It was eerily quiet for a beautiful spring afternoon. Several cars traversed the small, narrow roadways. There were several people doing yard work. Both Highland Beach and the approaching bay were calm. Monroe double-checked his directions and headed toward the address Ambrose had provided. On the way, he passed by the Frederick Douglass Museum and Cultural Center, which was housed in the summer cottage that was built for him. Monroe made a promise to himself that he would come back to visit it. He never did.

Locating the house where the gathering was being held, Monroe was surprised that there was a large gravel area for parking on the property. The structure, like many of the homes in the neighborhood, was wooden. There were two stories and, like the Town Hall building, it had a gable roof, but with two single-hung windows facing the front and two on both sides. The first floor extended well beyond the dimensions of the upper level with multiple horizontal windows on all sides. As he stood before the venerable structure a sudden sense of dread overcame him. Monroe let out a long, heavy sigh. *Let's get this over with.*

20

WALKING UP A BROAD FLIGHT of wooden steps that led to the porch, Monroe arrived at the door and was greeted by the sound of Teddy Pendergrass' "I Don't Love You Anymore." The somewhat muted volume indicated that it was serving more as background music. He knocked on the door once before realizing it was open. Monroe entered and immediately spotted Ambrose, who was across the room helping a very attractive woman move a table.

As the door opened and closed, Ambrose turned, greeting him with a warm smile. Having finished his task, he glided over to offer a handshake and a hug. Suggesting that Monroe have a drink, Ambrose escorted him through a hallway, past the dining room, and into a large adjacent area where people had gathered. While it wasn't meant to be a large affair, there were more people than he had anticipated, among them several high-profile figures.

As usual, Garland was holding court, regaling a small group in all manner of tales. His laugh was unrestrained and coarse. The latter was probably a result of his many years of smoking before he finally gave it up. He was truly reveling in the moment as he motioned Monroe over. Garland offered him an excessively enthusiastic introduction to the huddle of listeners. It was almost to the point that Monroe wanted to look around to see who he was talking about. He greeted each and shared a word before walking over to the makeshift bar to order his usual Jack on the Rocks.

Although he was in the midst of what should have been a pleasurable social activity, all of the turmoil that was surrounding Gamers incessantly nagged at him. Monroe decided to look for a chair near a window so that he could enjoy the light, cool breeze that traveled through the room on what had morphed into a surprisingly warm April day. He took a long sip of his drink and began to succumb to the thoughts of concern that were commanding his attention when Ambrose quietly took a seat next to him. His face carried a stern expression, and in his hand was a perspiring bottle of Heineken that he'd just opened. Ambrose turned to engage Monroe directly.

"Glad you could make it," he said, tapping his right arm.

"This is just what I needed. It's been one helluva week, man," Monroe responded.

"I bet. You guys been goin' through some shit," he said.

"I guess you could say that."

"So, my man, do the police have any idea who killed Dixon?" Ambrose asked with more than a hint of curiosity.

"Nah. To be honest, I don't have a clue about what they know. The detectives investigating the case are being tight-lipped."

"Have you talked with them yet?"

"Yeah. Standard shit. They were trying to rule me out as a person of interest, I suppose."

Ambrose abruptly sat up straight in his chair. He took a long swig of his brew and looked away momentarily, seemingly in search of his next words. He turned back toward Monroe. His eyes darted as if he was trying to locate an elusive thought.

"We should talk," he said, finally breaking his brief silence. "Wait here."

What the fuck? Now Monroe's curiosity was aroused. He was anxious to know where this was heading.

Ambrose returned shortly with a newly opened bottle of beer and a plastic cup with more Jack and ice.

"Let's walk," he said in a somewhat forceful tone while handing Monroe the cup.

Rising from his seat, Monroe poured what was left of his original drink into the one Ambrose had retrieved and set the empty glass on the table next to him. They stepped toward the door, and as Ambrose reached to grab the knob he turned to one of the women who was setting up the food table.

"We're going for a walk. Back in a few," he said.

The woman, whose name was Christine, barely acknowledged him. She seemed focused on her mission. They made their way down the steps and onto Bay Avenue and headed east. Instead of picking up the conversation where they left off, Ambrose delved into the town's history and recounted how Garland's family became property owners. With each house they passed, Ambrose offered up a story about who lived there. It was like he was the resident instead of Garland. Upon reaching Bruce Avenue, they made a left and proceeded toward the water. Despite the tranquil surroundings, Monroe was on edge. A cloud of suspense lingered over him as he awaited Ambrose's words.

The spring foliage was beginning to shadow the road as they trekked. At the end was Blackwater Creek, a serene body of water that flowed into the Chesapeake Bay. A long, wooden walkway led to a modest, squared river deck that held a small bench. Constructed of the same timber as the pathway, each had weathered countless seasons. They walked onto the platform. Monroe took a seat on the bench, while Ambrose leaned back against the railing adjacent to him and immediately unleashed several tales about fishing for crabs in the creek. Monroe felt his tolerance waning. He was ready for Ambrose to get to the point.

"All right, man," he said in a brusque tone. "You said we need to talk, so talk."

"Look here, bro. I don't know what your experience has been in trying to get into this casino business, but it's been fucked up on our end."

"How so?" Monroe responded more calmly.

"One huge problem has been that mothafuckin' Nimbus," he said with his standard disdain. "That punk-ass bitch told us he would make sure that we'd be part of one of the groups, but when all was said and done, he left us out in the cold."

"That sounds like a Nimbus move, but nothing's been awarded yet," Monroe reasoned.

"Yeah, but most of the agreements have been finalized, but that muthafucka told us that between him and somebody he refused to name, could get us into the one backed by Steptoe and Trimble or use your man Gordon's influence with Darnell and Dixon to get us into yours."

"Really?" Monroe said while trying to figure out who was playing who. "Did Nimbus explain how he was going to make that happen?"

"No, but the rumor is that they're going to cannibalize each group and form one made up of the highest bidders. We forked over 50 Gs to make sure that when the music stopped we had a seat."

"Hold up!" Monroe exclaimed, almost choking on his drink. "You and Garland paid Nimbus $50,000?"

"Damn sure did," Ambrose abruptly replied.

"Shit, that's a helluva number, Ambrose." Monroe never doubted that Nimbus was a duplicitous asshole, but fuckin' over Ambrose and Garland could touch off some actions that would have bad outcomes for everyone.

Ambrose continued, "Yeah, and that dusky muthafucka hasn't earned one dime of it. He says that we're good, but we don't have a damn thing in writing. He's also got us in the midst of some bullshit in Africa. But I'm sure you know about that since Gordon's the point man?"

There it is. Monroe tried to feign knowledge that he didn't have. "Just a little. Gordon and I haven't had the chance to have a real conversation with all that's happened," he responded while trying to conceal his surprise and building anger. "What's going on with that?" Monroe asked, knowing that he didn't have a clue.

"Nimbus and his crew have talked about pursuing gambling opportunities in Kenya and, when the ANC takes over, South Africa. With casinos and racetracks already in place, the consensus was that once political conditions were suitable, there was a fortune to be had. A group of us went over to the continent a few weeks ago to check things out. Didn't Gordon bring you up to speed?"

Not wanting to show Ambrose that he was being played, Monroe simply nodded. It was clear that Ambrose and Garland were engaged in a far different game than he was. For that matter, so were Gordon and Dixon. All of them weren't just tiptoeing around the margins; they were overstepping.

Ambrose continued. "But I guess Gordon has bigger fish to fry right now."

"What do you mean?" *There's more?*

"Word on the street is that he's only got days left to find new investors or Vogayer has an escape clause and can bring in new minority partners."

He was right. When they entered their deal with Voyager, Gordon and Monroe had clauses that would allow outs with 30-day notices, if Gamers couldn't meet certain financial obligations. Dixon's death and the loss of his funds met the criteria. To make matters worse, they would walk away with nothing and lose the investment capital that had been put up. The other members of the group would also be free agents in the process.

"I got no envy of Gordon's job," Ambrose continued. "Finding the kind of money he has to come up with on the fly has got to be a bitch."

"No doubt," Monroe responded, taken aback by everything that Ambrose had laid out.

"Too bad that young wife that Dixon's leaving behind won't play ball. I bet she can't wait to get her hands on his cash."

"How do you know that?"

"The grapevine, brotha. You know how people talk," he said with a snicker. "But a word to the wise. You need to watch your back. Somebody's serious about this shit, and Dixon might not be the first to go in all of this."

"Is that a warning or a threat?"

"Neither. It's just common-sense advice. I'm just telling you that somethin' or somebody ain't right, so you need to be careful."

"Appreciate it, Ambrose, but I'm a big boy."

"Monroe, that bravado you spouting don't mean a thing. Greed can push people to extremes. These are some cold-blooded muthafuckas that view you as a threat to be dealt with. My advice is to stay on your toes."

Monroe knew that Ambrose was right. With each shred of news that he learned, he realized his quest for treasure had become a curse and that forces beyond his control were conspiring against him, as he would soon find out.

21

THEY TALKED FOR A FEW MINUTES LONGER before deciding it was time to head back to the gathering. While walking, Ambrose reminded Monroe of his combat background as a Navy Seal, one of the few African Americans who served in that capacity during the '80s. He said that his expertise in marksmanship and close-quarters combat might serve him well in dealing with Nimbus' crew if they tried to screw him. There was no doubt that Nimbus was living in his mind, and he wasn't smiling when he imparted that veiled threat. Monroe was sure glad that he had stayed on Ambrose's good side. He could see the crazy in his eyes, and as events played out, he would be keeping an eye on him.

Just as they reached the house, Garland saw them and came over and lightened the mood. But for just a brief moment after Ambrose informed him that he had brought Monroe up to speed, a look of restrained anger briefly occupied Garland's face. It was apparent that he co-signed the feelings expressed by Ambrose. Quickly recasting himself back into affable host mode, he insisted that Monroe get another drink and enjoy the food and good company.

While socializing with a minimum of enthusiasm, Monroe found ways to steal a few quiet moments to unpack everything Ambrose had shared. While there was a lot that remained unknown to him, several pieces of the puzzle were beginning to come together. But even those few details couldn't prepare him for what lay ahead.

Monroe continued to rub shoulders for another hour or so before deciding it was time to head back to the city. Before leaving, Garland and Ambrose proposed meeting up with him and Gordon as soon as it could be arranged. Not knowing their intentions or what they hoped to gain from huddling with Gordon, Monroe saw it as an opportunity to uncover more facts, which could play to his advantage. He readily agreed to do so.

The more he learned, the more Monroe's instincts told him that unshackling himself from Gamers' operation and coming clean to the police was the smartest thing he could do. The chaos threatening to engulf him was the last thing he needed. But then again, since he'd been kept out of the loop regarding the group's recent activities, the choice to stay or leave might not be his to make if Gordon couldn't come up with the necessary cash or chose another path. Monroe was beginning to warm to the idea of distancing himself from the insanity. Sure, he would have squandered a lot of time and some money, but given his lifestyle, he believed he could handle that setback without much trouble.

But something Ambrose revealed struck a nerve. It sounded as if an agreement had been reached among the key players, rapidly narrowing the field of aspiring tycoons. But he also sensed that Garland and Ambrose were in better shape than even they realized. Nimbus was at least keeping them up to speed regarding whatever was being cooked up in Africa. But his tendency to double-cross

131

posed a threat. The trip to Highland Beach had been worth it. He knew a lot more, but he still had much more to uncover.

Monroe gave Malaika a call from his recently installed Motorola car phone. State of the art at the time, it had become an indispensable tool. While he still harbored reservations about the motives of the executives at her company, he was becoming enamored with her. But given everything that was going on, he would still have to be careful about what he disclosed. Monroe needed a confidante to talk things through and wanted it to be her, but he couldn't take that risk just yet. Little did he know that wasn't even in his control.

During their brief exchange, Malaika left the planning for the evening up to Monroe, which was what he was hoping for. He hoped to provide her with a special experience and had just the place in mind. Monroe suggested that she swing by his place at 6:30. This would give them time to have a couple of drinks and enjoy a few quiet moments before taking a taxi to their destination. Spending some time with Malaika would be a pleasant diversion.

Monroe walked through his apartment door just before 5:30, which gave him more than enough time to shower and get dressed before Malaika's arrival. His cleaning service, comprised of a Latina mother and daughter team, had come through while he was gone. The place was immaculate. One minute before their appointed time he received the alert that a guest was at the rear entrance. Monroe picked up. It was Malaika. He buzzed her in. Anticipation tingled through his veins, with each passing second feeling like an eternity. A swarm of butterflies fluttered within him, their delicate wings creating a wave of nervous excitement as he awaited her knock on the door. Taken aback by this rush of emotions, he briefly searched for what it meant—that was until he opened the door.

Malaika looked stunning. His only utterance was one word.

"Wow!"

"You like?" she sensuously purred.

"You never disappoint, do you?" he added, noticing that a garment bag and tote accompanied.

"I hope you don't mind, but I took the liberty to pack a few things. I thought that rather than drive home later, I could just stay over."

Is ice cold? "I was thinking the same thing, but I didn't want to get ahead of myself."

"I figured as much, so I thought I'd take the initiative," she said, flashing her brilliant smile.

Monroe offered her a seat and a glass of wine. They sat around and talked about almost everything that wasn't work-related. They also exchanged various forms of expressed and implied affection. After about an hour, hunger interrupted, so Monroe and Malaika headed out to make the walk through the complex to Maine Avenue. It didn't take them long to get a taxi, and in a little more than twelve minutes they were pulling up to Restaurant Nora located at Florida Avenue and 21st Street NW, unaware that dinner wouldn't be the only thing served that evening.

22

LTHOUGH IT WAS NEAR EMBASSY ROW and a commercial strip along Connecticut Avenue, the restaurant was relatively isolated in that it was the sole establishment within a couple of blocks in any direction. Nora, named after founder Nora Pouillon, an Austrian-born, self-trained chef, opened its doors in 1979. Restaurant Nora was organic before organic became a thing. Its touted reputation among food critics wasn't just due to the quality of its dishes; it was also celebrated for the use of mostly natural, pesticide-free ingredients sourced from local farmers. The eatery's seasonal menu attracted a devoted following of food connoisseurs. Since this was Malaika's first experience, Monroe was pleased with his choice. He had become aware of the place during a surprise birthday celebration arranged by an ex-girlfriend. Once it was on his radar screen, Monroe became an admirer and a semi-regular visitor.

The food was top-notch, as was the people-watching given the eatery's popularity with political and media personalities. After a short wait at the bar, Monroe and Malaika were escorted to a corner table in a discreet spot. The soft glow of candlelight provided a dim ambiance that was perfect for intimate dialogue. No sooner than they had been seated and their drinks placed on the table, a waiter appeared, describing the specials. Both Monroe and Malaika were famished, and each ordered the seafood entree.

The murmur of hushed conversations and the clinking of silverware against porcelain plates enveloped them. Waiters, clad in crisp black and white uniforms, glided seamlessly between tables, balancing trays loaded with mouthwatering gourmet dishes that filled the room with appetizing aromas. Following about ten minutes of pleasant conversation, the waiter returned with their meals. Their lively banter took on a slower but upbeat pace.

As they were taking their last bites, Malaika's demeanor turned a little more serious. Her dark eyes flickered with a mixture of determination and concern. She delicately sipped her wine while carefully searching for her words. A feeling of unease began to stir within Monroe as he observed her with a guarded expression. His gaze occasionally shifted to the bustling activity around them as he awaited her words. Just as she was about to speak, a waiter appeared to ensure their needs were being met. Monroe politely assured the server that things were fine. With the waiter within earshot, Malaika had skillfully steered the conversation toward a subject of innocence. Yet their words, disguised beneath the guise of normalcy, danced on the edge of the ominous revelation she was about to share.

"Monroe, I believe that the casino project is about to go in a direction that none of us counted on," Malaika said, her voice low and measured. "And there's something you need to know." She glanced around discreetly, ensuring their conversation remained shielded from prying ears. A pair of waiters passed by, their attention focused on delivering a lavish platter to a nearby table. Monroe leaned in, his expression sharpening with anticipation. Malaika continued, her words punctuated by the distant hum of background chatter and workers weaving between tables in synchronized chaos, their movements swift and purposeful.

"As much as we're friendly competitors, there's a darker game being played. Members of your group are being targeted and eliminated one by one. It's no secret that Gamers had the best proposal and overall deal. So to some of the other players, your group has to be discredited or eliminated."

"Go on," replied Monroe who was captivated.

"It goes beyond a business rivalry, Monroe. These people have political ties, and they're not fooling around."

The gravity of her words hung in the air as their discussion unfolded amidst the orchestrated activity of the restaurant. Monroe found it ironic that Malaika's disclosure, which held ominous undertones, was taking place in such a sophisticated setting. The line between business and danger was blurred, much like the shadows that flickered across the room.

As Malaika was delivering the unsettling news, a live jazz band in the corner filled the air with smooth melodies. The soft notes of the piano and mellow sounds of the sax created an interesting backdrop to the tension-filled exchange. Monroe, whose expression had taken on a mix of surprise and concern, looked around carefully to confirm that no eavesdropping was occurring. The restaurant was ideal as a sanctuary for such covert discussions.

"I wouldn't bring this up if it weren't serious, but the shit can hit the fan quickly," Malaika proceeded, her gaze unwavering. "I haven't quite figured it all out and neither have my colleagues. But there some diabolical bullshit going on and we all need to be cautious. Right now, anyone connected with Gamers appears to be in jeopardy. You've already lost Dixon, and other investors are throwing in the towel. But tomorrow it could be our group that's in the crossfire."

As the band transitioned to a soulful rendition of a classic jazz standard, the setting continued to mask the gravity of their conversation. Yet, the shadows seemed to deepen around them, casting a foreboding contour that extended beyond Nora's ornate walls. Monroe nodded, his mind already processing the implications of Malaika's words. The lively atmosphere clashed with their hushed conversation, adding an edge to the moment that bound their partnership to the dangerous road ahead.

A waiter approached with a silver tray that contained two more drinks. He also presented a dessert menu, momentarily distracting them from their conversation. While Monroe couldn't shake off the impact of Malaika's words, he did want to enjoy the remainder of his time with her, so he pronounced that all talk of work, casinos, and politics were off of the table for the remainder of the evening out. They could continue their discussion and compare notes later.

After what both agreed was an excellent meal and conversation that entertained and disconcerted, they headed down to U Street to hear more music at Utopia. As they were getting into the taxi he had hailed, Monroe noticed two men standing at the corner on Florida Avenue. He thought he had seen them when he and Malaika arrived. But he could have been mistaken, so he thought nothing more of it. After an hour or so at Utopia, Monroe and Malaika headed to his place. From the time they entered, clothes were coming off and in no time they were ravishing each other. All thoughts of danger disappeared.

Monroe awoke a little after 9 a.m. Malaika was still asleep but beginning to stir. He washed up and proceeded to the kitchen to make coffee and to prepare something light for breakfast. While the brew was dripping, he ran back into the bedroom to see if Malaika was up. She was and they made love again. Monroe had always enjoyed morning sex, and it was even better when it was with someone he had a connection with. Not wanting to be late for church, Malaika hurriedly arose from the bed. He handed her a cup of coffee and the bag she had requested as she was entering the bathroom.

Monroe went to the door to retrieve the Sunday *Post* that he had delivered weekly. He grabbed his mug from the kitchen counter and settled on the sofa to catch up on the news. He tried to concentrate, but his mind continually drifted toward Malaika. He was smitten. Monroe hadn't been in a steady relationship for a while and wasn't sure if he was ready to take the plunge again. But he was putting the cart before the horse. He didn't have a clue as to Malaika's desires or intentions, so he needed to slow down.

While reading the paper, he looked for any news on Dixon's murder. Crickets mostly. While there was a brief follow-up article, it provided little information that wasn't already known. The article did say that more would be released by the police as the investigation progressed. In the meantime, the MPD was asking anyone who had any information regarding the crime to contact them immediately. Also, there was a reward of $50,000 for information that would lead to the capture of his killer. *I wonder if the widow put the money up.*

Not satisfied, Monroe headed to the den and fired up his computer. Maybe one of the local papers had something new about Dixon's murder. He was sure the Black crime rag, *The Evening Whirl*, would, but they weren't online. Lucky for him, he had brought several editions with him from St. Louis, including the latest one. He'd dig into those later. For now, he scrolled through the *St. Louis Post-Dispatch* and the *Riverfront Times*. Both had articles mentioning

Dixon and the casino project, but there wasn't anything he didn't already know.

The *Riverfront Times* piece did toss out some speculation that Dixon's death might shake up the casino project. It also hinted that Dixon's widow wanted no part in continuing the effort. That made him wonder—what had Gordon heard? And, more importantly, what was he thinking?

After thirty minutes or so of searching for info on Dixon, Malaika emerged from the bedroom, and Monroe's eyes were diverted toward her. *Sexy church girl.* She wondered aloud why Monroe didn't offer to go with her. He told her that he didn't do Baptist. The last thing he needed was somebody "hollerin'" at him and then asking for money. She laughed. Malaika had parked on N Street, directly in the back of the building. Monroe quickly threw on something and walked her to the car. They embraced and shared a short, passionate kiss. She told him that she would say a prayer for him. And as things were transpiring, he would need that one and more.

23

S ITTING ALONE IN HIS APARTMENT after an eventful night with Malaika, Monroe found himself consumed by thoughts of Gordon's apparent dishonesty. Despite fatigue from a sleepless night, he was determined to uncover more answers since Gordon would be coming to town the next day. Deciding not to waste the rest of his Sunday stewing over his so-called associate, Monroe set his sights on the Martin Luther King Library at 9th and G NW. It had better research options and faster computers than the tiny branch near his apartment—the perfect place to dig into the questions that still haunted him. After a quick workout at the gym in his complex and a hearty lunch, he left at 12:45, timing it perfectly to arrive as the library opened its doors at 1 p.m.

The library was a modernist structure made of steel and glass, with a distinctive black granite facade that had been completed in the early '70s. The building contained four floors above ground with three situated below, with the lowest floor dedicated for parking. Monroe entered through the main entrance on the G Street promenade. Once in, he made a quick left for the reading room, which held a bank of computers. Quickly settling in, Monroe wanted to learn as much about the players in the expanding enterprise as he could. Maybe then their motives would become clearer.

One question that nagged him was the purpose of their junket to Botswana, Lesotho, and Swaziland, which is now known as Eswatini. It took only a few moments of digging. It had to be casinos. All three countries offered legalized gambling. Botswana had two relatively large properties, Gaborone Sun Hotel & Casino and the Grand Palm Hotel & Casino, while Lesotho and Swaziland maintained smaller operations. The other thing they had in common was that Botswana and Swaziland bordered South Africa and Lesotho lay within it. While Monroe was sure that Hancock and his conspirators were seeking opportunities in all three countries, everything he was learning suggested that South Africa had to be the ultimate prize.

The Republic of South Africa had legalized gambling in the Bantustans, which were nominally independent states created by the apartheid government, as well as in the so-called "White" areas of the country in the '70s. This included the Sun City Luxury Resort & Casino in the Bantustan of Bophuthatswana, which was open and extremely profitable. By the start of the '90s, more than 1,500 illegal casinos were also operating within the country.

While making sense of the information he was gathering, Monroe remembered that he had a friend, Clifford Basham, who had worked in the US Embassy in Lesotho in the '80s. He took a break to find a pay phone and gave him a call. Clifford had become a big shot of some sort at an international nonprofit and still played on the global stage. Fortunately, he was at home and was happy to share his thoughts with Monroe. The call to Clifford proved to be valuable. He was a wealth of information. But the biggest nugget he shared was a rumor that had been verified by his sources. Once the African

National Congress (ANC) took over the government they were going to legalize all gambling, especially since horse race betting had been legal since the '60s.

That's it! Hancock, who was steeped in the intricacies of African politics, would have been aware of the party leadership's secret decision. A silent and influential architect, he aimed to lend a hand in someone's bid to establish a footprint on that part of the continent. The hastily planned expedition whispered its ambitions, avoiding the watchful eyes of public scrutiny. The trip's concealed existence stood in stark contrast to the high-profile and well-documented global jaunts routinely taken by lawmakers.

After hanging up with Clifford, Monroe made several phone calls to contacts in St. Louis and the State Department in Washington. He learned that in addition to Hancock's usual hangers-on—Nimbus, Steptoe, and Prigmore—Gordon and Dixon were also included. Garland and Ambrose made the trip as well, but they traveled under separate itineraries to avoid any suspicion. As much as Monroe hated to admit it, this disparate confederacy would have been unthinkable to him mere days ago. Yet, a conspiracy of some sort appeared real, and money was at the center of it.

Monroe also dove into finding out what Hancock had been up to before the trip. He ran upon several articles related to his involvement in several issues of local concern. He also found two items that briefly mentioned Hancock's "fact-finding" mission to Southern Africa. Neither contained any real details of the trip other than the names of the countries he would be visiting and background information he already knew. He also came up empty when looking into the others.

Monroe reached into his bag to retrieve the copies of the *Evening Whirl* he had brought back from St. Louis, but hadn't read. While he had always enjoyed the paper's content, especially the over-the-top headlines, he figured that they might yield some valuable information. But since it's published on Mondays, there would be no news about Dixon's murder. However, when he opened the latest edition a headline in the lower right section of the front page jumped out at him. "Fuzz Put Black Capone in Hot Seat."

Accompanying the story was a photo of Chauncey Prigmore. The image was an early mugshot of Prig when he was probably in his twenties. The article described what police believed was an effort to bribe officials as the future of the downtown casino development project was being considered by the city. While there was no evidence that pointed to his guilt, the article revealed that he'd been caught on tape discussing ways to influence the people who would be making the decision. *Well, this just keeps getting better.*

What Monroe was learning triggered several thoughts. He knew that he needed to challenge Gordon, but with the details he was uncovering, he needed to be strategic about it. With Gordon arriving the next day, Monroe knew he'd have his chance—and this time, he'd be ready to press him. It was time to find out whether Gordon would finally come clean or keep dancing around the truth. While his ultimate goal was to find out who had killed Dixon, he wanted to take his time and get it right. Monroe also had to stay under Tyree's and Frazier's radar. He was sure that in their minds, he was still a person of interest.

Monroe felt a surge of exasperation. Following Dixon's murder and several revealing conversations, he was convinced that he was being handled. Determined to seize the moment during their meeting with Gordon at Union Station, he had gathered what he believed was a clear picture that would help him get to the bottom of what he viewed to be a fucked-up situation. He was intent on taking advantage of their time together. Packing his things, he set off for home, to devise a strategy for his showdown with Gordon, and finally get some quality sleep.

No sooner than he hit the door of his apartment his phone rang. His caller ID revealed that it was Gordon on the other end. He picked up almost immediately.

"Hello."

"What's happening, Monroe? Gordon casually offered.

"It's your world. What's up with you?" Monroe responded.

Gordon peppered Monroe with more questions about his meeting in Hancock's office. He was almost obsessive in asking about his impressions of Jerome Buford and Cleo Hancock, in particular. Monroe found that curious since he hadn't gotten around to telling him that she had attended the meeting. That meant that he'd gotten that tidbit from someone else on Hancock's staff or even Hancock himself, which was more likely.

Given all that he'd learned, Monroe felt that he was the one that should be asking the questions. But Gordon was unusually chatty, so he gave him the floor. Gordon was also eager to talk about Dixon's murder. He claimed ignorance when it came to knowing anyone who would want to hurt his wealthy partner. He also went out of his way to make it clear to Monroe that he didn't have a reason to see Dixon dead. It was like Gordon was using him as practice for the police.

After a brief silence, Monroe's demeanor and tone took a sharp and sober turn. "Okay, Gordon, what the fuck is going on?"

"What do you mean?" he asked.

"You know damn well what I'm talking about. You take a trip to Africa on gaming business, you start lining yourself up with Nimbus and his crew, and you're cutting deals with God knows who, all while leaving me in the dark."

"Let me tell you something," Gordon sternly retorted. "First, the Africa trip included several different deals we were looking at, and not just gaming. Two, given the situation I'm in regarding investors, I'm talking to anyone and everyone. And three, you're just a *tiny* part of all of this."

"Tiny?" Monroe said, with both surprise and anger. "All of the work that I put in, draining my savings in the process, and that's how you see things?"

"Afraid so, brother. As they say, nothing personal, just business," Gordon coldly added.

Taken aback by his partner's disrespectful tone, Monroe fumed but knew he had to keep his cool. He didn't want to let Gordon in on the fact that he knew more than he might expect. Adding to Monroe's suspicions was that he knew that Gordon was seeking new investors and that he knew that his denial of working with Ambrose and Garland was false. Dixon had gone on the Africa trip, so the investors for whatever this ring of greed was cooking up were set. Ambrose's admission of traveling with Garland to meet Gordon's group overseas was beyond question.

While Monroe continued to pursue answers, Gordon remained evasive. Complicating Monroe's effort to get at the truth was the repeated interruptions by one of Gordon's kids. Monroe resigned himself that he had gotten everything he could to that point. Before testily concluding his conversation with Gordon, Monroe confirmed his arrival information. He wanted to be there when Gordon got off the train. Gordon's arrogance struck a nerve with Monroe, and in his mind the battle of wills was just beginning, even if it proved to be brief.

24

MONROE WRESTLED WITH THE INSIGHTS he had uncovered over the previous thirty-six hours. He needed to figure out how he should use it all to his advantage. One thing was for certain: he had nothing to lose. Mentally, he had already checked out of the Gamers' project and would be completely done once he and Gordon cleared the air. He was also determined to find out who killed Dixon, all the while wondering if the same fate awaited him. With each passing hour, another shoe seemed to drop. But the game he was entering wasn't for the faint of heart. He'd just have to deal with it.

Monroe struggled to figure out Gordon's end game. All this time, he thought he and Gordon were on the same page about many things, but with the way matters had been unfolding, it seemed that was just an act. Although he could use the sleep, Monroe was restless. As he tossed and turned, one thing that was for sure occupied his mind, a misunderstanding of grand proportions was going to break out at the first sight of Gordon.

After a fitful night, Monroe arose early, worked out, and caught up on the news. There was nothing new on the Dixon front. Gordon's train would be arriving at 11:15 a.m., and he wanted to make sure that he would be at the Amtrak terminal waiting area when Gordon entered. Armed with a large coffee, Monroe nabbed a seat at the boarding and disembarking gate that Metroliner passengers use about ten minutes before the train's scheduled arrival. The adrenaline was pumping. Monroe was anxious to see if the arrogance that Gordon had flashed during their last call had traveled with him to DC.

Lost in thought, time passed quickly. It was now 11:40 and passengers from Gordon's train had yet to step into the station. It was nothing new for an Amtrak train to be late as they navigated the Northeast Corridor; it was always congested. But in looking at the monitor, he saw no indication of a delay or any other issue. Monroe felt his frustrations mounting. He knew that this unexpected disruption would only escalate his already simmering anger.

Suddenly, a group of paramedics rushed through the corridor that separated the gate and concourse areas from the train platforms. They were quickly followed by a crew of three men and one woman dressed in navy blue coveralls with the letters CSI emblazoned on the back. In short order, a group of MPD and Metro transit officers rushed through the crowd. Several uniformed officers began to section off the area using yellow crime scene tape and forcing bystanders, including Monroe, away from the entrance.

Several members of the media had magically descended upon the scene and were trying to get questions answered, which further added to the confusion. The designated entrance had been closed, and passengers arriving on Gordon's train were being spirited through a passageway two gates over, which was away from the commotion.

Gordon was nowhere to be seen, and Monroe wanted to find out what was happening.

A long line of emerging travelers made their way through the doors, some anxiously discussing an incident that had occurred on board. Still no sign of Gordon. Monroe approached a man in a gray suit who seemed somewhat flustered. Scurrying to get to his destination, the man paused just long enough to mention that a passenger had been found dead in the train car's bathroom. If true, the general assumption would be that the passenger's death was by natural causes. Monroe's first thought was that the bathroom on a train is a helluva place to die.

The steady influx into the terminal had slowed to a trickle and Monroe had yet to spot Gordon. Maybe he had slipped past him somehow. But if that was the case it would seem to reason that he would be waiting around somewhere nearby since they were scheduled to meet. That is unless Gordon was purposely trying to avoid him. After waiting a few more moments, Monroe decided to go out into the station's Main Hall to see if he might be there.

But as he walked toward the doorway, his curiosity got the best of him. Monroe altered his course and meandered over to the restricted area. Working his way through the crowd that had gathered he tried to get a glimpse of all of the comings and goings. Suddenly, two familiar figures walked hurriedly on the same path as the others. Although he shouldn't have been surprised, the men were Tyree and Frazier. Monroe knew enough to know that he should probably leave the premises, otherwise things for him might not end up well. Just as he turned to make his escape he was spotted by Tyree.

"You!" he shouted.

Realizing that if he ignored Tyree and kept walking he would create a scene, Monroe slowly turned and made eye contact with the detective. Pointing directly at Monroe, Tyree shouted, "Come here!"

"Me?" Monroe responded, placing his index finger toward his chest and striking a pose of innocence.

"Yes, you!" he responded even more tersely.

Shit! Monroe slowly ambled over. His face was plastered with dread.

Tyree met him just as he approached the crime tape that had been strewn from the gate entrance to the front of one of the stores that were situated across from the sitting area. He then raised the tape for Monroe to come under where he came face to face with the unflinching investigator. Frazier was busy talking to others who were nearby. Monroe still had no idea why they had pulled him out of the crowd.

Looking him up and down in a manner that oozed suspicion, Tyree gruffly asked Monroe, "What are you doing here?"

Monroe's first thought was to say none of your business, but common sense suggested that he not piss Tyree off. "I'm here to pick up my partner, Gordon Blackwell. He and I had a meeting scheduled.

"Did you know that he was meeting with us this afternoon?

"Yeah, he mentioned it," Monroe answered.

"So you two were going to get your stories straight before we got a hold of him?"

"Nothing like that. We had business to discuss."

Giving Monroe another look of skepticism, he said, "Uh-huh. Why don't you go over to that area on the other side of the tape and wait? Don't move until I get back."

Monroe turned, slowly ducked under the tape, and retreated over to a seat in the gate area that was being cleared out and guarded by

149

uniformed officers. He sat there finishing his now almost cold coffee and wondering what Tyree and Frazier wanted with him. Monroe had little doubt that his and Gordon's activities in St. Louis kept them on the radar regarding Dixon's murder. While he was gaining a lot of intel each day, he was well aware of the fact that the cops probably knew a lot more. A lot of people make the mistake of thinking that they're smarter when dealing with the police. Monroe wasn't going to take either lawman lightly.

As Monroe sat there, he kept an eye out for Gordon, though he doubted Gordon could get past the guards with the area sealed off. He resigned himself, knowing he was stuck until he finished up with Tyree and Frazier. One thing was certain: With homicide detectives on the scene, it was clear that whatever happened on the train was more than a random death. So he sat and waited, unaware that detectives and investigators from the medical examiner's office were on board the train, diligently taking photographs and gathering evidence for their probe and autopsy. For him, time seemed to drag on. After about an hour, Tyree and Frazier came into view, walking toward him.

"We need you to go with us," said Tyree without any hesitation.

Monroe offered no resistance. The trio made the short walk down the concourse and got on the escalator toward the station's secondary Metro entrance, which had been closed because of police activity. A station attendant who was standing outside of the booth near the fare gates noticed them approaching and opened the emergency entry and exit gate. They strode through and exited using the narrow entryway that led to First Street NE.

Police officers had formed a barricade, blocking access to that side of the facility, as a throng of reporters attempted to gather information. With the help of the patrolmen, the three men were escorted to a white 1993 unmarked Ford Taurus. Monroe was directed to get into the back seat. Frazier jumped in behind the wheel with Tyree riding shotgun. He quickly maneuvered the vehicle through the chaos and in no time they were off to MPD headquarters.

25

A PLAIN CONCRETE STRUCTURE that was built in 1941 during the New Deal, the Henry Daley Building, was clearly showing its age. Frazier drove right up to the front and secured a space designated for detectives. Tyree turned and looked at Monroe. He waved his hand as if to say "follow me." They entered the building. The security guards exchanged knowing glances and nods with Monroe's escorts as they made an immediate left and proceeded down the hall to a waiting elevator at its end. Upon exiting the elevator, they turned right and walked until the second door on the left was reached.

Leading the way, Tyree guided the men into a squad area that was abuzz with activity. Almost instantaneously, a quiet descended upon the room, and eyes followed the trio as they made their way to an adjacent interview room. Upon arriving at their destination, Frazier opened the door and instructed Monroe to go inside and sit down, explaining that they needed to gather some paperwork and would return shortly. Monroe took a seat in one of the metal folding chairs facing the door. Ever since his experience in Nam, Monroe had never been one to sit with his back to the door.

The windowless room itself was plain with spartan furniture that had seen more of its share of wear and tear. The only adornment was a recorder. The upper half of the wall was painted white and was separated from the drab fungus-green lower half by a maple-colored chair rail. As he would soon learn, the walls were soundproofed as a means of keeping annoying noises from interrupting any questioning and subduing any screams. Monroe was sure that a lot of people would take exception to that notion.

The detectives had been gone more than half an hour and Monroe was restless. He came very close to just walking out of the door but decided he wanted to get the questioning over with. After roughly ten more minutes the two men returned. Both were carrying spiraled notebooks and severe looks. Each abruptly took seats, opened their organizers, and almost in unison moved their chairs closer to him. For what seemed like an eternity, there were no words spoken, just stares. But Monroe was determined not to be intimidated.

He'd always operated under the belief that when in a verbal stalemate whoever spoke first lost. But after taking his circumstances into account, he broke the silence. "Quit beating around the bush, Detectives. If you got a point to make or question to ask, get to it."

"I'm glad to see you're in the mood to talk," said Tyree. "Did you see the stretcher with a body bag slapped on top that rolled by you back at the train station?"

"Yeah, so?"

"That was your boy, Blackwell."

"What?" Monroe blurted in disbelief.

"That was his body found in the bathroom in one of the train's toilets."

"How did he die?" Monroe asked.

Tyree and Frazier eyed each other as if to say "here we go again." "Right now we don't have a clue. One of the paramedics said it looked like natural causes, but we won't know anything until his remains are checked out by the medical examiner and we get a preliminary finding, which should be soon," he responded.

"Natural causes?" Monroe asked. "I never heard him complain about anything. He was kind of a health nut."

"That's what we heard too. Funny thing, though. His wallet was missing and there were no other documents on him. That tells me that someone was trying to hide something."

"If he had a bag of any kind, that was gone too," added Frazier. "Fortunately we had a photo of him as a person of interest in the Dixon investigation, so we were able to ID him on the spot."

"Dixon investigation?" Monroe uttered.

"Yeah, you know the one where we're trying to find out who killed your business partner," Tyree interjected sarcastically. "Now your boy Blackwell is dead and my nostrils tell me that something smells."

"And there wasn't a visible gunshot wound or any sign of strangulation," Frazier disclosed. "But I suspect we could have another homicide on our hands."

"Hold up!" Monroe exclaimed. "Killed? You mean to tell me that you think Gordon was murdered?"

"Fraid so, Sport," Tyree said. The seasoned cops gave Monroe a minute to take it all in with their intense gaze laser-focused on him. Silence enveloped the room. After collecting his thoughts, Monroe slowly raised his head. He knew Tyree and Frazier were making things up on the fly since any official findings hadn't been leaked. He decided to see if he could get a rise out of them.

"Let's say he was murdered. I'm the last person who would want him dead."

"Hold up, Chief," said Tyree. "You're putting the cart before the horse. Blackwell's corpse just showed up. Now we've got two dead bodies and one link—you. So don't try to play all innocent and shit."

"Just trying to be up front," Monroe quickly retorted.

"I know your kind. Think because you got a law degree that we're just dumbass cops. We'll know one way or the other real soon. And while we don't have any suspects, we have more than a fair share of persons of interest, and you're at the top of the list."

Monroe was now restless and decided it was time to push back. "Well, *Detective,* I'd have to be a damn magician to have killed Gordon, because I was home and not on the train," he said in a tone that dripped in sarcasm.

That caused Tyree to bounce from his chair and toward Monroe. Menacingly hovering over him, Tyree pointed his forefinger toward Monroe as if it were a weapon. "Don't fuck with me, boy! I'll put my foot ankle-deep in your ass and won't lose one goddam minute of sleep over it," he growled.

Frazier was fighting trying to suppress a laugh, but snickered. "If I were you and weren't involved, I'd worry less about who killed your friends and more about watching your back."

"So you think I'm in danger?" Monroe asked in an almost cynical tone, although he knew damn well that Frazier was telling the truth. He may have been one of the least important players, but many people outside the group didn't know it.

"I wouldn't make any long-term plans," Tyree grunted. "And let me say one more thing: If at the end of the day we find you under this pile of shit, you're going to pay big time. I can promise you that."

Monroe's first inclination was to tell both to go fuck themselves, but he decided against it. Instead, he just let Tyree's words dissolve into the silence without a response. But they weren't finished. For the next three hours, Tyree and Frazier bombarded him with questions ranging from his first encounters with Gordon and Dixon to details about the casino project. They had covered most of that ground before, but Monroe was sure that the two gumshoes were trying to see if his answers stayed consistent.

They also wanted details about the remaining investors in Gordon's group, and how well he knew members of other organizations competing for the gaming contract. They even did a deep dive into his relationships with the family and friends of both Gordon and Dixon. As they went through this ritual, Monroe came to realize that he knew very little about Gordon or Dixon.

Tyree and Frazier continued their interrogation, repeatedly asking Monroe the same questions with slight variations. Frustrated and weary, Monroe felt that this alleged interview had run its course. He had nothing more to contribute, at least nothing he was willing to share. Unexpectedly, there was a knock on the door and a female officer entered. Walking over to Tyree, she handed him a brown letter-sized envelope. The officer left as suddenly as she had arrived. Tyree laid the packet on the table, and the eyes of all three men were fixated on it. Monroe's first thought? *It's on now.*

26

STILLNESS BLANKETED THE ROOM where accusations and denials had been vigorously exchanged. With his eyes casting a look of mistrust toward Monroe, Tyree slowly slid the envelope toward him. Picking it up, he began to unravel the string that secured the packet's button holder. Reaching inside he removed a sheet of white paper. As he perused it the brow over his right eye arched. Looking at Monroe, he passed the note over to Frazier.

"Well, well, well," Tyree said with a trace of satisfaction in his voice. Redirecting his eyes toward Frazier, he continued. "It looks like we might have ourselves another murder investigation."

Weighing in, Frazier offered, "Now this just got interesting."

"How so?" Monroe asked

"The ME was ready to declare Mr. Blackwell's death a heart attack—that was until they found what they determined to be a small needle mark in his neck. They're doing toxicology tests as we speak. For now, the ME will label the manner of death as "Undetermined," but I'd bet cash money that Blackwell was murdered by injection."

"They also found impressions of what appeared to be a taser on his shirt and traces of burn marks on the side of his body," said Tyree. "That would seem to show that he was incapacitated before he was injected."

"Still doesn't have anything to do with me," Monroe asserted.

"Maybe, maybe not," Tyree shot back. "There's all kinds of ways to be involved in a murder, and the way I see it, you got plenty of motive. Know this, we're just getting started."

Reaching back into the envelope, Tyree pulled out what appeared to be a photo.

"Okay, my man, for the record, do you recognize this person?"

Taking the photo from the detective, Monroe gazed at it intently. Gordon was positioned on a long metal table. His body lay bare with only a sheet covering the lower half of his body. "That's him," he replied.

"Who?" countered Tyree, wanting Monroe to utter the name since the session was being recorded.

"Gordon Blackwell," he affirmed.

"Now was that so hard?" asked Frazier as their attention toward Monroe intensified.

It was approaching six hours since Monroe had entered police headquarters. He was hungry, spent, and pissed. He hadn't even been offered a sandwich or soda from one of the nearby vending machines. He'd had enough and was ready to go, but he got the sense that they were just getting started.

Monroe knew he had to remain composed. One wrong word said or any physical tell would be misconstrued. He had to take control to get out of there. He hadn't done anything, at least by commission, and they had no evidence of a crime on his part. He knew that they had no reason to hold him. So Monroe decided to call their bluff.

"Here's the deal, *Officers.* First, let's get a couple of things straight. Yes, the three of us were business partners, but like I told you in every way possible, I only became familiar with Dixon about three or four months ago, and while Gordon and I had become friends, I'd known him for less than a year. And as far as money, my stake in this wasn't large, only about five percent."

"Yeah, but that's still a lot of dough," chimed in Frazier.

"It is. But it's not worth goin' to jail or dyin' for," Monroe quickly responded.

"To be quite honest, I think you're bullshittin' us," said Tyree.

"*Gentlemen*," he said, with a subtle edge in his tone. "I have one solid alibi and another that should also be good. If you took the time to think about it, without Dixon and Gordon, absent of a miracle, the deal that we were working on is dead."

"Well maybe they were going to cut you out and you got your panties in a bunch and decided to take 'em out," said Frazier.

"Enough of this bullshit!" Gimme a lie detector test," Monroe said angrily.

"Are you sure you want to do that?" asked Frazier.

"I didn't stutter, did I?"

Frazier and Tyree quizzically eyeballed each other and retreated from the room. Moments later a polygraph expert entered and began to hook Monroe up. The fact that he appeared on the scene so quickly was a sign that they were going to ask him to take one at some point. But by beating them to the punch it threw them off guard. After completing the test and a ten-minute wait, Tyree and Frazier reentered the room.

"Well, Mr. Gray, it looks like you passed the test," said Tyree with a grunt.

Game, set, match. Monroe began to gather his things to leave when Tyree added, "Not so fast, Ace."

"What now?" Monroe asked testily. His patience had worn beyond thin, and Tyree's ongoing disrespect by not using his name only added to his rising annoyance.

"It seems that you showed some deception on the question of whether you arranged for Blackwell and Dixon to be killed."

"Deception? Get the fuck out of here."

"This isn't a joke," said Frazier.

Fed up at that point, Monroe donned his jacket and headed for the door. "Unless you're going to charge me with something, I'm outta here." He opened the door and turned back to look at the two men. "When you get serious and want to see if I can help, give me a call. Right now, I'm going home. I've got things to do. You both have a nice mothafuckin' evening!"

Stepping out of police headquarters, Monroe welcomed the cool evening breeze as it gently brushed against his face. It was a refreshing contrast to the stale confines he'd just left. The sun was dipping below the horizon, and dusk was casting a soft, calming glow over the city. Monroe chose to walk the thirty minutes back to his apartment, hoping that the solitude and the rhythmic pace of his steps would clear his mind after the day's events.

Monroe's thoughts raced as he walked, fixating on the disturbing fact that both Gordon and Dixon were murdered by entirely different means, yet their bodies were left in similarly humiliating states. Dixon, naked and bound, was abandoned in the center of a hotel room bed, while Gordon was left sprawled on the floor of a train car bathroom. Was this a calculated choice or a random occurrence? Monroe's resolve to unmask the mastermind who was behind these killings deepened, even as the stakes for his own survival became increasingly clear. He had no idea just how perilous the path ahead would be.

27

FEELING THAT HE HAD HELD HIS OWN in his sparring match with Metro DC's finest, Monroe decided it was time to ramp up his effort to find out who'd killed Gordon and Dixon. Gordon's demise was slightly more personal, but terminating Dixon had a financial impact. With the news of the murder on Amtrak only beginning to get a lot of play, Monroe tried to come up with a game plan.

The walk home from the Daly Building was much needed and gave Monroe some time to think. He stopped briefly at the neighborhood Safeway to pick up pasta sauce and linguine to make a quick dinner. Although he knew the *Post* wouldn't have any coverage of Gordon's murder until the next morning, he picked up a copy anyway, having been in news exile all day. He also hoped someone with information might have called.

While Monroe had numbers for Tyree and Frazier, he had more than his share of both for one day. Keeping a low profile was crucial. The lie detector results were meant to ease their suspicions, but they still had him in their sights due to the inconclusive final question. Any further contact with the duo would be restricted by design.

Monroe crossed the threshold of his unit around 6:30 p.m. After setting his groceries on the counter, he grabbed the remote and turned on the television, hoping for any updated reports about Gordon. With the evening broadcasts on the four major local stations ending by 7 p.m., he switched to News Channel 8, which focused exclusively on news from D.C., Maryland, and Virginia and operated 24/7.

Sure enough, one of the station's crime reporters was on the scene near the gate area that had been sealed off earlier, close to the seat Monroe had occupied. In an almost melodramatic tone, the reporter announced that, according to his sources, 'the body of a Philadelphia-area man had been discovered in the bathroom of an Amtrak Metroliner train that arrived in D.C. from New York.' He continued, stating, 'The victim has been identified as Gordon Blackwell, a businessman and former partner in a Philadelphia law firm.' The reporter concluded by noting that the MPD would hold a press conference at 9 a.m. the following morning.

Few facts that had gotten out, but he knew it was only a matter of time before the real story would emerge. Just who was behind all of this? That was the mystery to Monroe, though he had his suspicions. He was certain the casino deal lay at the heart of the matter, but he had no idea who the culprits were. For his money, however, all roads led to Nimbus Bushrod and his unsavory crew of urban desperados. But he had no proof. Then again, would they be that stupid to commit a crime that would clearly put them under the microscope? On second thought, the answer to his own question was probably yes.

If you had asked Monroe just a few weeks ago, he would have been quick to praise Gordon's character. He was well-liked, and

Monroe believed he had few, if any, skeletons in his closet. But now, after uncovering his partner's underhanded dealings, Monroe saw him in a different light. Gordon's obsession with money, which he constantly talked about, now seemed glaringly obvious. Monroe realized he had been drawn in by Gordon's straight-laced demeanor, overlooking the telltale signs of his narcissism. In hindsight, he recognized that the pursuit of those gaming licenses had consumed Gordon, possibly driving him to make reckless decisions. All that seemed to matter to him was the potential windfall.

After washing up, Monroe began to prepare his dinner. But when his eyes drifted to the answering machine, the blinking light caught his attention. Walking over, he noticed he had twelve messages waiting—a surprising number for his home line. But then again, since he hadn't been in the office, anyone who really needed to contact him would have used that number. After the day he'd experienced, Monroe figured it was wise to check who had been trying to reach him.

He played each message, listening intently. Most were from friends wanting to catch up, unaware of his connection to Gordon. A few were from smaller investors or acquaintances who had heard about Gordon's death and were fishing for details. It seemed everyone was looking to him for information. Returning those would have to wait until the next day—he wasn't up for it just yet. Besides, he needed to come up with a response that would satisfy their curiosity without giving away anything meaningful.

But two calls quickly seized his attention. The first was from Jacob Weiss, Gamers' general counsel, who expressed concern about Gordon, noting how unusual it was that he couldn't reach him. Jacob had initially been Darnell's personal attorney, which made him a prime target for Gordon to recruit as Gamers' legal head. But Jacob's reputation as an exceptionally skilled and well-respected lawyer also made him invaluable. Knowing that he was aware of Gordon's travel plans, Monroe was eager to connect with Jacob, not just to discuss the situation but also to get some of his pressing questions answered.

The other call was from Tyree. Monroe guessed that his abrupt departure prevented the surly investigator from getting in the last word. His message instructed Monroe not to leave town without informing him. Tyree also warned him to keep his mouth shut regarding what he knew about Gordon's murder until the police made an official announcement. Monroe was just happy that he didn't ask him to call him back. At the conclusion of Tyree's message, Monroe gave his answering machine the middle finger. That summed up his feelings.

But as happened a lot with him, Monroe's overwhelming sense of curiosity got the best of him. Walking back toward the phone he placed a call to his *favorite* detective, who was still in his office. True to his nature, he answered gruffly.

"Tyree."

"Detective, this is Monroe Gray."

"Well, well, well," he said with more than a hint of derision.

What an asshole. "I was returning your call."

"You hauled ass gettin' outta here this evening. You didn't like our company?"

"Okay, Detective. You and your partner already fucked up my day. Now what?"

"I think my message was clear. Keep your mouth shut and your ass in town. Ya hear me?"

"Yeah, I hear you, but I have two trips to make this week, so that isn't possible."

"I don't think you heard me, Chief," he snapped.

"Look, Detective, it's only right that I attend Dixon's funeral on Wednesday, and I have to attend a mayors conference in New York this weekend for business."

"Hmm. Alright, but you had better give me the info on your whereabouts, leaving out not one detail," Tyree commanded. "And by the way, are you the one that leaked Blackwell's name to the press?"

"No!" Monroe said emphatically. "Besides, I was with you most of the day. Are you and your partner that clueless?"

"Boy, don't fuck with me! I'm not as nice as Frazier—I'll put a foot in your ass. You just make sure you do what I said and stay the fuck out of our investigation."

"Okay, Detective, anything else?" Monroe asked, now regretting his call.

"That's it. Watch your step, Ace."

Dickhead! Monroe didn't need Tyree to tell him to keep quiet. That had been his intention all along. He knew that he would be making a lot of calls the next day, and his goal would be to extract more information than he gave. Monroe believed he had an advantage. He knew the details of both murders, almost as much as the police. So anyone he talked with who knew anything about them would have to be considered a suspect.

Monroe was starving. While rice became a staple in his diet during his tour in Vietnam and trips to other parts of Asia, he had recently been on a pasta binge. He grabbed the linguine he had just purchased and added chicken meatballs and broccoli to his sauce. Just as he was preparing his plate, the phone rang. Monroe walked over to retrieve the handset and saw Ambrose's name on caller ID.

Ambrose had known Gordon was coming to town because he had asked Monroe to set up a meeting. Despite the last-minute request, Gordon had agreed to meet them for dinner. But that was moot now since Gordon was lying in the morgue. Despite Ambrose's best efforts, Monroe still harbored suspicions about him. He was a bit too inquisitive for Monroe's taste, which suggested a hidden agenda. Ambrose's display on the dock in Highland Beach also left Monroe with the impression that there were no limits to his actions. *Should I?* After a brief internal debate, his spirit of inquiry once again prevailed. He picked up on the fourth ring.

"Hello."

"Monroe.

"Ambrose."

"Man, this is getting old, but I hope you'll accept my condolences."

"Thanks, I guess," Monroe said. "Look, Ambrose, I'm tired and hungry and my day has been quite fucked up."

"I hear you, man, but I may have some info that could maybe turn your fortunes around."

"Really?" Monroe said as he took a seat on his sofa.

"But not on the phone," he advised.

"What do you suggest?"

"Can you be available tomorrow around 4 p.m.?"

"I guess I can."

"Good. Let's meet up at the Channel Inn between 4 and 4:30. Whoever gets there first, grab a table away from the bar. I'll fill you in then."

"Okay, Ambrose. I hope this won't be a waste of my time."

"It won't, I can assure you of that. See you then."

As Monroe hung up, his resentment of Tyree exited his thoughts, replaced by the anticipation of Ambrose's revelations. Starving and mentally drained, Monroe prepared to eat in silence as he struggled to make sense of it all. Little did he know that what he thought he knew was only the tip of the iceberg compared to the vast unknown that awaited him.

28

WITH DIXON AND GORDON OUT OF the picture, Monroe's dreams of striking it rich had vanished. Now, his primary concern was that he might be the next target. The thought of being hunted unnerved him, and he knew he needed to be prepared for whatever came next. He walked to his bedroom, retrieved his gun case from the closet, and laid it on the bed. As he opened it, the cold, black metal of his Glock 17 greeted him.

Despite his military background, Monroe didn't consider himself a gun enthusiast. He kept a gun because he knew that, in a country awash with firearms, there might come a day when he would need one. Guns were illegal in DC, so whenever he needed to brush up on his skills, he would head to a friend's farm in Virginia. Monroe had always lived by the motto that it was better to ask for forgiveness than to seek permission. Having the gun at hand gave him a sense of security, knowing that if things went south, he would do whatever it took to survive. He would have to leave it behind when he headed to St. Louis, but beyond that, until his ordeal was over, his gun and extra magazine would be his constant companions.

Monroe closed the case and carried it and his cleaning kit to the dining area. His meal had cooled to the touch. Monroe took a bite of the tepid pasta, grimacing at its lack of warmth. Despite the unappetizing temperature, he was too hungry to reheat it and kept eating. After dinner, he began the process of cleaning his gun, and slowly a course of action was coming into view. But any final plan would have to wait until after his meeting with Ambrose and his trip to St. Louis. By the time his head hit the pillow, Monroe felt like for the first time the situation and a plan to deal with it was coming together.

Monroe awoke at 6 a.m. surprisingly invigorated as any man could be given the stress he was under. For whatever reason, he felt like he was on the verge of a breakthrough in finding out who killed Gordon and Dixon. But there was a lot Monroe didn't know and the upcoming forty-eight hours would be crucial to his efforts. He had a lot to get done over the course of the day before his meeting with Ambrose. He was eager to get started.

Monroe hit the fitness center in his building for a quick workout before heading back to his apartment to make coffee and breakfast. Once the kitchen was cleaned up, he set about making a few calls. He reached out to some of the smaller investors again. With Gamers' collapse looming, most had already come to grips with their financial losses. There was also an undercurrent of fear, likely spooked by what had happened to Gordon and Dixon. One common theme was their insistence that they knew nothing. After a couple of fruitless hours on the phone, Monroe shifted gears to tackle some overdue client work.

By the time Monroe glanced at the clock, it was already 3 p.m., and his meeting with Ambrose was fast approaching. He'd managed to make headway on his upcoming cases, but now his focus shifted to devising a strategy for his next crucial encounter. With bodies turning up and no obvious suspects, Monroe couldn't help but wonder just where Ambrose and Garland fit into this chaotic puzzle.

They had been making their rounds in St. Louis for months, but for what purpose? Was their conflict with Nimbus and his associates authentic, or just a smokescreen? Their lack of formal ties to any group competing for gaming licenses made Monroe question their true intentions. The timing of Ambrose's latest call only deepened Monroe's suspicions.

Monroe had a few theories about Ambrose's meeting proposal, which he felt was motivated by several self-serving reasons, likely orchestrated by Garland. Monroe suspected that he was actually pulling the strings. They probably wanted to understand how much Monroe knew about the deaths of Gordon and Dixon and the larger conspiracy.

With the situation becoming more precarious, Ambrose probably needed to determine where Monroe's loyalties stood. Unaware of the fractured relationship between Monroe and Gordon, he was probably interested in whether or not Monroe might be seeking revenge or answers. Ambrose could also be aiming to misdirect Monroe, pointing him toward the wrong targets or, even worse, forcing him into silence through threats.

As a cascade of thoughts soaked his mind, Monroe quickly showered and dressed for the brief walk to the Channel Inn. He had thought long and hard about his strategy for the upcoming meeting and chose to follow the advice a seasoned salesman once gave him when it came to gathering information, "Ask plenty of questions and listen carefully. Eventually, people reveal everything you need to know." Dressed and ready to go, Monroe headed out the door. With both him and Ambrose digging for answers, there was no doubt in his mind that the meeting would be anything but ordinary.

29

MONROE ENTERED THE CHANNEL INN just shy of 4 p.m. All was quiet. The hotel desk near the entryway was unattended. As he walked into the lounge, a few early patrons were already at the bar, swapping tales. The usual crowd of regulars—typically federal and D.C. government employees—had yet to arrive. On many evenings, the crowd could also include notable Black politicians, such as the mayor, members of both the city council and Congress, and their staffs.

At the Channel Inn, many of the men could be considered "seasoned," and a "young girl" meant a woman forty-five to fifty-five—a fact that earned the bar the nickname "Jurassic Park." It was the kind of place where a convicted felon, his attorney, and the judge who sentenced him might end up seated together at the bar, where departed regulars were remembered fondly, and where you didn't need to mind your own business because everyone else did it for you.

Monroe surveyed the room. Fortunately, most of the tables were unoccupied, and since Ambrose had yet to show, Monroe selected one in an area far away from the bar that would offer maximum privacy.

Equipped with his suspicion of Ambrose's motives, Monroe intended to probe him with open-ended questions and look for any inconsistencies. Maybe Ambrose would unwittingly reveal useful information. Regardless, Monroe was determined to be cautious in engaging him. In his view, he was there to listen.

Just as Monroe was getting comfortable, a waiter of Ethiopian descent, wearing a white formal shirt and bow tie but no jacket, approached him.

"What can I get you, sir?" he asked in an accented voice.

"Jack on the Rocks," Monroe replied almost immediately.

Before the waiter could turn around, Ambrose hurriedly strode over. Wearing a light blue suit, a navy and white striped shirt, and shoes of skin that was once a gator's, he quickly grabbed a seat opposite Monroe. Before even greeting him, Ambrose sought the waiter's attention.

"I'll have whatever he's having," he directed. The look on the waiter's face seemed to indicate that he didn't care for the tone of the request. "Monroe, sorry for being late. I appreciate you meeting me on such short notice."

"No problem. I live in the area, so it was an easy ask. But time is what I don't have a lot of, so let's get right to the point. What's this about? You said it was urgent."

"It is. Look, man. I know that you've got a lot on your mind now, with the two most important men in your bid dead and a company that has met the same fate."

"It seems like being associated with Gamers isn't good for one's health," Monroe said in a deadpan manner. "You're not telling me anything I don't know."

"That's precisely why I wanted to talk to you. With Gamers out of the picture, there's a lot up in the air—especially concerning the casino licenses in St. Louis."

With his interest stirred, Monroe asked, "And where do I fit into this, Ambrose? By now, I'm sure you know I was never in the inner circle with Gordon and Dixon."

"True, but you're a smart man. You understand the stakes here, and you know the politics." Ambrose paused, searching Monroe's face for a reaction. "And with Nimbus Bushrod and his crew under suspicion for this mess, it's only a matter of time before things start falling apart for them, too."

Their drinks arrived. Both men gave a quick stir, Monroe with a finger and Ambrose with the small plastic straw that he'd retrieved from a holder on the table.

Monroe frowned. "Are you saying Nimbus is behind Gordon and Dixon's deaths? That's the first I've heard that theory."

Ambrose shrugged nonchalantly. "I'm not tellin' you anything official. But you know how the street talks. The word is Nimbus wanted more control, and Dixon was in the way. Now, with Dixon out and Gordon... It's interesting timing, wouldn't you agree?"

"It might seem that way. But why come to me? What are you proposing exactly?" Monroe asked, leaning back and striking a thoughtful pose.

Ambrose glanced around and then back to Monroe. "Look, Monroe, with Gamers crumbling, that means fewer players with 'juice,' if you know what I mean."

"No, I don't know what you mean. School me."

"Bullshit, Monroe. You know exactly what I'm talking about. Everyone's been trying to find the right person to put their thumb on the scale, including Dixon and Gordon, so don't play dumb with me."

"You'd be surprised what I don't know," Monroe replied with a slight grin.

"Save all of that 'I'm just a low man on the totem pole' shit for somebody who doesn't know any better. I know all about you."

"You do? Enlighten me."

"I've got no time for fuckin' around. Here's the deal. All of the licenses in St. Louis are up for grabs. Garland and I—well, we see an opportunity. Not just here, but connections that could extend our reach into Africa. Prosperous connections. We could use someone like you."

Monroe's eyes narrowed. "And in return?"

"Stability. That's what we're offering. A chance for you to be on the winning side when the dust settles. Plus, a stake in what comes next. We're talking about significant international deals." Monroe leaned closer as Ambrose continued. "You wouldn't want to miss out because you were aligned with the wrong people."

"You make it sound like you're offering me a lifeline, Ambrose," Monroe countered, smirking slightly.

"Call it whatever you want. You're a sharp guy, Monroe. You know it's better to be out front in situations like this. So, what do you say?"

"I'll need to think about it, Ambrose. This isn't cut and dried. And if what you're implying about Nimbus is true, it could get more complicated."

"Sure, take your time and think it over. But don't overthink the situation. Opportunities like this are fleeting, and they don't stay on the table for long." Both men downed the last of their drinks before Ambrose rose from his seat. He reached into his pocket and retrieved a wad of bills. Plucking a $20 bill from it, he laid it on the table and extended his hand, "My treat."

Shaking it, Monroe said, "Alright, Ambrose. I'll be in touch."

Monroe reclined slightly, his gaze fixed on Ambrose as he departed. His expression was reflective as he processed the implications of their discussion and examined his next steps. By not committing and promising to consider Ambrose's proposal, Monroe believed he had bought valuable time to explore the murky waters he was navigating. He would leave the meeting more skeptical than he was when he entered. He was especially troubled by the cryptic mentions of the influential figures behind Ambrose and Garland. The encounter had raised more questions than it had provided answers. Determined, Monroe knew he needed to dig deeper to uncover who was truly behind the murders of Gordon and Dixon. He had no idea of the depth of the deception.

30

ONCE AGAIN, SLEEP WAS NOWHERE to be found for Monroe as he replayed the events of the week in his mind. During his conversation with Ambrose, his suspicions about Nimbus, Steptoe, and Prigmore being involved in the deaths of Gordon and Dixon were seemingly confirmed. Yet, trusting Ambrose was another matter. Could it all be a setup? Delaying his decision could buy Monroe the time he needed to uncover the truth.

With only five minutes left until his alarm clock was set to ring at 4:30 a.m., Monroe decided to get up and prepare for his 6:30 a.m. flight to St. Louis. Fortunately, his apartment was less than ten minutes by taxi from National Airport, so he knew he had sufficient time to arrive at his gate without any hassle. He prepared a quick breakfast of a bagel with lox and cream cheese, accompanied by coffee, which would hold him over until later. Since he intended to return the same day, he had little to pack. In addition to his briefcase, Monroe partially filled a tote bag with essentials just in case of an emergency.

Monroe arrived at the airport well ahead of his flight time and learned at check-in that he had been upgraded to first class. He looked forward to the prospect of maybe getting some sleep in the more spacious first-class seating. Traveling to St. Louis without Gordon felt strange. They had always coordinated their travel plans, usually sharing a ride using a prearranged car service.

While his feelings toward Gordon had become more complex and strained, he still felt sympathy for Gordon's family, which was left to grapple with the aftermath of his actions that were bound to become public. The inability to directly confront Gordon about his involvement in the unsettling venture irked Monroe. Still, he reminded himself that he would have enough time to seek answers once he was back on the East Coast.

Monroe's flight touched down in St. Louis at the scheduled time of 8:00 a.m. CST, parking at the gate next to the one used by TWA's arriving flight from New York, which Gordon would have taken. They would normally catch up over breakfast in Lambert's terminal, discussing the day's agenda before going to find their ride. While his reflections were pleasant, the nostalgia was short-lived and soon gave way to recollections of his last difficult encounters with Gordon, once a trusted friend. But Monroe knew he'd have to shed any emotional baggage, at least on this day. Staying sharp was essential if he was going to come away with any useful information.

As usual, Monroe stopped by the shoeshine stand after deplaning. His well-worn routine now carried an unfamiliar strain—he'd always made this stop with Gordon by his side. On this day, he was alone. He approached the stand, nodding at Moses and Sham, the two leather groomers who had polished his shoes and swapped stories with him and Gordon on countless visits.

"Monroe, good to see you," Moses greeted, his voice carrying its usual warmth. "Where's your boy?"

Monroe hesitated, not sure of how much he should share. He stepped up onto the platform, placing his size twelves on the foot rest. "Gordon… didn't make it," he said quietly, watching their reactions closely.

Sham, who was setting out his brushes, froze mid-motion. "Didn't make it? What do you mean?"

"He was murdered," Monroe said, the words coming out somberly. "Two days ago."

Moses dropped the rag he was holding, his face a mask of shock. "Murdered? Damn shame. We heard some talk, but… damn. Gordon was a good man."

Sham shook his head slowly, picking up a can of polish. "We knew things were heating up around that casino deal, with Carlton Dixon's murder. But now your man Gordon? That's a whole other level."

Monroe leaned forward slightly, his voice dropping to a near whisper. "What have you heard?"

The two men exchanged a look, as if deciding what they should disclose. Moses finally spoke, his tone cautious. "Just whispers, you know? Folks saying there's a lotta money changing hands, people getting in over their heads. Can't tell you much more than that."

"Yeah," Sham added, his hands working methodically on Monroe's shoe. "Things been strange. A lot of suits coming through here lately. Nervous-looking types. Not like Gordon or you."

Monroe filed their comments away, nodding. "Appreciate the heads-up."

"We'd tell you more if we could," Moses said, resuming his work. "But you be careful, Monroe. Sounds like trouble's closer than you think."

Monroe sat back as Sham buffed his shoe to a mirror shine. The men didn't know much, but their unease was palpable, and it added another layer to the storm clouds gathering in his mind. As he stepped down, both men gave him a firm handshake and a quiet, "Take care of yourself."

Monroe couldn't shake the feeling that even the shoeshine stand—his usual safe haven—was now veiled by the shadows of danger. Just as he reached for his wallet, a young woman holding a sign with his name approached him. Monroe had called Darnell to let him know he would be attending solo, so arrangements had been made for one of his people to pick him up. Tasha Bennett, a woman of medium height and proportionate build, wore a black pantsuit that accentuated her curvaceous figure. Her rouge blouse matched her lipstick, complementing her walnut-colored skin. Her deep brown hair was styled into a ponytail that fell to the lower part of her neck.

After she had greeted everyone, Moses and Sham wasted no time pulling out their old player lines from back in the day, trying to mix it up with Tasha. She displayed a wicked sense of humor and outmatched them with each exchange. Judging from their reactions, they enjoyed every minute of it. Tasha came across as down-to-earth, with few pretensions. Monroe liked her right away. Once he settled the tab, he and Tasha were off. Anxiety was building; Monroe was ready to see what the day would bring.

Probably because Tasha worked for Darnell and the city owned the airport, she was parked in a VIP space near the entrance. The black 1993 four-door Mercury Marquis looked as if it had just rolled out of the showroom. It even featured a sunroof, which was an uncommon luxury. As they approached the car, Monroe noticed Tasha putting on her sunglasses, adding a touch of mystique that seemed tailor-made for such a classic sedan. Monroe settled into the plush leather seats in the back, and they were on their way.

The drive in was quiet, except for Tasha's occasional small talk. "I heard about Mr. Blackwell," Tasha said hesitantly. "Such a shock. I remember seeing you both on several occasions during the campaign. We were even introduced once.

Looking at her further, Monroe recalled seeing her around Darnell's headquarters but knew little about what she did.

"Always thought you two were like night and day, she continued."

Monroe nodded, choosing his words carefully. "We had our differences, but we made it work."

"And Mr. Dixon..." Tasha trailed off, glancing at Monroe through the rearview mirror. "I didn't know him personally, but I heard he was... a complicated man."

"That's putting it lightly," Monroe replied with a dry chuckle, then quickly redirected. "How long have you been driving for Darnell?"

"A while. He's good to work for," Tasha said, clearly sensing Monroe's preference to keep the conversation light. "But enough about me. How'd you two end up working with Mr. Dixon?"

Monroe tilted his head slightly, his mind racing. "It's a long story. Mostly business. You know how it is."

Although she appeared trustworthy, Monroe remained cautious. For the time being, he preferred to keep any and all insights to himself. He wasn't about to divulge sensitive information to someone he had only just met. Since Tasha worked directly for Darnell, he knew he had to be careful about what he said around her. He shifted the conversation to more innocuous topics for the remainder of the ride. In seemingly no time at all, Tasha pulled up to their destination, the First Baptist Church of St. Louis.

This house of worship was built in 1903 in the Richardsonian Romanesque style used by many churches at that time. It featured a large bell tower with a steep roof, as well as rounded arches and a mix of stone and brick in its construction. Several renovations and additions over the years resulted in an appearance that probably differed from its original design. It was impressive.

As one would expect the church was extremely crowded and the mood was somber. The sanctuary offered a spacious and simple design with a raised platform or pulpit at the front of the room. There was both a piano and an organ on each side for musical accompaniment during services. Above that were two choir lofts whose seating lay opposite one another. There were three rows of pews facing the platform, with two aisles separating them. There were windows on both sides, but those on the left were larger, with one grand aperture that was situated toward the front that illuminated the room on its own. The walls were decorated with religious artwork or symbols, and the stained-glass windows featured biblical scenes or figures.

Just as Monroe settled into his seat, the grieving widow and her entourage made their entrance. Clad in a black ensemble that expressed her mourning yet subtly highlighted her natural beauty, she was the embodiment of what men used to call a PYT—Pretty Young Thing. Something seemed oddly familiar about her to Monroe, but he couldn't put his finger on it. She was undeniably fine, making Monroe question what inner demons Dixon must have wrestled with despite having such a woman waiting for him at home. Of course, he reminded himself, he knew nothing of what was happening behind closed doors, so he was in no position to judge. But being a young widow with the cash she stood to inherit, options would be in abundance.

Monroe had always despised funerals, and his discomfort wasn't lessened by the fact that today's service wasn't for someone particularly close to him. He struggled with the reason behind his feelings until he realized that he preferred to remember people as they were when alive and vibrant, not as lifeless figures dressed up for one last showing. It was always jarring to hear someone remark on how good the deceased looked. "Good? They're dead." His other peeve came to fruition on this day. Adding to his annoyance were the endless, glorified tributes that were so extreme that Monroe thought about verifying whether the body in the coffin was Dixon.

Discreetly sitting in the back row, Monroe quietly slipped out of the church just after the funeral party passed by. He noticed Darnell among the pallbearers but didn't approach him. This wasn't the right moment for the kind of conversation he needed to have with him. Monroe carefully watched as mourners began filing out to take their stock. His contacts, who had worked countless homicides, always insisted that killers often return to the scene of their crime or the victim's funeral, seeking some twisted form of satisfaction. Whether it was a need for recognition, a desire to gather information, or an attempt to manipulate, there was a good chance Dixon's killer could be lurking among them.

Lost in thought, Monroe was suddenly approached by Jacob Weiss, the general counsel for Gamers. They exchanged a few pleasantries, and Jacob quickly got to the point, suggesting they needed to talk. Aware of the gap between the formal repast at the church and the gathering at Dixon's home, Monroe saw an opportunity to probe him for information. He proposed to Jacob they meet at Duff's in the Central West End in twenty minutes. Jacob readily agreed. As Monroe turned away to look for Tasha, he anticipated that their discussion might yield significant revelations. Little did he know it would exceed his expectations.

31

MONROE SPOTTED TASHA WAITING BY the car, which was double-parked in front of the church. As he slid into the back seat, he quickly asked if she was familiar with the locations of Duff's and Dixon's home. She verified that she was. She also mentioned to Monroe that Darnell had tasked her with escorting him for the day and driving him to the airport afterward. With his stomach reminding him that he needed to eat, they set off toward the restaurant.

Monroe had planned to make time to run down a few people in his search for answers. But as luck would have it, he ran into Jacob almost immediately, which proved to be very beneficial since he likely knew as much about Gordon's affairs as anyone. Monroe invited Tasha in and told her to order whatever she wanted but asked her to sit at the other end of the bar so he could have private time with Jacob. She readily agreed, happy to enjoy her meal and the copy of *Essence* magazine she had brought along.

Within minutes of Monroe being seated, Jacob strolled through the door. The pair of owners also came over to greet Monroe, who, as a friend of Darnell, had patronized the place on more than one occasion. Jacob, a straightlaced Jewish man from Lake Forest, Illinois, might not have been the trendiest guy around, but he had a certain coolness about him and was well-regarded by everyone who knew him. After taking a seat, both Monroe and Jacob took on looks that expressed the urgency of the moment.

"I think that this might be the first time I've seen you without Gordon," Jacob said.

"Now that you mention it, you're right," Monroe responded. "I don't know everything that he was into, but he didn't deserve to end up dead."

"I've got to tell you, I'm still in shock," Jacob added.

"I'm sure. What have you heard?"

"Only what's been on the news. Was he really murdered?'

"It looks that way."

"I'd been trying to reach him several times on Monday and most of yesterday, but now I understand why I wasn't able to connect with him. I knew something was up when he hadn't checked in," Jacob added.

"Checked in about what?" Monroe asked.

"I've got to be honest with you. You're a good guy, and I think you deserve to know."

"Know what?"

"Gordon stopped looking for investors a couple of days after Dixon was killed. He had been approached by Gateway Players about merging his effort with theirs. With Dixon no longer in the picture, he became the majority stockholder based on an agreement that the two had."

Both Malaika and Yvonne were right. "No shit," Monroe said as he attempted to act surprised.

"I wasn't happy about it," Jacob admitted. "I cautioned Gordon not to do it, but his mind was made up."

"What concerned you?"

"I knew that getting fresh money would be tough, but I wouldn't trust anyone associated with the Gateway group as far as I could see them. But I guess he viewed the 25 percent he was being offered better than nothing."

"But now that he's dead, where does it leave his shares?"

"They're in limbo for now, but word on the street has it that Shantelle Dixon is making moves to take over what's left of Gamers."

"Where does that leave you and me?" Monroe asked.

"We're out. Both of our percentages were separate agreements with Gordon. So once Gamers is dissolved or taken over, they no longer exist," Jacob explained.

"I thought it was well-known she wanted nothing to do with putting her newfound wealth in a gambling venture."

"That's what I heard too. But I think someone might have gotten to her. There's a clause in the shareholder agreement that gives her a thirty-day window to change her mind."

"This whole thing is insane."

"But that's not the half of it. He was working with them to secure the rights on properties in Swaziland, Lesotho, and South Africa."

"Working with who?" Monroe asked.

"Gateway, I presume."

"I'd heard that, which was a surprise to me," Monroe said. *Okay, so where do Garland and Ambrose fit in?*

"The problem arose when this group of Black Americans started making bold business moves on the continent, certain local power players with considerable influence were not pleased to see a bunch of outsiders attempting to enter their turf," Jacob explained.

"Gordon was doing a lot of backdoor dealing."

"I warned him. But he told me that he knew what he was doing. So I left it alone. His dying is a shame, but the dollar signs in his eyes kept getting bigger every day. Someone out here is operating with sinister motives and he was making a lot of enemies."

"Man, I didn't have a clue," Monroe added.

"I'm going to have to leave. I have an errand to run before I go over to Dixon's. But let me give you some advice. Be very careful; you may be a loose end that needs to be tied up. Also, I don't know how she fits into things, but you should look into Tammy."

"Darnell's Tammy?" Monroe said with obvious surprise.

"I've heard she's the primary person pushing Shantelle into the gaming deal for whatever reason."

'I'll give it a look. In the meantime, keep me posted on anything you hear. I intend to find out who killed Gordon and Dixon."

"Good luck with that," Jacob said with a wry smile.

The men talked for several more minutes about Gordon, sharing some personal thoughts and about the status of several of the other investors. Everyone but Shantelle Dixon, by way of her husband, had folded their tents.

"I'll be in touch," Jacob said as he stood. He then ambled toward the exit, offering a wave to the owners as he left.

Monroe left his meeting with Jacob more curious and driven than ever to unravel the complexities of the plot, especially the connections to Africa. Tammy's name had come up before, but he had dismissed it as mere chatter about her role as Darnell's protector. But now, her involvement in persuading Shantelle to enter the casino business raised his suspicions. Fueled by these revelations, Monroe felt an urgency to intensify his search for the truth while hoping to stay one step ahead of any danger directed his way.

LAWSON BROOKS

32

MONROE TOOK A FEW MINUTES after Jacob left to reflect on matters. He was bothered by the fact that the forces behind these murderous acts felt that there was no other way to get what they wanted. But then, insatiable greed can never be underestimated as a motivating force. Gamers undeniably had a competitive proposal and seemed well-connected politically—at least at first glance. But was Nimbus the architect of this madness behind this chaos, as Ambrose had hinted and Monroe had started to believe? The more he thought about it, the simpler that theory seemed. While he was morally dubious and certainly an asshole, Monroe was skeptical of his, Steptoe's, or Prigmore's ability to devise and execute such an elaborate plot. He was left wondering what he was missing.

Monroe paid the bill and signaled to Tasha that it was time to leave. They reached Dixon's residence in under ten minutes. Located in the southern tip of the Central West End, the neighborhood was home to some of the city's most affluent Black residents. The house was an impressive two-story brick structure. Upon entering, guests were led through a spacious atrium and two sizable rooms to the backyard, where a vast tent had been erected. Tables with a variety of dishes were spread about and two bars were situated on both sides.

Monroe's earlier detour had allowed time for people to gravitate from the main repast to the burial site to Dixon's home. The atmosphere at the funeral reception was somber yet charged with underlying tension. The first familiar face Monroe encountered was that of Tammy Treadwell, who was solemnly working the crowd. They acknowledged each other with subtle waves. Monroe turned away to see if he could locate Darnell when Dixon's widow and her entourage came into view. It must have been a whirlwind for her—the funeral, the interment, and two reception events, all while she mourned her husband.

Although she was clad in traditional and conservative funeral wear, Shantelle Dixon still projected a sultry aura. Her simple yet stylish black silk dress with long sleeves and modest neckline fell just below her knees. She wore a matching pillbox hat that held a classic veil, which covered part of her face and added an element of privacy and mourning. Her jewelry was minimal. A pair of pearl earrings and a matching pearl necklace were understated and elegant. Simple black pumps completed her outfit.

As the group filed past, Monroe took the opportunity to introduce himself and express his condolences. Her handshake was gentle, and the warm, inviting look in her wide, hazel eyes captivated him. Monroe found himself holding her hand a moment too long, hoping to spark a recognition of where he had seen her before. However, she had a long line of mourners waiting and couldn't linger. Just before she moved on, she gave him a playful wink and purred, "How you doin', sugar?" The word "sugar" jolted Monroe with a sudden rush of familiarity, stirring a blend of surprise and excitement. In an instant, it hit him—they had once shared an intimate encounter. The image in his mind became as clear as it was unexpected, stirring emotions he thought he'd left behind.

***

It was the previous fall during one of his and Gordon's many trips to St. Louis. They had checked into the Mayfair Hotel and Gordon was waiting for Tammy to come by for a brief meeting. He suggested that Monroe come downstairs because she would be bringing a friend with her. The thought was that while he and Tammy met, Monroe could entertain her companion. As the four convened in the hotel lobby coming from opposite directions, her friend was introduced only as Telly.

Monroe had observed her moving through the room with the lithe grace of a seasoned runner, which, it turned out, she had been in college. Her presence was commanding yet subtly inviting. Standing at an impressive five-foot-eight, her physique melded athletic firmness with an enchanting curvature that suggested both strength and softness in equal measure. Her short black hair was styled in a chic, straight coif that framed her striking face, accentuating her sharp cheekbones and a gaze that flickered like warm, amber light. Her eyes, a mesmerizing shade of hazel, seemed to shift from green to brown as they caught the light, revealing depths that hinted at untold stories. *I may not have liked Dixon, but damn if he didn't hit the romantic jackpot.*

They enjoyed a round of cocktails in the hotel bar. At Gordon's suggestion, they retreated to his suite for a little more privacy. He ordered more drinks and appetizers to be delivered there. After an hour or so, Tammy, who had engineered the meeting, stated that she and Gordon had a matter to discuss privately. To his knowledge, Gordon had remained true to the one woman-man image he projected, so Monroe thought nothing of it. Given the sobriety of their tone, their need to talk appeared to be strictly business. Monroe and Telly slipped off to his room next door to wait with drinks in hand.

They engaged in idle conversation for several minutes while seated on the sofa. But during an awkward moment of silence the sexual tension that had been present, but repressed, erupted with a vengeance. Telly and Monroe thrust themselves toward each other and embraced in a long, passionate kiss. Her outfit was a one-piece knit job. While caressing her soft lips with his, Monroe began to raise her skirt with his left hand so that he could palm her taut, yet supple ass cheek. *No panties!* With his right hand, Monroe lowered her top to reveal two of the most beautiful breasts he had ever seen. His mouth descended, pressing his lips to one, taking it into his mouth with a slow, deliberate motion that made her gasp. After about five minutes of passionate foreplay, Monroe unbuckled his belt and lowered his pants. When without warning that wonderful moment was interrupted by a knock on the door. *Oh, hell no!*

The pair scurried to get their looks back in order. Telly ran for the bathroom to straighten out her dress and reapply her lipstick, while Monroe pulled up his pants and buckled his belt. He cracked the door, exposing his head. It was Gordon and Tammy. For whatever reason they had wrapped up their business in short order. Their faces wore looks of restrained amusement as if they knew that Monroe and his new friend had been up to something. After exiting the bathroom, Telly took his hand, kissed his cheek, and said, "Are you comin' downstairs with us, sugar?" She looked back and offered a seductive wink as she stepped across the threshold and into the hall.

Still partially hiding behind the door, Monroe explained that he had several phone calls to make and that he would meet them in the lobby shortly. Tammy said that she and Telly had to go and she would see him another time. Gordon said he would wait in the bar for him. With that, they turned to head for the elevators. After closing the door, Monroe couldn't avoid looking at his reflection in the mirror that occupied the wall to his right. It was the look of an exasperated man with a dick that was harder than Chinese arithmetic. In a strange way, that may have been the best sexual encounter that Monroe never had.

***

Shantelle slowly made her way to the area prepared for her and her group. Two thoughts haunted Monroe: Was she truly the aggrieved widow she so eloquently portrayed? In the months since their meeting, she had undergone a few cosmetic changes—a different hairstyle, new makeup—and the veil only added to the mystery. Monroe had met countless people during that time, including being involved in more than a few late-night encounters, which blurred the details of memory. He couldn't shake the feeling that he'd been slipping. Maybe it was the whiskey that day, but he should have put two and two together much sooner.

Why hadn't Gordon told him that Telly was Shantelle Dixon? That could also be the reason behind his mischievous grins on the occasions whenever Monroe mentioned the friction between him and Dixon to Gordon. If Dixon had somehow discovered that Monroe had canoodled his wife, that would have been more than reason enough for him to hold Monroe in contempt. And maybe, just maybe, armed with that knowledge, Gordon was trying to compromise him by creating a divide between the two veterans.

All of those thoughts swirled in Monroe's mind as he watched her flawlessly engage with guests. The glimpse of her voluptuous body as she moved through the small crowd that had gathered around her once again triggered another mental replay of that evening that gave rise to an enamored smile.

Unexpectedly, a raspy and familiar voice summoned his ear.

"Like that, huh?"

Monroe's muscles tensed as he slowly turned to confront Detective Otis Tyree, who was eying him with a smug look that oozed the self-satisfaction of a hunter who'd just trapped his prey.

Can't a brother catch a break?

33

ONROE TOOK A STEP BACK TO CREATE some distance before responding to Tyree who had a habit of invading personal spaces.

"You again?"

"I saw you, Chief," the grizzly lawman uttered while staring directly at Monroe without a blink of an eye. "You were eyeballin' her like she was the last piece of pie at Thanksgiving dinner."

Keep your cool.

"Some men will do some unholy things to get next to a woman like that," Tyree continued. "And now she's rollin' in big money? Well..."

Monroe was aware that Tyree was pulling his chain, but he knew he needed to maintain his composure and not give him the satisfaction of some ill-advised off-the-cuff reaction. Tyree's Columbo act was growing thin.

"The name is Monroe, not Chief or Ace or any other of your pet names, and why don't you get your head out of the gutter? A man was just buried and is being mourned."

He leaned back and chuckled. "I could use a drink. Let's walk and talk."

Tyree was the last person Monroe wanted to have a drink with, but his desire for one overpowered his reluctance. Besides, refusing the offer would only fuel Tyree's suspicion that he was avoiding him. With Dixon's murder unresolved, Monroe recognized that both Tyree and Frazier would be inescapable presences for the foreseeable future.

Compounding his unease was the knowledge that if they ever discovered he had been the first to find Dixon's body, their scrutiny would only deepen. On the flip side, having a drink with Tyree might also present an opportunity to get his hands on some useful information. Resigned, with Tyree leading the way, they sidled up to the bar.

"Let me buy you a drink," Tyree said in an attempt at humor, knowing that the bar was open.

"Jack on the rocks," Monroe uttered to the bartender.

"Well whadda ya know. Great minds think alike. Same for me," Tyree said, looking directly at their server.

"You and your partner must be using up the MPD's travel budget on this one case," Monroe tartly remarked. "Where are you staying, Motel 6?"

Turning back toward Monroe, he retorted, "Don't be a smartass. You're already on thin ice."

The pair seemed to have gotten comfortable exchanging insults. Maybe their adversarial relationship was thawing. So Monroe decided to test that theory.

"When you first came to my apartment and I asked you how did Dixon die, you wouldn't say. So what can you tell me now?

"I'm not obligated to share any details with you. Let's just say I'm in a good mood, and to prove I'm not all bad, here's a little something to chew on. Dixon was bound tighter than a hog before slaughter, with a ligature around his neck. Every time he struggled to break free, he was strangled a bit more—a slow, torturous end."

So tell me something I don't know.

"You do know you're still a person of interest, don't you?"

"I don't know why," Monroe quickly answered. "I didn't have a reason to see Dixon dead."

"You sure? It looks to me that you've got the hots for his widow," Tyree said, hoping to get a rise out of Monroe. "You know what I think, Gray?"

"No. What do you think, Detective?"

"I think that you and the widow Dixon been knockin' boots and now you're looking for a more permanent arrangement with her and all of that cash."

"Bullshit. You have one helluva an imagination. Have you ever thought of writing for Disney?"

"It makes sense to me, based on the glad eye I saw you give her."

"Please. Including today, I've only met her briefly twice," Monroe retorted, leaving out the details of his first encounter. "As I told you before, he was worth a lot to me alive and I'm going to make it a point to find out who killed him."

Monroe sensed that Tyree had suspicions about him knowing more than he let on, yet lacked the evidence to confirm it, which Monroe found reassuring. Although Tyree still seemed unaware of his actual involvement, Monroe knew it was crucial to divert his and Frazier's attention elsewhere.

"I've told you before, don't go messing around in our investigation. If you fuck it up, I'll fuck you up!"

"I'm just trying to help," Monroe said.

"If I needed your help, I'd ask for it. You had better watch your goddamn step."

Monroe, tired of Tyree's groundless accusations, flashed a tight smile and said, "Detective, it's always a pleasure. Excuse me, but I need to speak with some other guests. Have a good day." As he turned to leave, he paused and looked back. "Oh, and one more thing—you might want to consider who benefits most from Gordon and Dixon's deaths. Just a hint: it's not me."

Tyree leaned back against the bar, his elbow propped up casually, a self-assured scowl playing across his lips. He clearly believed he had rattled Monroe—and to some extent had. But Monroe saw through the facade—the ongoing efforts to connect him to the Dixon case were a sign of desperation and suggested they lacked a solid suspect. Their visit to St. Louis was nothing more than a tree-shaking expedition to see which apples fell to the ground. Reflecting on this, Monroe realized he might hold as many cards as Tyree and Frazier, at least for the moment. He was also sure that his last statement to Tyree would serve as the breadcrumbs that would spur them to use a wider lens in their investigation.

As he retreated from the bar area, Frazier made his way over to meet up with Tyree, who offered Monroe a grimaced smile. His ears burned knowing that he was the topic of discussion between the two cops. Shaking off any discomfort, Monroe spotted Tammy Treadwell wrapping up a conversation with Alderman Steptoe. He waited for a moment until Steptoe moved on, then approached her guardedly.

"Tammy, I couldn't help but overhear bits of your conversation," Monroe smoothly lied. "Sounds like the waters are getting pretty choppy around here. How are you holding up with everything going on?"

"It's a juggling act, as you can imagine," she acknowledged with a smile and look that indicated the wheels in her head were turning. "Every day brings a new challenge. But we do what we must, don't we? How about you, Monroe? How are you holding up with the breakup of your group and the loss of your associates?"

"Just trying to stay ahead of the storm, or at least keep from getting swept away. Speaking of storms, the winds seem to be shifting directions frequently these days. Have you noticed any new developments that might be of interest?" Monroe subtly probed.

"Well, in times like these, alliances can shift quickly. It's all about staying connected with the right people. I haven't seen you since election night. Any particular reason?"

"You know how it is—sometimes you find yourself on the outside looking in. But I'm trying to find where the lines are drawn. Speaking of which, have you had any recent interactions with Nimbus or his group that might enlighten someone who's out of the loop?"

Tammy paused and seemed to be measuring her response. "Nimbus has his hands in many pots, as usual. But Monroe, you should be more concerned about the bigger players. Sometimes the real moves are hidden behind the most charming smiles. Look beyond the obvious, Monroe. That's where the real game is."

"Since you raised the subject of hidden games, there's a lot of talk about new players from outside the city making moves. Anything you think I should watch out for?"

"Everyone has an agenda, and not everyone's is as transparent as you might hope, including mine. Just remember, not all threats come holding a dagger. Some come bearing gifts. Or then again, maybe you should just cut your losses, go back to DC, and do your legal thing."

"Thanks for the advice, Tammy. It's always enlightening to get your perspective. I'll keep my eyes wide open. The last thing I'm going to do is get caught with my pants down."

"That's all any of us can do, but watch out. I heard that they come down pretty easily," she responded as she walked away.

Okay, lady. It's on now.

That exchange triggered Monroe's belief that Tammy was in some way a key player and not just a bystander. Her last remark was thrown in for spite. She no doubt was aware of the details of his interrupted tryst with Shantelle, and he was confident that she would hold it as a trump card for future use. While his conversation with her left Monroe with more questions than answers, it motivated him to dig deeper into the connections and alliances Tammy hinted at.

Monroe continued his stroll through the clusters of mourners, his eyes scanning for any familiar faces that might offer clues. Monroe tried engaging several key figures possibly linked to the murders. He even briefly conversed with Nimbus and Steptoe, but got nowhere. Their silence was ironclad, but to Monroe, it spoke volumes. He wanted to approach Congressman Hancock but he was far too busy reveling in his status as a big shot to make time, although they exchanged eye contact several times.

With options dwindling, Monroe's attention shifted to Cleo Hancock, who was effortlessly wading through the crowd. She was dressed in a sophisticated black crepe dress with a subtle floral lace trim at the cuffs and hem, adding a unique touch to her respectful, somber attire. Her look was completed with a delicate silver locket and matching earrings, which lent a quiet elegance. Her drink caught his eye—a Cosmopolitan, which is what the mystery lady who'd visited Dixon's hotel room had ordered. The lipstick she was wearing seemed to be a similar shade to the lip print on the glass that was on the table.

Monroe knew he needed to speak with her. But just as he was about to make his approach, he was intercepted by an enigmatic stranger who would ultimately lead him down a path he never anticipated and send him off into newer and more dangerous directions.

34

"**M**R. MONROE GRAY, I PRESUME?" His voice was even yet resonant, the kind that suggested a background of authority.

Monroe turned to find a man standing a few paces away, who appeared to be in his mid-to-late-thirties. His posture was upright but unforced, the stance of a man equally comfortable in solitude or under scrutiny. Yet he smoothly blended into the gathering, exuding a quiet intensity. His tailored charcoal suit, crisp white shirt, and black tie struck a perfect balance between respect and refinement. His polished leather shoes caught the fading sunlight, an obvious testament to his attention to detail. The faint shadow of stubble lining his jaw added a rugged edge, contrasting with his composed demeanor. Dark brown eyes, keen and observant, locked onto Monroe with a determination that seemed to pierce through the noise of the crowd.

Surprised, Monroe quickly assessed the man before speaking. "You've got me at a disadvantage. Who are you?"

"My name's Oswald Dixon. Carlton Dixon was my uncle," he said, extending a firm hand, his movements as calculated as his advance.

"I wasn't aware Carlton had a nephew," Monroe said, shaking his hand. "My condolences for your loss."

Oswald nodded appreciatively. "Thank you. Though, to be honest, my uncle and I weren't exactly close."

"Really? Why was that?" Monroe asked.

"Let's just say I was viewed as a little too principled for my uncle's business practices."

Monroe was intrigued. "Interesting. So, what can I do for you, Mr. Dixon?"

"Oswald, please. It's more about what I can do for you," the young man replied as he glanced around to ensure they weren't being overheard. "I know you're looking into my uncle's murder and the web of corruption that may surround it. I believe I can help."

Monroe leaned in slightly. "I'm listening."

"The game you're playing in is much more complicated than you realize. Congressman Pressley Hancock isn't just taking bribes from one source. He's on multiple payrolls."

"Go on."

"First, he's been accepting bribes from several casino companies eager for him to step in on their behalf regarding the available gaming licenses here in St. Louis. They want his influence to tip the scales in their favor."

Monroe nodded thoughtfully. "That squares with some things I've heard."

"But that's just the tip of the iceberg," Oswald continued. "He's also in bed with someone known only as 'The Investor.' This person is keen on entering the African market and sees Hancock as the key to unlocking lucrative deals there."

"The Investor...any idea who that might be?"

Shaking his head, "Not exactly. But I know they're powerful and have deep pockets. Hancock is also receiving funds from an African casino mogul aiming to partner with US operators expanding into Africa. It's a tangled web of mutual exploitation."

Monroe's eyes narrowed. "That's a lot of self-dealing. He's on a path where he's going to disappoint somebody and his ass is going to be on the line."

"Greed blinds people to risks. But there's more. Do you know about Tammy Treadwell's history with my family?"

"I know her father lost his shot at a congressional seat years ago under scandalous circumstances."

"It was a smear campaign manufactured by my uncle and Hancock. They connived to falsely implicate her father in a corruption scheme. It paved the way for Hancock to take over the seat he holds today. Tammy's been harboring a deep-seated hatred ever since."

Surprised, Monroe responded, "That explains a lot about her...motivations, but murder?"

"I can't go that far, at least not yet. But she's been quietly maneuvering to position my uncle's widow, Shantelle, to take over his casino interests. But it's not just for Shantelle's benefit. Tammy intends to use her to potentially fund Darnell Mayfield's long-term ambitions not only as a local but a national power broker. And Tammy would be the woman behind the man and the central player."

"So Darnell gains control over the casino operations without directly involving himself, thanks to Tammy's actions," Monroe said, connecting the dots.

"Exactly. And while all eyes are on Nimbus Bushrod and his associates, the real puppeteers are operating unseen. But there are others in the mix who are working behind the scenes for Hancock. They were responsible for bringing in The Investor."

"Do you know who these individuals are?"

Oswald paused, choosing his words carefully. "I have my suspicions. Two men—Garland Bentley and Ambrose Pinkston. They come off as almost cartoonish wannabes, but don't let that fool you. From what I've been told, they're street-smart and devious as shit. They know when to keep a low profile but I think they're deeply involved in all of this intrigue. I don't have concrete proof yet, but I'm working on it."

"Why tell me all this? What's your angle?" Monroe asked pointedly.

"I want to see justice served," Oswald said with a look that projected sincerity. "My family's legacy is tainted, but I refuse to be part of their corruption. If exposing them means setting things right, then so be it."

"You're taking a considerable risk," replied Monroe.

Looking earnestly at Monroe, "So are you, Mr. Gray. But I believe together we can unravel this conspiracy."

"Agreed," Monroe said, extending his hand. "Let's keep in touch, but we'll need to tread carefully."

Oswald shook Monroe's hand firmly. "I'll be in contact soon. Stay vigilant."

As Oswald disappeared into the crowd, Monroe wrestled with the implications of the new information confronting him. It was almost 7 p.m. and his flight was scheduled for 8:25. It was time to head for the airport. In a sense, he regretted that he wasn't staying overnight. A visit to Gene Lynn's—a local nightclub popular with both Black and White patrons, including local politicians—might have allowed him to gather more intel.

But Monroe needed to get back home. He had several ends to tie up before he left for New York and he was anxious to get started. Monroe found Tasha, and after saying a few quick goodbyes, they headed for the airport. The puzzle pieces were beginning to form a clearer picture, but the image they revealed was more uncertain than he anticipated.

35

MONROE SAT AT HIS DESK, the morning light casting a warm glow through the window of his DC office, which was located at 1025 Vermont Avenue NW. He'd been there for a couple of years now and liked the proximity to the K Street Corridor. The sound of rustling papers was the only noise in the quiet space as he leaned back in his chair, reviewing files that had been collecting dust since he'd become embroiled in the complex mess surrounding the casino murders. He sighed, aware that clients would soon begin asking questions if he didn't address some pressing matters. With that in mind, he dove in. After several hours, he felt as though he had regained control over his client agenda. Now, he could return to the mystery that had been haunting him.

Next to him stood a whiteboard filled with a chaotic mess of notes, ideas, and diagrams that somehow seemed organized. His eyes drifted to the scrawlings he'd just made—a chart listing all the players:

Carlton Dixon: Gamer's primary investor (*dead*)

Gordon Blackwell: The deal's chief architect (*dead*)

Congressman Pressley Hancock: Corrupt schemer, role unknown

Nimbus Bushrod: Point man for Gateway Partners

Tammy Treadwell: Darnell's right hand

Darnell Mayfield: Mayor and political beneficiary regardless of who wins the deal

Demetrius Steptoe: Bushrod flunky #1

Chauncey Prigmore: Bushrod flunky #2

And now: Oswald Dixon ???

Monroe moved to the board and, gripping a red marker, began drawing lines, connecting the dots.

"Dixon gets killed, Gordon's tied to the casino deals... Hancock's taking bribes left and right. And Tammy's hatred of Hancock... It all comes back to that damn seat her father lost," Monroe recited while thinking aloud. He paused, uncapping a blue marker, and drew a big circle around "The Investor," the faceless entity that seemed to loom behind every major deal. "But who's pulling the strings behind the strings?"

Monroe stood back, staring at the tangled web he'd charted. He shook his head, frustrated. Pieces were starting to fall into place, but the full picture still eluded him. As he gazed at the board, Monique, his sharp and always well-put-together assistant, peeked her head into the office.

"Mr. Gray, I was just finishing up. Do you need me for anything else today?"

Monroe glanced at the clock. It was nearly 2 p.m. He had no problem with her leaving early. He appreciated Monique's dedication and knew she had been working hard lately. Besides, his day would consist of mostly paperwork and puzzle-solving.

"You've earned some time off, Monique. Go ahead and enjoy the rest of the day. I'll handle the phones for now."

"Are you sure? You've got a couple of client calls scheduled for tomorrow, and I can reschedule them if you want."

Monroe smiled. "Do that. Remember, I'm heading to New York. Tell them I had a family emergency and will get back to them first thing Tuesday morning."

Monique smiled. It wasn't the first time she'd covered for her boss, and she knew it certainly wouldn't be the last. Clearly grateful for the early exit, she gave him a knowing look, well aware that he'd been involved in more than just business as usual.

"Alright, boss. Just...make sure you don't stay locked up in here all night again. You need a break too."

Monroe nodded. "Don't worry, I'll grab a bite to eat in a few. Thanks."

As she left, the office felt quieter than before. Monroe turned back to the whiteboard, absorbing the names, the connections, the tangled web of lies, money, and murder. His stomach growled, reminding him he hadn't eaten since early that morning. It was time for a break.

Monroe left his office and strolled down to the small deli that occupied the street-level space of his building. The place wasn't fancy, but it served the best turkey Reuben sandwich in town. As he ate, his mind kept returning to the whiteboard. The more he thought about the connections, the more the feeling grew in his gut that something big was on the horizon. He finished his sandwich, paid the tab, and took a short walk before heading back up to his office, his mind still running over details.

When Monroe returned around 3 p.m., the office was quiet. The afternoon sunlight had dimmed, casting long shadows across the room. He glanced at his desk and noticed a blinking light on the answering machine connected to his private line. His brow furrowed. Only a few people had that number—personal friends or trusted clients.

He walked over and hit play. It was Hancock's Chief of Staff and Monroe's newfound friend, Yvonne Montgomery. Her voice crackled through the machine, her tone frantic and fearful.

"Monroe! It's Yvonne. Listen to me... I think—I think I'm being followed. I need you to come over to my place now! Please. I don't know what's going on, but it's bad."

Monroe's heart rate quickened as her voice wavered, a tangible panic in her words.

"They've been watching me all day. I'm scared, Monroe. Please, you have to come. And if—if anything happens to me, or I'm not here—" her voice faltering slightly, "check the microwave."

The line went dead. Monroe stood frozen, gripping the edge of his desk. He hit the button to replay the message.

"Microwave...?" he muttered aloud.

While he'd only been acquainted with Yvonne until recently, he knew one thing: she wasn't the paranoid type. If she thought she was in danger, she was in danger. He felt a sick knot forming in his stomach.

Monroe briefly paced his office, playing out scenarios in his head. What if something had already happened to her? What if he was too late? He thought about calling Nitro Blue, but time felt too precious to waste.

No time to hesitate. If she's in trouble, I need to go now!

Ominous thoughts clouded his mind as he grabbed his coat and keys. Fortunately, he had driven to the office that day instead of taking the Metro. Monroe exited his office, locking the door behind him, and hurried down the hallway. Anxiety gripped him as he waited for the elevator. After what seemed like an eternity, it finally arrived. He exited at the garage level and dashed to his car. Within moments, he was speeding north toward Maryland, pushing his car as fast as it would go.

Monroe now faced a ticking clock and a vital clue—Yvonne's fear-stricken voicemail and her cryptic message about the microwave. He tried to devise a plan as he drove. Yvonne was likely caught in the same dangerous web they both sought to untangle. He would have to proceed with caution—whoever had been following Yvonne might still be watching her place. The question of what was in the microwave continued to plague him. But more importantly, would he be too late to help her?

Monroe bolted through the early rush hour on Georgia Avenue, threading his way through the thickening flow of vehicles with a sense of urgency. Fortune seemed to favor him as the traffic lights cooperated, each turning green just in time, allowing him to reach downtown Silver Spring far faster than he'd expected. When he spotted her street, he swung a sharp right, but instead of parking near her house, he executed a quick U-turn, pulling into a spot a quarter of a block away. He didn't know what awaited him, but he needed the advantage of escape. Reaching under the passenger seat, Monroe grabbed his Glock 17—his constant companion in recent days. He threw open the door and sprinted toward the house, adrenaline surging through his veins. As he neared the porch, his heart clenched. The door was ajar. With a steady hand, he pushed it open, bracing himself for whatever lay inside—and his worst suspicions were confirmed.

36

MONROE SAT QUIETLY IN THE DARK, continuing to take comfort in the glow of the US Park Police District 3 Station. The building was barely visible through the trees, and while it provided temporary safety, he knew it wouldn't last. The adrenaline from discovering Yvonne's body still surged through his veins, making it difficult to think straight. He ran a hand through his hair, exhaling slowly.

What the hell did you get into, Yvonne?

With his mind in overdrive, Monroe realized that the implications of what he'd just witnessed made the world feel even more dangerous than it had an hour ago. He glanced at his phone, contemplating who he could reach out to for advice—someone who could help him manage a situation that was growing more uncertain with each passing moment. He shook his head, realizing what had to be done. Nitro Blue was the only person who could help him make sense of it all. Nitro had a reputation for being... unconventional, but he was the sharpest guy Monroe knew, and this called for a mind like his.

Alright, Nitro. Time to get you into the mix.

Monroe placed a quick call to his friend to give him a heads-up. With a turn of the key, the engine rumbled to life, and Monroe made his way toward Brookland. He didn't look back at the station as he drove off—it wouldn't offer him answers, just questions he wasn't ready to face yet.

***

Monroe had met Nitro Blue at a veterans' support group several years back, and the man had left an impression. He'd heard stories from other vets—rumors that Nitro had been an explosives expert who was more than a little into his work. Some even joked that he hadn't quite given up the passion, which explained the nickname. To this day, Monroe didn't know Nitro's real first name, which he figured was intentional. He never asked. With Nitro, some things were better left unknown.

Nitro Blue's house was like a hidden oasis of controlled chaos. The two-story bungalow, weathered but sturdy, stood out amidst the recently renovated homes surrounding it. As Monroe pulled up, he noticed the flickering glow of various computer screens inside, the faint hum of activity signaling that Nitro was in his element.

Before Monroe could knock, the door swung open. Nitro appeared, grinning widely, his wild hair sticking up in different directions and wearing a worn Lakeside t-shirt from a concert that had likely been years earlier. A tall, lanky man with an angular face and high cheekbones, Nitro exuded a restless energy that made him seem incapable of standing still. His deep brown skin contrasted with the streaks of silver in his scruffy beard, and his expressive eyes were always in motion, taking in every detail. His hair, a thick cloud of tight coils shaped into a modest, uneven afro, perfectly matched his chaotic brilliance.

"Monroe Gray, the man of mystery. What kind of trouble did you bring to my doorstep this time?"

With a look of anxiousness, he stepped inside. "You know I wouldn't show up if it wasn't serious."

"If it's as urgent as that look on your face, we better get you a drink," Nitro said while closing the door.

The inside of Nitro's home was a cluttered marvel—half workshop, half surveillance hub, with gadgets Monroe couldn't name scattered across the room. Stacks of old vinyl records sat precariously near an array of computers, and blueprints covered the walls alongside faded concert posters. He poured two generous glasses of whiskey and handed one to Monroe, who sat heavily in an old leather chair. The warmth of the drink didn't ease the cold knot of fear tightening in his chest.

Nitro took a seat across from him. "So, what's going on, man? I know that look—someone just kicked the beehive, didn't they?"

Monroe sighed. "You have no idea. It's bad, Nitro. Yvonne's dead."

Nitro sat up straighter, his grin fading as his brow furrowed. "Yvonne? The one who works for that crooked congressman? Jesus… How?"

"Execution style," Monroe said in a subdued tone. "I found her in her house earlier. Whoever got to her, they wanted to send a message."

Nitro's eyes narrowed. "That's not your average murder, Monroe. What the hell was she mixed up in?"

Monroe took another sip, the gravity of it all crashing over him. He explained the tangled conspiracy he had been piecing together— Dixon's and Gordon's murders, the casino licenses, Hancock's bribes, and Tammy's behavior. As Nitro listened, he started pacing the room, his mind already working through the puzzle.

"So you think they killed her because she knew too much?"

Monroe nodded. "She left me a message, panicked, right before it happened. Told me to check her microwave."

"Wait—what? Microwave?" Nitro asked, stopping dead in his tracks. The hell kind of clue is that?"

"I found the key to her safe deposit box," Monroe said, leaning forward. "Whatever Yvonne was hiding from them, it's in there. She must have been collecting evidence, tracking all of it."

Despite the seriousness of the situation, Nitro grinned slightly. "Yvonne, smart girl. She knew they were coming, and the last place the intruders would look for anything was the microwave. So, you have the key—what's the plan?"

"First thing tomorrow, we get into that box and see what she left behind. If I'm right, it'll be enough to blow this thing wide open. Payoffs to Hancock, backdoor deals in Africa, maybe even proof of who killed Dixon, Gordon, and her."

"Alright, but you need to be careful, Monroe," he said as he walked back over to the bar for a refill. "These guys already took out Yvonne, and Lord knows who else. They'll come after you, too, if they think you're on to something. We need to play this smart."

Monroe leaned back, exhaustion occupying his voice. "That's why I'm here. You're the only one I trust to help me unravel this mess."

Nitro paused, the grin returning to his face. "You know I've always loved a good mystery. I'm in. Tomorrow, we get to the bottom of this. But tonight, you stay here. You're not going back out there until we figure out who's hunting who."

37

THE NEXT MORNING, THE AIR WAS THICK with unease as the duo neared the bank. Nitro, ever cautious, urged Monroe to park a block away from the bank as he scanned the area for any signs of trouble. He didn't like taking chances, especially not now. The plan was simple: get in, retrieve the contents of the safety deposit box, and get out—no lingering, no mistakes. They were walking a fine line now, and the stakes had never felt higher.

"You remember the plan, right?" Nitro asked, glancing at Monroe. In and out, no lingering. This isn't a social call."

"Yeah, yeah. Let's just get this over with."

They approached the entrance of the bank, located on Capitol Hill. Nitro took up a position outside to keep watch while Monroe went in. The air inside was cool and sterile. Monroe approached the teller, forcing himself to appear calm like this was just another day at the office.

The young woman behind the window wore a neatly pressed pale blue blouse, and her red hair was shoulder-length. Her expression was attentive, and her demeanor professional. "How can I help you today, sir?" she asked.

Monroe held up the key. "I'd like to access my safe deposit box, please."

The teller nodded and motioned to a nearby bank officer to come over. After introducing himself, he led Monroe to a secure room. As the door clicked shut behind him, the silence was deafening. Monroe's hand trembled slightly as he inserted the key into the box's lock. With a click, the lid opened to reveal two cassette tapes, a thick envelope filled with documents, and a handwritten letter in Yvonne's unmistakable handwriting. He took the letter first, carefully unfolding the fragile paper.

Yvonne's words leaped off the page.

Monroe, if you're reading this, it means I'm gone and there was no escape. The forces behind this shit are beyond corrupt! Inside this box, you'll find proof—proof of everything Hancock's been doing, the bribes, the deals in Africa, and the murders. One of the tapes is a conversation between Hancock and someone called "The Investor." The other is between Tammy and Gordon, planning how to take down Nimbus and Steptoe. Be careful, Monroe. You're in deep now. Don't trust anyone—especially not Hancock.

Monroe's pulse quickened as he took the tapes and the documents. Everything Yvonne had been killed for was in his hands. He stuffed the evidence into his briefcase, locked the box again, and hurried out. As he exited the bank, Nitro was leaning casually against the side of a nearby building, eyes scanning the area.

Nitro pushed off the wall. "You get what you needed?"

"I got it," Monroe affirmed.

"Good. Now let's get the hell out of here before anyone figures out what we just took."

Nitro slid into the passenger seat with Monroe back behind the wheel. The two men were off, their vehicle blending into the morning traffic as the city churned around them. Yet Monroe's thoughts were far from the city's daily bustle. What he'd just uncovered had the potential to blow everything wide open. But with that knowledge came danger: if he hadn't been a target before, he was one now.

"This changes everything, Nitro."

"Yeah, and not for the better. A lot of people gonna want a piece of whatever we just pulled out of that box."

His jaw tightened. "You don't think I know that."

As the sun crept higher in the sky, the duo sped past monuments and office buildings, with the treasure that they'd retrieved settled in the briefcase on the floor behind Monroe's seat. The contents that had been inside that safe deposit box could be the evidence that would expose a vast network of corruption. Little did they realize the magnitude of it all.

"We gotta be smart about this," Nitro said, glancing out the window and shifting uneasily in his seat. "The feds might have their sights on the same people, but right now, no one knows what we have. That keeps us in the game."

"For now. But Tyree and Frazier aren't going to let this slide. Yvonne's dead, and you can bet they're putting my name at the top of their list of suspects...again."

"Yeah, I'd bet money they're looking for you already. You gotta lay low."

As the car rolled west to head back toward downtown, Monroe came up with an option. His gut told him that he knew the perfect spot, but he needed to make a few preparations. If the police—or worse, the people behind Yvonne's murder—were after him, he needed to be ready.

Exiting Pennsylvania Avenue NW, he drove for two more blocks. With rush hour just over, spaces by meters were momentarily plentiful. He neatly pulled into a parking space in front of Woodward

& Lothrop, a department store at 11th & F Streets NW—or as it was known locally, "Woodies."

Startled, Nitro said, "Your new plan—a shopping spree?"

"I always keep a change of clothes in the trunk for unexpected opportunities," Monroe offered with a smug grin. "But I need more than that. I'll grab some essentials since I'm not going back to my place before leaving for New York."

"Okay, I'll watch out."

"Back before you know it. Don't let that case leave your sight."

"You do know who you're talkin' to, don't you?" Nitro said with a mischievous smile.

Once inside the store, Monroe wasted no time, quickly grabbing a couple of shirts, slacks, and socks. He moved through the checkout line with precision and made his exit without attracting any unnecessary attention. From there, he headed straight for Peoples Drug Store on 15th & G Street NW, where he picked up deodorant, shaving cream, and some aspirin. His head throbbed under the weight of everything closing in on him. Roaming the aisles, he tried to remain inconspicuous, though his mind was in overdrive. Scenarios played out in rapid succession as he calculated who might be after him and how much time he had before the noose tightened.

Once back in the car, Monroe tapped his fingers against the steering wheel, mentally running through the steps ahead. He decided that The River Inn would be a good place to set up camp for the day. Ever since he had recommended it to a client, he had liked the property. Located on 25th Street NW just a few blocks from the edge of Georgetown, the River Inn was off the beaten path. It was tucked away on a mostly residential street, and except for the extended yet narrow hotel awning with the property's three-word name, it could pass for a dwelling that few would notice.

"No one will look for us there," Monroe insisted. "At least for now."

"Yeah, but don't get too cozy. It's just a pit stop, not a solution," Nitro retorted, still nervously scanning the street.

"I know, but it will give us the space and time to plan our next moves. I was scheduled to leave for New York tomorrow, but I need to push my trip back by a day. I can't leave town with all this going on and without a plan."

Nitro offered a dark laugh. "Yeah, I don't think a little mayor's conference is high on the priority list right now."

"I beg to differ, my man. Most of the players in this game will be there and so will I. That's where I'll find answers. I just need to be ready."

They drove in silence for a moment before Monroe broke it.

"What do you think the next play is, Nitro? We've got this dirt on Hancock, but the deeper I dig, the more it feels like I'm still missing something."

Nitro sighed. "First, we really don't know what we have yet. But I got a feeling that whatever is in that case is enough to light the match, but the whole thing is gonna blow if we're not careful. Hancock's just one piece of the puzzle. Whoever's funding all this— 'The Investor'—is still out there, pulling strings. We have to set a trap, bait the big fish."

Monroe nodded. "Agreed. But first, we gotta figure out how to get Tyree and Frazier off my back long enough to make our move."

Just as he pulled up in front of the hotel, a parking valet was waiting. Before handing over his keys, he retrieved the briefcase and the bags of items he'd just purchased from the back seat and glanced around. They quickly walked down the steps and into the lobby, which was located several feet below street level.

"Let's get inside and regroup," his voice low as he turned toward Nitro. "I'll call Amtrak and reschedule my trip to New York until Saturday. We need every second we can get to plan—no room for slip-ups."

They entered the room, and Monroe swiftly shut the curtains, the late afternoon sun disappearing behind the heavy fabric. He tossed his bags onto the floor as Nitro started pacing, his mind working overtime, thinking through next steps.

"I've gotta keep Tyree and Frazier off my back, at least for now," Monroe muttered, half to himself. "If they get a whiff of where I am, or what I'm up to, it's game over before it even starts."

Nitro stopped pacing, a sly grin forming on his lips. "We'll cross that bridge when we come to it," he said, with a confidence that almost bordered on cocky. "If I need to, I've got some tricks I haven't used yet. But you—you better be ready for New York. From the time you get there to the time you leave, it's checkmate or nothing."

"Yeah...if I make it that far."

They exchanged a knowing look, neither needing to say more. The next few days were going to decide everything—whether Monroe would come out alive, whether the truth would finally be exposed, or whether the outcome would veer dangerously off course.

"We need to loop in the feds, and fast," Nitro said, his tone growing more urgent. "If they crash the party too soon, we'll be up to our necks in trouble."

Monroe didn't disagree, but a sinking feeling told him they were already on borrowed time. Neither of them realized just how prophetic Nitro's words were about to become.

38

ONROE AND NITRO SETTLED INTO the room at the River Inn, the low hum of the city outside muted by the thick curtains. Monroe had chosen that particular hotel for its spacious and well-appointed apartment-like suites, which provided a comfortable, lived-in feel rather than the sterile atmosphere of a standard room. The location was also tucked away— just enough off the grid to stay under the radar of any possible stalker, but not so secluded that access to major arteries and commercial establishments wasn't a concern.

The coffee table was now covered with the contents of Yvonne's manila folder. A cassette tape sat in the middle, like a relic from a different era, and beside it, a stack of papers: handwritten notes, Xerox copies of bank transactions, and internal communications.

Nitro leaned back on the couch, rubbing his chin. "Feels like we've been handed the keys to the kingdom here," he said, grinning widely.

Monroe was focused, flipping through the papers. "Yeah, but we're still blind in a lot of ways. The more we uncover, the more this thing unravels."

Monroe set aside the Xerox copies—bank transactions showing deposits in Switzerland and Panama, made to shell companies linked to the names of figures he didn't recognize. As he tapped the paper, his eyes narrowed.

"These deposits...they're not small. Whoever's behind this has been funneling money for years, setting up shop in Africa. The money seems to be coming mostly from Morrocco, France, and South Africa, with a few transactions from New York. "

Nitro nodded. "Fits the timeline. These kinds of operations don't pop up overnight. That means they've been laying the groundwork, making connections, building the right relationships."

"According to Yvonne's notes, Hancock's the recipient of a lot of these and is probably using an alias as the owner of one or more of the shell companies. Neck-deep in it."

"I think we need to listen to the tape," Nitro suggested.

Monroe slid the cassette into a small portable player Nitro had brought and hit play. The tape crackled to life, distorted for a moment before the voices emerged—Hancock's oily tone was unmistakable to Monroe's ears. The other man was speaking with what seemed to be a French accent.

"It seems like everything's lined up on our end. Once we lock down the casino licenses in St. Louis, we'll be in position to make a run at other cities," Hancock boasted. "That's where my political connections will make all the difference."

"Everything is on track in Botswana, Lesotho, and Swaziland, and when the ANC takes over in South Africa, we can pursue our opportunities there," said the French voice. "But we must move quickly and carefully as a new government is being formed. There will be many eyes on this.

"True," Hancock responded. "But I think we're in good shape."

"And these characters, Ambrose and Garland—they are useful, but only for now. They are...expendable."

"I understand," Hancock said with an evil chuckle. "That's the beauty of it. Those muthafuckas don't even know it yet. But when the time comes...we'll deal with them. Quietly."

"One last thing—this is the first and final time we speak," warned the French voice. "From here on, anything that needs to reach me will go through 'The Broker.' Are we clear?"

"Crystal clear," replied Hancock. "We've been on the same page from the start. From where I sit, he has things under control."

Monroe paused the tape. The silence that followed hung in the air, thick with tension. Nitro leaned forward, eyes sharp, locking on Monroe. "'The Broker'—who the hell is that?"

Monroe frowned. "I don't know. But it sounds like he's running the show behind the scenes for 'The Investor.' Could be someone we haven't even clocked yet."

"Or maybe it's someone familiar, just wearing a different mask. Either way, they got control of the city's casino licenses and all that money just waiting to be made."

"Hancock and this French guy have bigger plans in motion—multiple countries in Africa and St. Louis, with more cities on their radar. They've got Ambrose and Garland thinking they're part of the master plan, but when the time comes, they'll drop them like a bad habit—or worse."

"Typical. When the heavy lifting's done, the pawns get wiped off the board," Nitro remarked.

"Exactly. But what's worrying me is, who's this guy? He's gotta be 'The Investor,' right? French accent, talking like he's orchestrating everything alongside this 'Broker.' It has to be him."

Nitro leaned back and exhaled. "Yeah, that's gotta be 'The Investor.' He's the money man behind this whole operation. St. Louis is just a piece of the puzzle—Africa's the big score. They've been working on this for years, Monroe. And now they've picked up the pace and people are dying as a result."

"Yeah, it's like they're tying up loose ends and greed is the accelerator," added Monroe.

They both stared at the notes on the table for a moment. Monroe's mind was working through the implications, the connections, the risks. Then, he picked up the papers again, flipping through Yvonne's notes.

"She didn't know much about the murders. But look at this," he said, handing Nitro a note where Yvonne had written down her thoughts, a kind of diary entry.

Carlton Dixon and Gordon Blackwell...there's something off here. Different methods—Dixon strangled, Blackwell poisoned. Feels like two different hands were involved. But why? Why would the same people kill them in different ways unless there's something else at play?

"Two different assassins?" Nitro queried.

"I don't know how Yvonne got wind of the way Dixon and Gordon were killed. Maybe she overheard something. One thing is for certain, she was right," Monroe blurted. "Strangling someone is up-close, personal. Poisoning is...cleaner, more detached. And a gunshot to the forehead would signal that a professional was used."

"Right," Nitro affirmed with a nod. "And it makes sense. Dixon was the big fish, so maybe they wanted to send a message with how they took him out. But Gordon?"

"He was playing on both sides of the fence," Monroe interjected. "Maybe they caught on to his bullshit and just wanted him gone quickly and quietly."

Monroe paced. "Yvonne was on to something. She didn't have all the details, but she knew there was more going on behind the scenes," he said with a grim voice. "You know, I should have seen this and it's probably the reason why I haven't been cleared. The police probably believe that there's more than one killer on the loose."

"Maybe Dixon's murder was about control—eliminating a threat—and Gordon was a loose cannon who needed to go before he could double-cross them."

"But if we've got two different killers working under the same operation, that means this conspiracy is even bigger than we thought and somebody may have gone rogue."

"Yeah. And I'm guessing they've still got a few more surprises for us," Nitro said, wincing.

Monroe stopped pacing, his eyes locked with Nitro's. "We need to identify 'The Broker,'" Monroe challenged. "Whoever this mystery man is, they hold the key to solving this puzzle."

"Agreed," Nitro retorted. "But first, we need to determine who we can trust. Because the deeper we dig, the more we're surrounded by sharks. And it feels like they're closing in."

"Most of the players will be in New York at the conference, which only ups the risk for me," Monroe stated with a tinge of concern creeping into his voice.

"Relax, my man. We got this," said Nitro.

"We?" Monroe asked with a raised eyebrow, surprised.

"C'mon, you didn't think I was going to let you have all the fun, M.G.?"

"Seriously, man, you don't need to do this. It's not going to be a picnic."

"Look, brotherman, you're not doing this alone," Nitro insisted. "I'm catching a taxi home, getting my gear sorted, and we'll meet up tomorrow. And yeah, it's time we brought the feds in before we get out of town."

"I appreciate the backup, but I won't hold it against you if you change your mind."

"Let me worry about me. Just don't go driving around the streets tonight. If you get spotted, it could ruin everything."

As the two of them sat there, surrounded by incriminating evidence and tangled threads of conspiracy, they realized the forces they were up against. They knew time was running out—a showdown was looming, and the key players were about to make their moves. But Monroe and Nitro were determined to stay one step ahead, even if it meant walking into the lion's den without a clear escape plan. The truth was going to come to light, and with it, the danger grew. Every detail they uncovered pushed them further into a web of corruption and murder, with no guarantees they'd make it out alive.

39

THE EVENING AIR IN GEORGETOWN WAS CRISP, with a light breeze rolling down the cobbled streets. The faint glow of streetlamps reflected off the storefront windows, casting long shadows. Monroe kept his head down as he walked, his hands tucked in his pockets, keeping a low profile. He reached Paper Moon, a small Italian bistro tucked just below M Street NW, its warm lights spilling out onto the sidewalk. The restaurant was intimate but casual, with a mix of well-dressed patrons and locals enjoying a relaxed evening.

After Nitro left the hotel, Monroe's restlessness got the better of him. He knew his friend's advice was solid—driving around wasn't a smart move when both the police and the thugs from the previous day were likely looking for him. Yet, he craved a way to release the pent-up tension that flowed through his body.

Monroe decided to take a chance. He reached out to Malaika, hoping she would be free. To his delight, she was available and agreed to meet him for dinner. As he headed out, Monroe couldn't help but anticipate the possibility their meal together would be just the beginning of a longer night, one that ended back at the River Inn.

After entering the restaurant, Monroe scanned the crowd inside. His eyes landed on Malaika, already seated at a table toward the back of the restaurant away from the bar. She was dressed in a soft gray blouse, her hair pulled back, a look that was both understated and effortlessly elegant. For a brief moment, Monroe's tension eased. Maybe tonight wouldn't be about conspiracies and corruption. Maybe, just maybe, he could let himself indulge in a little normalcy.

Monroe slid into the chair opposite her, giving her a warm smile. "You're early."

Malaika smiled. "You're late."

He chuckled, reaching for the drink menu. "Alright, I'll give you that one."

They ordered drinks—bourbon for Monroe, a dry martini for Malaika—and the conversation began easily enough, flowing with casual remarks about the crowd and the day. Monroe's mind, however, was anything but casual. The intensity of the past twenty-four hours sat heavily on him, and despite the charm and chemistry between them, he couldn't stop thinking about what he and Nitro had uncovered.

As the drinks arrived, Monroe tried to push those thoughts aside. He leaned forward, giving Malaika a look that he hoped conveyed something deeper than just friendly conversation. Summoning up his best provocative gaze, he said, "You know, I've got a place not too far from here… Could be a good spot to unwind after dinner."

Malaika, playing coy, smiled and took a sip of her drink. "Unwind? I didn't realize I needed unwinding."

Monroe leaned back, grinning. "Maybe not, but I could definitely use a little…relaxation. And you're the best company any one man could have."

She laughed, but for some reason, his proposition didn't quite land. Monroe noticed the flicker of something—hesitation, maybe? Or was it something else? Before he could probe further, their food arrived. The conversation turned lighter as they ate, discussing nothing in particular: the food, the ambiance, even a couple of inside jokes they'd shared from past encounters.

But as they finished the meal, Monroe couldn't help himself. The stress of everything gnawed at him. He needed to share something, at least a little, with someone he trusted—or thought he could trust.

"So, something happened recently," he said, leaning in to get closer. "And I haven't told anyone this yet."

Malaika's eyes flickered with interest, though she kept her expression neutral. "Something? Do tell."

Lowering his voice, Monroe revealed, "Yvonne Montgomery. I found her…dead. In her house. Looked like an execution. And she left me a message before she died, telling me to check her microwave for a key."

He had Malaika's attention. "What? Wait a minute. Executed? What makes you say that?"

"She was shot point blank in the forehead. No other explanation as far as I can see."

"Damn! And? Did you find what she wanted you to?" she asked with more than a little interest.

Monroe nodded slowly. "Yeah. A key to a safety deposit box. My friend Nitro Blue and I opened it this morning. There was a lot in there—bank transactions, notes, recordings. Yvonne was close to blowing this whole thing wide open."

Monroe stopped short of revealing the full extent of what he'd found, still holding some of his cards close to his chest. He was testing Malaika, gauging her reaction. She set her fork down and took a long sip of her drink, her expression unreadable. When she finally spoke, her tone had shifted—serious, but not alarmed. More…calculating.

"Monroe, I need to tell you something." He leaned in slightly, his brow furrowed.

Malaika exhaled, "I've been waiting for the right time, but it seems like now's the moment. I learned about Yvonne's death last night. I'm also not the company executive you think I am. I'm...I'm with the FBI."

Momentarily stunned, Monroe exploded, "You're—what?"

"I've been undercover for a while now. The agency embedded me in the firm where I "work" several years ago to investigate political corruption in targeted cities around the country. With states legalizing gambling, greed is running rampant and the players range from local hacks to organized crime. The very conspiracy you've found yourself tangled in. That's my case."

Monroe leaned back, trying to process the revelation, "I thought we were building something real. You had me fooled."

"I didn't want to lie to you," Malaika said softly. "I wanted to understand you—get to know the man."

Monroe shook his head as a feeling of betrayal overwhelmed him. "You used sex to get close to me. What else was a lie?"

"Not everything!" Malaika pleaded. "My feelings for you were...are real. I just...but the job complicated everything. But I cleared you before we had sex."

"What do you mean, cleared me?"

"I knew that you weren't corrupt and that you didn't kill Dixon or Blackwell. And don't ask me how. That's my job. Let's just say, I needed some stress relief too."

Monroe took a deep breath, his expression a mix of anger and hurt. "You should have trusted me enough to be honest. Now I don't know what to believe."

"I know this is a lot to take in."

"No shit! So this isn't a joke."

"Not even. This is serious business, Monroe. I've been gathering evidence for months, piecing together the players—Hancock, Dixon, Gordon—and now you're telling me Yvonne stumbled on what sounds like is incriminating evidence? I had a feeling something was wrong with her silence these past few days, but I didn't expect…this."

"What? Yvonne was working with you?"

Sighing, Malaika continued, "Not really. But we had talked on a couple of occasions and I was hoping to bring her in to help. Obviously, she had more confidence in you than me."

Monroe's mind raced. Had Malaika been playing him this whole time? His instincts told him to be cautious, but another part of him, the part exhausted by the events of the last few days, wanted to trust her.

"So, what now? You're here to take me in?" he asked cautiously.

"No. I'm here because you're in over your head," Malaika replied softly. "You're a target. The people behind this—they won't hesitate to come after you. You need protection."

Monroe scoffed. "Protection? No thanks."

Malaika leaned in, her tone firm. "This isn't about you trusting me. It's about survival. You think you can handle this alone, but these aren't street-level thugs we're dealing with. This is international. You're talking about people with connections in Panama, Switzerland, Africa—this is big. And the FBI is already onto it."

Monroe's heart raced. This changed everything. His mind flicked back to the tapes, the conversations about Africa, "The Investor," and the murders. If Malaika was right—and he had no reason to doubt her now—then he was a small piece in a much bigger puzzle.

"I don't know, Malaika," Monroe replied in a hushed tone. "This is bigger than what the FBI can handle, isn't it? You really think you can protect me?"

Malaika nodded confidently. "We can. And we will. But I need you to trust me. We can work together, Monroe. You're good at this—figuring things out, connecting the dots. But we have resources, manpower. You give me what you know, and I'll make sure we get to the bottom of this. You're in the thick of it now, but if we pull you out too early, we could lose our shot."

Monroe exhaled, rubbing his temples. "Damn. I didn't see this coming."

They sat in silence for a moment, the magnitude of the situation settling between them. Monroe could feel the importance of a decision pressing down on him. He was used to playing lone wolf, taking matters into his own hands. But this? Maybe she was right. This was too big.

Malaika reached across the table, her hand resting on his arm. "Monroe, you're good at what you do. But this is the endgame. You can't go to New York without backup. You can't face these people alone."

Monroe met her gaze. "I wasn't going alone. My partner Nitro would be with me."

"Doesn't matter, you both would be lambs among wolves," she quickly retorted.

"And what happens if I don't play ball with the FBI?"

"If you don't cooperate…someone else will get to you first. Do you really want to end up like Dixon, Gordon, and Yvonne?"

Monroe stared at her, weighing his options. He knew she was right. The stakes were too high to go it alone anymore. But trusting her? Before her revelation, yes, but now? Yet there he was, cornered by the very people he thought he could handle.

Monroe slowly nodded. "Alright. I'm in. But we do this my way, and I don't give you everything right off the bat. We're in this together, and I want to see who's pulling the strings before the hammer comes down."

"Deal," Malaika said softly, shaking his hand. "We'll get them, Monroe. All of them."

"So I guess sex is off the table now," he said dryly. Malaika responded with a look that adequately answered his question. He would be going back to his hotel alone. With an understanding in place, they clinked glasses, though the tension still hung in the air. Neither of them knew what lay ahead in New York, but for now, they were on the same side. And together, they might just stand a chance.

40

THE HOTEL VALET PULLED UP in Monroe's car shortly before 8 a.m. Since his train to New York didn't leave until one, he would have plenty of time to plot with Nitro and touch base with Malaika. He had been in some tight spots in his life, especially in Nam, yet this predicament was unlike any he had encountered since returning to civilian life.

He made the turn onto K Street. His destination was the Florida Avenue Grill, where he was to meet up with Nitro. Despite the emotional rollercoaster of the last few days, his appetite was still intact. Although his stomach growled in protest, Monroe knew there was one more stop he needed to make. This brief detour could determine the outcome of his mission and possibly keep him alive.

***

In a bid to stay under the radar, Monroe parked on 11th Street, just north of Florida Avenue, rather than the restaurant's lot. He locked his car and began the short walk toward the restaurant when he spied Tyree and Frazier stepping out. Monroe should have known. The Grill drew a diverse crowd, including government officials and numerous celebrities whose autographed photos adorned the walls.

To make matters worse, with it being a Saturday morning, the place was packed.

Stopping dead in his tracks, Monroe took refuge behind a tree that would shield him from their view if they looked his way. Fortunately, they didn't. The two men made their way to the parking lot. After a tense moment, Monroe watched as their car pulled out, turning right onto 11th Street and heading toward downtown. Bullet dodged. He hurried toward the entrance to see if Nitro was there.

Monroe squeezed through the crowd of patrons that surrounded the door, most of whom were waiting for tables or seats at the counter. Monroe's nostrils were immediately introduced to the rich aroma of a variety of southern comfort foods, instantly stirring his hunger. The diner was bustling with the morning crowd, a mix of local regulars and visitors who seemed to enjoy the welcoming atmosphere.

Spotting Nitro standing near a booth toward the back, Monroe made a beeline in his direction. His pulse quickened as he settled next to him. Nitro looked up, his expression shifting from casual interest to concern as he noticed Monroe's tense demeanor.

"You look like you just saw a ghost," Nitro quipped. "What's going on?"

Monroe glanced around nervously. "More like two. I almost ran into Tyree and Frazier on the way in."

"The detectives?" Nitro asked with a raised eyebrow. "Here?"

Monroe hesitated before answering. "I shouldn't have been surprised. Look around. This place is a melting pot, and those two assholes have to eat too."

"Hold on," Nitro said, rubbing his chin thoughtfully. "Was one kind of fit and the other looked like he wasn't missing any meals?"

"Yeah, why?"

"I spotted them when I came in. First thing I thought was they had Five-O written all over them. I don't think they even noticed me."

"I doubt they were on the lookout for me, but I'm certain they wouldn't have minded crossing paths," Monroe said. He let out a breath, running his fingers through his hair. "I can't risk being seen by anyone right now, especially not those two."

Before another word could be uttered, the waitress handling the carryout orders called out Nitro's receipt number.

"You ordered?" Monroe asked with a quizzical look.

"Man, you can see this place was a madhouse. No telling when we would have been seated, so I ad-libbed."

They walked over to the counter and the waitress handed over a large bag with what appeared to be two orders.

"Here you go, baby," she said with a warm smile. That was the standard pet name used by all of the female waitresses or servers for any customer. Nitro grabbed the bag and they headed for the door.

"What are we eating?" Monroe queried.

"Eggs over easy, salmon cakes, home fries, and wheat toast."

"My man. Just what the doctor ordered. Let's get a move on it."

Nitro had taken a taxi to the restaurant, planning to ride back to his place with Monroe. They quickly made their way to the car, cruising down Florida Avenue toward Howard University, and eventually making their way back to Brookland. The aroma of the food filled the car, prompting Nitro to open his container and sample a small piece of salmon cake—only to nearly choke on it when Monroe revealed that Malaika was a federal agent. Despite Nitro's shock at the revelation and the chaos surrounding them, the rest of the drive was unusually silent. Each man was lost in his own thoughts, envisioning what might lie ahead.

As they pulled up in front of Nitro's house, Monroe gathered his belongings, his mind racing with anticipation and anxiety. Nitro jumped out first, quickly unlocking the door and carrying the food into the kitchen. Monroe soon followed after retrieving some additional items from his trunk. In no time, they were at the kitchen table, devouring their food. As both men were finishing up, Monroe leaned back. "This is going to be an interesting two days. I just hope I'm up for it."

"Don't worry. I'll do everything I can to make sure you are. I just hope that Ms. FBI has her shit together."

"I'm sure that she will," Monroe said almost wistfully.

"That girl had you pussy-whipped," Nitro chuckled, unable to hide his amusement.

"Fuck you!" Monroe shot back, though a small smile tugged at his lips.

"That's all you got?" Nitro laughed, shaking his head.

"Yeah, okay. I was digging on her, but this FBI thing hit me hard."

"So she was using you to get information?" Nitro pressed, his tone turning serious.

"You and I talked about this last night. I don't know. I thought we had a connection, and I gotta say, the sex was great," Monroe said, rubbing the back of his neck, a gesture of uncertainty. "But now? I'm not sure I can trust her, although for now, I have to. Everything seems twisted." He paused, staring blankly out the window.

"Look, I know that she wants you to come alone, but none of these people know me or what I look like. Maybe I'll stay in the background and see what I can dig up."

Monroe turned to Nitro, considering his friend's suggestion. "You know that's actually not a bad idea. We've got a couple of hours. Let's go over everything and come up with a Plan B that's tight. If the shit hits the fan, we'll be ready."

41

THE ROOM WAS CLUTTERED BUT COZY, with a worn couch and a small coffee table stacked with files and documents. Sunlight filtered through the curtains, casting a warm glow. Monroe sat forward in his seat, hands clasped, studying the collection of information left by Yvonne. Meanwhile, Nitro rummaged through what he called a wardrobe, selecting a suit and a couple of shirts to take along.

"Make sure your socks match," Monroe added, "and pick out a tie from one of the last two decades."

Nitro needed to blend in and not attract unwanted attention. The last thing Monroe wanted was for Nitro to arrive in New York looking like he was homeless. Maybe he could pull off an eccentric professor look. That could probably work.

After about ten minutes, just as Monroe reached to open one of the documents, Nitro came bounding down the steps with his usual energy. He entered the room dressed sharply in a tailored black two-button suit that hugged his lean frame. The crisp white shirt beneath, with its clean, classic collar, added to his polished look, though there was still an air of unpredictability about him—like a man who could go from business to chaos in an instant.

Monroe turned, his eyes widened in mock disbelief, and quipped, "Who are you, and what have you done with Nitro?" He examined his friend's sharp outfit as if searching for any sign of the disordered man he knew so well beneath the polished exterior.

"Real funny," Nitro said with a roll of his eyes. "Had to go to a family funeral a couple months back, and Mama said I wasn't allowed to show up unless I looked presentable."

"Now if you'd just do something about that jungle on your head you call an afro," Monroe said, eyeing Nitro's wild hair with amusement.

"Don't worry about me; the Nitro man will be together when I make the scene."

"Man, sit your ass down here and let's get serious for a minute."

Nitro removed his jacket and placed it on the back of an adjacent chair. "Let's get it on, bro."

"We went over everything at the hotel, but we got so wrapped up in trying to figure out who our two mystery men were that we didn't finish listening to the tape," Monroe admitted, his frustration evident.

Nitro, always one for action, reached across the table, grabbed the recorder, and hit play without hesitation. The cassette whirred to life, and the now-familiar French Voice, who they had pegged as "The Investor," took center stage. Monroe and Nitro exchanged glances as Hancock's voice followed, full of bravado, boasting about all the global deals he had his hands in. The conversation seemed to dance around power, money, and control—the usual chest-thumping. But then came the first real shock. Hancock's voice lowered as he casually mentioned his future plans.

"Once all these deals are locked down," his voice crackling through the speakers, "I'll step down from Congress. Let the boy take the seat. After that, I'll spend all my time…spending my money."

"So, he's just going to stiff-arm Cleo?' Monroe said, taken aback. "That's fucked up."

The cassette continued to spin, unleashing more of their ambitions into the open. The scale of their intentions was astounding and, to Monroe, alarming. The more they listened, the more unsettling the scope of the operation became—power plays that reached far beyond the US, all linked by bribes and corruption, and a plan to leave a trail of bodies behind them.

"What about those three clowns who are in your employ?" asked the French Voice, his tone frigid and calculating.

"Who? Nimbus, Steptoe, and Prigmore?" Hancock answered.

"Whoever," the French Voice replied dismissively. "What's your plan?"

"We won't have to worry about them. One of my people has funneled enough shit on them to the cops. Those stupid muthafuckas will be old men by the time they see the light of day again."

Unimpressed, the French Voice's response was sharp. "I'd prefer a more permanent solution. I'm going to get 'The Broker' on it. You just keep your distance so nothing comes back to you. Do you understand?"

"I understand."

"Damn, that's cold!" Nitro whispered, shaking his head.

"Ssshhh," Monroe blurted, eyes fixed on the recorder.

"And what about the last two loose ends—the mayor and his right hand?" the French Voice continued.

"That's easy. They're just looking for a piece of the St. Louis casino deal," Hancock responded.

"And that can be done without them being ensnared in some type of corruption scandal?"

"Yeah, no problem," Hancock assured him. "They'll use Dixon's money, channeled through his unsuspecting widow. She'll be the face of the whole thing."

There was a long, heavy exhale on the other end of the tape before the French Voice spoke again. "I'll leave that in your hands, but make no mistake—we'll do whatever is necessary to protect our interests."

"It will all work out, I assure you," maintained the congressman.

"One final thing. I want you to organize a meeting with all of your principals in New York. I want to make sure everyone is on the same page. And by the way, 'The Broker' will be in attendance as my proxy."

"Okay, I'm on it," replied Hancock.

At that point, there was a click and the conversation ended.

The cassette tape clicked off, leaving a heavy silence in the room. Monroe sat back on the sofa, running a hand over his face. Nitro continued to lean forward, staring at the recorder as if willing it to reveal more words.

"So, that's it," Monroe finally said, his voice low. "Hancock's up to his elbows in graft and everyone else has got their hand out. That French guy, 'The Investor,' and 'The Broker' are orchestrating everything."

Nitro, who'd been unusually quiet, crossed his arms and leaned back. "And now we're stepping into the unknown, Monroe. It should be interesting. All the players in one place, each with an agenda. This will be tough."

Monroe nodded. "Yeah, our job is clear: blend in and find out everything we can before I meet with the FBI."

"Absolutely," Nitro declared, his eyes gleaming with mischief. "I'll be moving in the shadows, picking up what I can since I'll be an unseen presence." He reclined back in his chair, exuding an air of confidence.

"First things first," Monroe continued, a serious edge creeping into his voice. "You'll need to come up with a cover and spend as much time as you can at the bar in the Milano Royale. According to Darnell, that's where he and most of his entourage were staying. Because he'll be there, everyone with an interest in the development deal will be hanging out there. The only reason Nimbus and his crew are going is to stay close to Darnell and attend Hancock's meeting."

Intrigued, Nitro asked, "What's your angle?"

"Since Gordon and I had planned on being there and to spend time with Darnell, I'll just play it straight. But one thing I have to do to make all of this work is to get into that negotiation."

"That's going to be tough," Nitro responded. "How are you going to make that happen?"

"I don't know just yet, but I think that the key to getting in might just be Ambrose. He's asked me to join his and Garland's effort recently. Maybe he's still open to it. But once I get there, I'll stick close to Darnell, pretend nothing's changed."

Nitro grinned, his usual bravado emerging. "Don't worry about me. I'll be like a ghost—no one will even see me coming." He stood up, stretching his arms, his lanky frame filling the room with energy. "You ready for this?"

Monroe glanced down at the scattered papers on the table, then back up at Nitro. "I don't have a choice, do I? We're in this now, but we'll make it work."

"We're not amateurs," Nitro replied, stepping to the window and peeking through the blinds. "I'll call a couple of cabs and we'll head to Union Station separately. No sense in drawing attention to ourselves. If our paths cross on the train, we're strangers."

Monroe agreed, glancing at the old clock on Nitro's wall. Time was slipping away. "Stick to the plan. I'll keep things looking as normal as possible. I'm supposed to be Gordon's partner, right? If I act off, they'll smell blood in the water."

"And I'll be at the hotel bar soon after I check in at the Sheraton," Nitro added, grabbing his jacket from a nearby chair. "You just stay cool, M.G."

Monroe offered a dark laugh, organizing the contents on the table and placing them in a gym bag to stow in Nitro's front closet under a pile of clothes for safekeeping. "Easy for you to say. You're the one who'll be invisible. I'm the one who has to face down these sharks without getting eaten alive."

Nitro, always quick with a comeback, winked. "Hey, I'm the brains. You're the charm. Just smile, shake some hands, and let me do the dirty work."

"And remember, the feds will probably have the phone in my room bugged, so if we need to talk, I'll call your room from a public phone," Monroe added. "You can also leave me a note at my hotel if needed."

"Sounds good," Nitro quickly said.

Monroe retrieved his briefcase and a small overnight bag. "Alright," he said, checking his pockets for his ticket. "We'll split up now. I'll take the first taxi."

"You got it," Nitro affirmed, already dialing a cab company. "I'll be about five minutes behind you."

As Monroe headed toward the door, he paused and turned to Nitro one last time. "Be careful out there, alright?"

Nitro gave him a reassuring smile, but his eyes were serious. "Same goes for you, M.G. Stick to the plan, and we'll both walk away from this. Now let's get outta here before anyone catches wind of us."

The two men exited the house and stood by the curb, waiting for their separate taxis. The street was quiet, almost eerily so, as if the city itself was holding its breath.

A Diamond Cab pulled up in front of Monroe, the driver idling while Monroe tossed his bag into the back seat. "See you when I see you," Monroe said, turning to Nitro before sliding into the car.

"Yeah, man. We've got this," Nitro replied with a quick wave. He watched as Monroe's taxi took off, disappearing down the street before another cab approached for him. Each man headed off into the unknown, walking a fine line between caution and courage, understanding that one miscalculation could lead to disaster or worse.

42

U NION STATION GREETED MONROE with its usual energy, well ahead of the daily surge of government workers and other commuters crisscrossing the Grand Hall. That cushion allowed him the time to purchase a decent meal and a drink to carry on board without wait. Monroe was traveling on Amtrak's Metroliner, the high-speed alternative to regular trains. When the service was introduced, it was advertised that trips between Washington and New York would take roughly two and a half hours; it often stretched to four. On this trip Monroe arrived in just over three.

It was a little after 5 p.m. when Monroe stepped down onto the platform at Penn Station. Although it was Saturday, the place was a madhouse. Like ants at a picnic, travelers were scurrying to make their connections not just with Amtrak, but also with the Long Island Rail Road, New Jersey Transit, and the various subway lines that were connected to the transit center. Once outside, the lines for taxis were long. Patience might be viewed as a virtue, but in this situation, it was a necessity. No need to create any additional anxiety. Sooner than he expected, Monroe had been scooped up and was on his way to the hotel.

The front desk of the Milano Royale was adjacent to the entrance of the hotel bar, which was occupied by a lively group of patrons.

Monroe quickly checked in and made his way to the elevator without looking in to see if he knew anyone who was taking part in the revelry. Besides, he wanted to unpack and organize his room before kicking off his evening. As soon as he entered his suite, the former soldier meticulously arranged his clothing and other items.

His eyes drifted to the desk, where the phone's red light blinked rhythmically like a silent heartbeat. A message waited. Darnell's voice crackled through the receiver, bearing good news—Monroe was officially on the guest list for the welcome reception at Gracie Mansion, hosted by New York City's first Black mayor. Monroe smiled.

It got even better. Darnell mentioned that a pair of well-connected investment bankers, eager to talk about some lucrative bond work in St. Louis, would be picking them up in a limo. Under different circumstances, Monroe would have been stoked by the way the evening was to play out. But he reminded himself what he was there for and the risks that were involved. He made it a point to keep his emotions in check.

Wary of the possibility that Malaika and her FBI team had his phone wired, Monroe decided to play it safe and head down to the lobby to find a phone to reach out to Nitro at his hotel before hitting the bar. After freshening up and donning his jacket, Monroe walked briskly down the hall toward the elevator, the pulse of anticipation quickening with each step. Since he had no control over the night's itinerary, he would be improvising. As the elevator doors opened, he spotted a sign to his left, pointing toward the restrooms and phones. He wasted no time, heading over to place a call. The Sheraton's hotel operator connected him and Nitro answered on the first ring.

"Yo, Monroe?" Nitro asked, sounding sharp and alert.

Monroe leaned against the wall, phone pressed firmly to his ear, scanning the lobby out of habit. He glanced around, still on high alert despite the casual tone. "What up, Nitro." His voice was low but steady. "I see you made it in okay."

"Yeah, everything's cool." Nitro's reply came quickly, his confidence almost contagious. "All good on your end?"

Monroe exhaled, his fingers tightening slightly on the phone. "As well as can be expected," he muttered, a flicker of anxiety creeping into his tone, though he tried to mask it.

Nitro, ever the steadying force, didn't miss a beat. "M.G., it's all good." His voice was calm, almost reassuring. "We'll be fine, and by the way, I've got a surprise for you."

Monroe raised an eyebrow, a mix of curiosity and wariness flickering across his face. "Surprise? Okay, but remember, we can't acknowledge each other," he reminded, his voice hardening slightly as he shifted his weight, the tension in his shoulders unmistakable.

Nitro laughed softly, clearly unconcerned. "I know, but I can't wait to see the look on your face."

Monroe's eyes widened, taking on a look of wonder as he considered what Nitro had in store. He glimpsed at the crowded bar just down the hallway. His jaw clenched as he kept his eyes moving, instinctively checking his surroundings. "Look here, man. No time to chitchat. The bar's full." His voice dropped, becoming more urgent. "I'm heading in now for about an hour. I'll be with Darnell most of the evening, so hopefully I can learn a little something."

"Excellent!" Nitro replied eagerly. "I'm only a block away, so I'll be there shortly."

Monroe gave a slight tilt of his head, more to himself than to Nitro. His heart raced as he prepared for the next move. "Watch your back," he added, his voice soft but firm, knowing the night was just getting started. Monroe hung up the phone, took a deep breath, and headed toward the bar.

Entering the bar, Monroe was welcomed by an atmosphere thick with celebration. Darnell was at the center of it all, surrounded by a mix of familiar and unfamiliar faces, hanging on his every word. Aside from Butch Ollie, the only other recognizable figures were Michael Hill and David Harris, the two investment bankers who would be escorting Darnell around town for the evening. Locking eyes with Monroe, Darnell motioned for him to come over and join the group. Turning to the bartender nearby, Darnell ordered, "Whatever he wants, put it on my tab."

As he waited for his drink, Monroe scanned the various faces that filled the room. Those gathered around Darnell resembled sharks circling their prey, each one with hidden intentions. The mayor-elect was being approached as if he were handing out cash, with many eager newcomers and opportunists hoping to do business with his city.

By being in New York during the conference, they not only had access to Darnell but also to other mayors and their teams in a neutral setting. You would think that Darnell would have felt overwhelmed by the onslaught of pitches coming his way, but to the contrary, he seemed to revel in the attention. Michael and David had calculated well. With Monroe and Butch Ollie as the only other companions, they ensured that they would get quality time with Darnell. The pair had already hosted him for breakfast the previous morning. Since Michael's firm held a seat on the New York Stock Exchange, he had arranged for Darnell to ring the bell at the opening of the market. Points scored.

Michael and David were exceptionally sharp brothers, among the few Black investment bankers thriving in the municipal bond market thanks to their well-cultivated relationships within African American political networks. Michael, a substantial man over six feet tall, carried his size well with dark skin, a closely trimmed beard, and an infectious smile that matched his gregarious nature.

In contrast, David was effortlessly cool, turning heads with his striking looks and charming personality. His caramel-colored skin, neatly cropped mustache, and wavy jet-black hair complemented his slender six-foot frame, dressed impeccably in designer clothes. Despite being married, his appeal attracted his fair share of admirers.

In 1993, big-city mayors, particularly Black chief executives, were finally in control of urban centers and were spending millions on various development projects, leading to significant successes for Black bankers across the country. With their skills and political connections, these asset managers thrived, challenging the status quo and causing discontent among their white counterparts, who ultimately complained and prompted rule changes that favored them once again.

However, the shift at the time was undeniable; Black faces became essential in city halls for companies hoping to compete for municipal contracts. Darnell, intent on building a legacy from his modest upbringing, understood this dynamic and aimed to provide genuine opportunities for others to succeed—though he was known for swiftly cutting ties with anyone who brought any hint of dishonesty to the table—at least that's what Monroe thought. It seemed that these very interactions might have laid the groundwork for the corruption that had now cast a shadow over him.

After about thirty minutes of organized madness, Monroe felt a surge of relief when Darnell gave the nod that it was time to depart. Once the last glass hit the bar, the group slid into the waiting limo and set out for the evening. To Michael and David, it was just another

Saturday, but as they drew closer to Gracie Mansion, Darnell, Butch, and Monroe began to realize that this night held something special in store.

43

L OCATED AT EAST END AVENUE and 88th Street in the Yorkville neighborhood of Manhattan, Gracie Mansion was built in 1799 and was one of the oldest surviving wooden structures in the city. For the previous three and a half years, it had been occupied by the city's first Black mayor, who was hosting the conference. He was also in the midst of a bitter reelection campaign. But on that night, he would enjoy the company of others like him, men and women who had similar roles, but on smaller stages. Attendance was the largest in the history of the organization, largely due to the fact that the mayor's name was attached and the gathering was in New York.

The mental portrait of such a meeting brings to mind the legendary big-city mayors of the era. Although many of the attendees were well-known figures, most of the present mayors represented smaller cities and towns, particularly from the South.

In states like Alabama, Georgia, and Mississippi, and others, a host of cities and towns boasted significant Black populations, with African Americans holding a large number of municipal offices. Monroe might not have been acquainted with many of these towns, but the officials he engaged with displayed an impressive level of knowledge and ambition. He also crossed paths with a few who stood out as genuine characters, in a positive sense.

True to Monroe's expectations, the reception was impressive. The food was excellent, the alcohol was top-shelf, and the entertainment in the form of two nationally noted jazz artists was stellar. The event was also peppered with stars from Broadway, television, film, and music. What struck Monroe was the mutual fascination between the celebrities and the politicians. Living in DC, he had long believed that these two groups shared a kinship, and on that night it was abundantly clear. Depending on one's point of view, the essence of charm or stench of narcissism was in the air.

Monroe detected Hancock almost immediately upon his arrival and made it a point to keep an eye on him throughout the evening. The congressman was busy mingling, glad-handing as many guests as possible. Yet, what really caught Monroe's eye were the two times he saw Hancock and Darnell engaged in a spirited conversation about what he didn't know. If he'd tried to get closer, they would have more than likely changed the subject. But, it was apparent there was a conflict of some sort in their exchange.

A couple of hours into the reception, Michael and David suggested taking Darnell to some popular spots where Black New Yorkers frequented—first to B. Smith's on 8th Avenue and 47th Street, and then downtown to Lola, located on East 22nd Street between 5th and 6th Avenues. Monroe was familiar with both venues from his periodic visits to the city. While they attracted somewhat similar crowds, the atmospheres were distinct.

After having a round at each, the decision was made to go somewhere to dance. Leaving all entertainment options to Darnell and his new friends, they ultimately ended up at a club somewhere back in Midtown. The place was live with energy as they walked in. "Hip Hop Hooray" by Naughty by Nature was blasting, and without missing a beat, Darnell spotted an attractive young woman in a short red dress and was on the dance floor in an instant. The party had officially begun.

About an hour later, the group made the decision to return to the hotel and close down the bar. Monroe had worked all evening to give off the impression that he was having a good time; after all, the trip had intended to be a celebration of Darnell's win and Gamers' impending casino success. With everything that had transpired over the last eleven days, Monroe was consumed with an avalanche of contrary thoughts. Apart from witnessing the tense exchanges between Hancock and Darnell, he had made little progress toward his real objectives.

Feeling a sense of pessimism, he hoped that some of the key players he wanted to encounter would be on site upon their return, which would allow him the opportunity to salvage the evening. He also needed to check in with Nitro to see if he had made any headway. As the group approached the entrance to the lounge, surprisingly the scene inside was perfectly set: not only were Garland and Ambrose there, but so were Nimbus, Steptoe, and Prigmore. At that moment, Monroe felt a surge of excitement—things were about to get interesting. Little did he know that this gathering was the spark that would set everything in motion.

44

THE BAR AT THE HOTEL WAS DIMLY LIT, a perfect setting for shadowy conversations and whispered deals. Monroe, having struck out at every turn earlier, felt his pulse quicken as he entered the bar. While the crowd had thinned over the course of the evening, there was still an ample number of patrons occupying seats at the bar or the tables scattered around. Ambrose and Garland sat at a table near the window, while Nimbus, Steptoe, and Prigmore were gathered in a small nearby corner booth. Despite the cordial expressions they wore, there was an undeniable tension rippling through the group. Also, at the table with Ambrose and Garland were two attractive White women and a man standing with his back to Monroe.

True to form, Ambrose and Garland were the life of the party, their laughter echoing through the bar, much to the delight of the two women and the curious bystander. In an instant, Monroe concluded that the two striking blonde ladies were of Eastern European descent, either Polish or Czech. Ambrose and Garland were dressed in matching black tuxes, while their companions wore short black sequin dresses that showcased their long, smooth, porcelain-colored legs. While he tried to reserve judgment, Monroe's instincts told him that the ladies were likely high-end escorts who frequented upscale hotel bars.

Monroe squared his shoulders, knowing he had to play this just right. While his attention had been distracted in scrutinizing Ambrose and Garland, he suddenly noticed Darnell slipping into the booth occupied by Nimbus, Steptoe, and Prigmore. A wave of envy washed over Monroe; he would have preferred to be a fly on that wall, taking in every detail of their conversation. Yet, he had to focus; building rapport with Ambrose was paramount. Tomorrow night's meeting loomed large in his mind, a pivotal moment where he hoped everything would finally come together.

As he made his way across the room, Monroe caught a glimpse of Ambrose speaking with a tall, lanky man whose back was turned to him. The man was dressed in a sharp suit, and his close-cropped haircut gave him an air of meticulousness. Something about him seemed oddly familiar. Ambrose spotted Monroe approaching and his face lit up with forced enthusiasm. "Monroe! Good to see you, man."

Monroe smiled in return, but his gaze lingered on the man standing next to Ambrose. When the stranger turned to greet him, Monroe's heart skipped a beat. It was Nitro, looking nothing like himself—clean-shaven and impeccably dressed.

Ambrose placed a firm hand on Nitro's shoulder, grinning widely. "Monroe, this is a new friend of mine, Seymour Pettigrew. Seymour, meet Monroe Gray." Monroe recovered quickly, extending his hand and locking eyes with Nitro. No flicker of recognition. Not a hint of familiarity. Nitro's performance was airtight, flawless even, but inside, Monroe felt tinges of amusement dance around the edges of his composure. Monroe blinked once, his face neutral, as his brain scrambled to catch up. Nitro—or Seymour, as it were—stood there, the epitome of calm and smooth confidence.

Seymour Pettigrew? Seriously? Monroe almost had to stifle a laugh. That was the name of Harold Nicholas' character from the old flick Uptown Saturday Night. The absurdity of it nearly made him crack a smile, but he kept his cool. Well, he supposed, as far as fake identities went, it wasn't half bad.

"Pleasure to meet you, Mr. Gray," Nitro—or Seymour—said smoothly, his voice calm and rich like a seasoned jazz singer, as though they were two complete strangers crossing paths for the first time.

"Likewise," Monroe replied, keeping his tone steady and light, all the while marveling at how deep into character Nitro had gone. It was like watching a masterclass in deception.

"When I told Ambrose that I was from DC, he asked if I knew you. Unfortunately, our paths never crossed before, but I'm sure we probably have some common acquaintances," Nitro added, the lie rolling off his tongue with perfect ease.

"No doubt," Monroe responded, impressed by his friend's acting chops. He was pulling this off without breaking a sweat. "Are you enjoying the conference, Seymour?"

"You have no idea," Nitro answered, flashing a sly, almost mischievous smile. There was a hidden layer in his words, a private joke between them that Monroe couldn't help but catch. Nitro's undercover work was practically performance art.

"Who's your friend, Ambrose?" one of the women at the nearby table called out, her voice laced with curiosity.

Ambrose turned and gave a wide, almost theatrical smile. "This is another friend from Washington, Monroe Gray."

One of the women, striking and golden-haired with a cat-like gaze, smiled invitingly. "Well, hello," she purred, her voice dripping with that familiar note of intrigue. "I'm Alinka, and this is Esterka," she added, gesturing to her companion, who smiled in polite acknowledgment.

"Polish, I take it," said Monroe.

Alinka's eyes widened slightly, clearly impressed by his guess. "How did you know?"

Monroe chuckled. "I have a friend in Baltimore who is Polish. Ironically, her name is Esterka too."

"Small world," Esterka responded, her voice soft, but with an edge of playful invitation. "Why don't you join us for a drink?" she added, her smile widening, her eyes flitting between Monroe and the seat next to her.

Monroe's grin was genuine, but he had other priorities. "I'd love to, but I've got some business I need to take care of." He turned his attention back to Seymour and Ambrose, trying to keep the conversation from derailing.

"Seymour, I'd love to hear more of your impressions about the conference sometime." Monroe glanced at Nitro, his tone casual but laced with a subtle hint. "But if you'll excuse us, I need to have a quick word with Ambrose. We need to catch up on some things."

Nitro gave a knowing nod. "Absolutely. Handle your business." He cast a quick, discreet glance in Monroe's direction before casually sliding into Ambrose's now-vacant seat at the table with Garland, Alinka, and Esterka.

As soon as they were far enough away, Monroe turned to Ambrose, lowering his voice to a firm but hushed tone. "Ambrose, we need to talk," Monroe began, leaning in slightly. "I've been on the sidelines too long. I know there's a lot happening, and I want in."

Ambrose raised an eyebrow, pretending to be caught off guard. "In? On what? You're already on the inside, Monroe."

Monroe let out a short laugh, his eyes narrowing. "Don't play me, Ambrose. I know you and the rest of the crew are gearing up for something big. I'm talking about the meeting tomorrow night. I need to be in that room."

Ambrose shifted uncomfortably, his eyes flicking toward the group at the booth, who were still in their tense conversation. "I don't know if that's a good idea, Monroe. The group's tight-knit, and things are moving fast. You've been out of the loop—there's a lot you wouldn't understand. And besides, how did you hear about it?"

"Come on now. You of all people should know that I've got my sources," Monroe affirmed. "Not to mention, I'm a quick study." His tone hardened. "Look, you need someone like me. Someone who knows how to get things done on the sly. Someone who's already got ties to the right people."

Ambrose studied Monroe for a moment, his face betraying nothing. "Why now?" he asked. "You played it cool when I offered you an opportunity. Why the sudden interest?"

Monroe leaned in closer, his voice dropping to a near whisper. "Because I know what's at stake. I've heard the whispers, Ambrose. About Africa, about St. Louis. I've been keeping tabs, and I know the players involved. Don't think I haven't been paying attention. You need someone who can maneuver the political side of this. Someone who will have your back in case things don't go as planned. I can help you."

Ambrose frowned, clearly weighing his options. He glanced over at the group once more before turning back to Monroe. "This is risky," he said slowly. "I'm not saying I can make any promises, but…if I get you into that meeting tomorrow night, you'd better be ready for what's coming. Things are about to get a lot more involved."

Monroe didn't flinch. "I'm always ready, Ambrose. You know that."

There was a long pause. Ambrose's eyes darted toward the group again, lingering on Seymour Pettigrew (Nitro), who was deftly consorting with Nimbus and Steptoe. Finally, he let out a resigned sigh. "Fine," Ambrose muttered, his voice low. "I'll talk to the others and see what I can do. But you'd better be ready to play ball, Monroe. Once you're in, there's no backing out."

Monroe nodded, his face set. "I'm in."

Ambrose straightened up, plastering on a more casual expression as he clapped Monroe on the shoulder. "Alright then. Let's grab a drink and keep things light. I'll get you in tomorrow night, but keep your head down until then."

Monroe forced a smile, but inside the tension was building. Tomorrow was going to be the turning point. Everything he and Nitro had been working for hinged on what would happen in that room. And now, thanks to Ambrose's reluctant agreement, he'd be right in the middle of it and so would Malaika.

They rejoined the group, but Monroe's pulse quickened when he caught Seymour's eye across the room. In that fleeting glance, they shared an unspoken understanding. The plan was falling into place, piece by piece. Tomorrow, they would either bring the conspiracy crashing down or find themselves drowning in its wake. Monroe decided to relax, allowing himself to enjoy what was left of the evening, while still keeping his ears open for any stray bits of intel. He couldn't help but marvel at how quickly Nitro had forged new connections. If he didn't know better, it would be easy to believe that Nitro was one of them.

After about an hour, the lights in the lounge flickered—a subtle signal from the staff that the night was winding down, and that they could go anywhere in New York but there. Just as Monroe was considering his next move, his eyes met Darnell's. He recognized that familiar gleam, one that always came after Darnell had knocked back a few too many cognacs. Murmuring something to the others at the table, Darnell got up and strode purposefully toward Monroe.

"Come on," he said intensely. "Let's take a ride."

Monroe said his goodbyes and trailed after Darnell. As they stepped out of the hotel, Darnell got the attention of a waiting cabbie and the duo quickly jumped in with barely a pause. Darnell leaned toward the driver and announced without hesitation, "*Angels on Poles.*" *I should have seen this coming.* Monroe was in no position to resist at that point. Darnell's enthusiasm and resolve made it impossible for him to bail. He simply accepted the fact that the remainder of his night or now early morning would be filled with bare tits, shaking asses, and glitter. *It could be worse.* But Monroe had no idea that *worse* was lurking nearby, looking for an opportunity to pounce.

45

ONROE AWOKE TO THE HARSH LIGHT of morning that filtered through the heavy curtains of his hotel room. The relentless throbbing in his head felt like a marching band rehearsing for a parade. He squinted at the digital clock on the nightstand; it was already past seven. Memories of the night before flooded back: Darnell, a parade of dancers, and the stench of cheap cologne mingling with cigarette smoke. Monroe had never enjoyed strip clubs, but the magnetic pull of Darnell's exuberance always managed to draw him in. This time, though, he regretted it more than usual. His mouth felt dry, and his body ached as if he had run a marathon, not just sat through another of Darnell's wild out-of-town escapades.

Groaning softly, he swung his legs over the side of the bed, feeling the softness of the elegant carpeting beneath his feet. He took a moment to collect his thoughts, blinking slowly as he tried to shake off the remnants of the previous night's perversion. The suit he had worn the night before lay crumpled over a chair. He grimaced. With a sigh, he forced himself up, the effort of standing making the headache even worse. After reaching the bathroom sink, he splashed cold water on his face, wincing as it sent sharp jolts through his temples. "You're getting too old for this," he muttered to his reflection. The bags under his eyes were evidence of the late hour and poor decisions.

As he dressed, the fabric of his shirt felt constricting against his skin, and he fought the urge to button it all the way up. He opted to forego a tie and instead go for the open-collar look. Each movement was deliberate and slow as if he were trying to buy time before facing the day. He took another look at himself in the mirror, running a hand through his ungroomed hair that begged for a comb and a brush.

On the way back to the hotel, Darnell mentioned he had a prayer breakfast on his schedule, which meant he was already up and out the door. Monroe found it astonishing how effortlessly Darnell could tap into so much energy at the drop of a hat. Despite his inner turmoil, Monroe recognized that it was time to step up. The fallout from the night before had to be put out of his mind. A series of unexpected challenges lay ahead, and he needed to be fully prepared.

Just as he was reaching for the door handle, the hotel phone rang, slicing through the stillness. He picked it up, his heart racing as he recognized the voice on the other end. It was Malaika. "Monroe, no time for chitchat. You need to come over to Brooklyn as soon as possible. We have to discuss the FBI's surveillance plan," she instructed, her tone brisk and no-nonsense. "I don't want to risk being recognized if we meet at your hotel. It's too high-profile."

He could hear the urgency in her voice, and it pushed him into action, shoving aside the remnants of his hangover. "I'll be there," he said, adrenaline cutting through the fog in his head. "I have one important stop I have to make. Does 11 a.m. work for you?"

"Not a moment later," she firmly replied.

No goodbye? This was a Maliaka he hadn't seen before, and it was one he wasn't sure he liked. With a final glance at his reflection, he steeled himself for the day ahead, aware that he would be stepping into situations where every move counted. Quickly adjusting his jacket, he took a deep breath to quell any feeling of nausea. One thing he knew as he ambled down the hotel corridor, his first stop would be the restaurant's carryout. He needed caffeine.

After paying for his coffee and a Sunday *New York Times*, Monroe set out for the Sheraton. The one-block walk felt longer than it should have, each step resonating with the rhythm of his headache. The city was waking up, the streets buzzing with early morning wanderers, and he could smell the faint aroma of coffee and pastries from a nearby café.

He took in the sights, forcing himself to focus on the mundane— a bus rolling past, the sound of laughter from a group of tourists, the honking of horns—anything to distract himself from the collision of thoughts flooding his mind. Despite the ebbing pain in his head, a sense of purpose began to form. He was ready to confront whatever lay ahead, determined to piece together the puzzle that had been laid before him.

Monroe entered the Sheraton's lobby, the scent of fresh coffee mingling with the distant chatter of early morning guests. The clock on the wall read 8:30 a.m., and though the sun was just beginning to peak through the city's skyline, the air felt charged with urgency. He spotted Nitro—Seymour, his New York alias—seated at a corner table in the hotel's café, his demeanor calm yet alert, eyes scanning the entrance.

"Morning," Monroe said, easing himself into the chair opposite Nitro. He noted the untouched cup of coffee in front of his companion.

"Morning. Damn, bro, you look like you had a rough night," Nitro replied, a slight grin on his face.

"Darnell was intent on hitting a shake joint, and he doesn't do anything alone. When we left you and the others at the hotel, I had no idea where we were going until the taxi had taken off. Hell, I could have been flying solo, for all it's worth. That niggah spent most of our time there in the Champaign Room. But that's another story. You said you had news?"

Nitro leaned in closer, his breath barely above a whisper as he lowered his voice, his eyes darting around to ensure no one was eavesdropping. "Here's what I got so far. Whatever is being planned, it's something big. Just like we heard on the tape, Hancock is driving it. The meeting's set for tonight at 10 p.m. at an office building just a stone's throw from your hotel on 51st Street." He paused for effect, letting the weight of his words settle. "Like a lot of buildings in New York, the recession and the real estate collapse have left it with a slew of vacancies, making it the perfect location for a clandestine gathering. They've paid off the doorman and the maintenance crew. Once inside, they'll have the entire floor at their disposal, operating under the radar with no questions asked."

Monroe raised an eyebrow, intrigued. "I read an article in the *Times* a few weeks ago that talked about the glut of office space in Manhattan. What's the draw?"

"They will be making the final decisions on the casino opportunities and assigning territories," he said, his tone grave, each word punctuated with urgency. He leaned in closer, lowering his voice as if the very walls might eavesdrop. "Rumor has it the 'Broker' will be there, and they're using the virtually unoccupied building because it's off the radar—a place where no one would think to look."

Monroe felt a chill run down his spine at the implications. "I'd bet the farm that the FBI will set up surveillance equipment there, if they haven't already. I also wouldn't be surprised if they have a confidential informant somewhere. Maybe even in the group."

He leaned back in his chair, contemplating. "Well, the good news is that Ambrose is getting me into the meeting."

"Excellent!" Nitro exclaimed, taking a robust sip of his coffee, steam curling up around his face. "What's your plan?"

"Well, I won't fully know until after I meet with Malaika. She called just before I came over here and wants me to come to Brooklyn to discuss whatever it is the feds want me to do. I wish I could get you in as well, but I've barely got my foot in the door."

"No problem. I can probably be more helpful on the outside anyway."

"After we eat, I'm going to head over to Brooklyn and get whatever's gonna happen started. Let's meet back here in your room about 3:30 to finalize our end. What's your room number?"

"516."

"I'm going to try to catch up with Ambrose and Garland around noon. I'll see if I can come up with any more information about The Broker. If he does show, it could change everything."

"Right. We need to tread carefully. I only hope the Feds aren't going to try to wire me."

"Hey, man, after last night, I know you're hungry as shit. Go ahead and eat. I'm going to head up. I had planned to have breakfast in my room.

Monroe gave Nitro an extended once-over, his expression turned to one of skepticism. "Oh, hell no!"

"What?" Nitro shot back, standing and deliberately avoiding eye contact.

"Alright, which one?" Monroe pressed, a teasing glint in his eyes.

"What are you talking about?" Nitro asked with a look that was cheaper than a $50 suit.

"Alinka or Esterka?"

With a hint of embarrassment creeping onto his face, Nitro mumbled, "Esterka."

Monroe erupted into a fit of laughter, the kind that had been pent up for days under the pressure of his situation. "Man, I ain't mad at you. That's probably the first woman you've had since a woman had you," he teased, relishing the lightness of the moment.

"All I can say, Monroe Gray, is fuck you," Nitro jokingly snapped. "I hope you choke on your meal. See you at 3:30."

As Nitro walked away, Monroe realized he needed that good laugh to relieve the tension swirling within him. Yet, in an instant, a rush of adrenaline surged throughout his body. The stakes were rising, and he was ready to dive headfirst into the danger that awaited. The clock was ticking. Soon they would be face-to-face with all of the players in this surreal drama, including the enigmatic "Broker," in a strange environment where shadows lurked and secrets whispered.

46

THE WALK BACK TO THE MILANO ROYALE seemed shorter than his earlier trek to the Sheraton. The persistent inner turmoil that Monroe was experiencing may have been a factor. Monroe entered the lobby with a focus that shielded him from any distractions. He had learned more in the previous forty-eight hours than he had in the past few months, and every bit of it led to the big meeting that was on the horizon. But first, he needed to check for messages before heading to Brooklyn for his briefing with the feds.

Just as he approached the front desk, a familiar voice stopped him cold. "Mr. Gray, fancy running into you here." His stomach tightened as he turned, and there, leaning casually against the wall, were his two favorite detectives. Tyree displayed his consistently smug look, while Frazier stood beside him, arms crossed, eyes locked onto Monroe with his all-too-familiar suspicion.

Tyree and Frazier stood out like sore thumbs. Usually, they were immaculately dressed—for cops, that is. Tyree, the slightly more put-together of the pair, had on a tan trench coat and a dark suit that still had a crease from where it had been hastily thrown over a chair. Frazier wore a brown leather jacket over a faded shirt with the top button open, his tie askew. Both were wearing shoes that hadn't been introduced to polish lately. It was clear they'd been tracking Monroe for hours.

"Out for a morning stroll?" Tyree asked, his voice dripping with sarcasm.

"Not my lucky day, I see," Monroe muttered under his breath, plastering on a smile. "Detectives. What brings you to the Big Apple? Sightseeing?"

Tyree chuckled, but the sound was without humor. "You might say that, except you're the main attraction," Tyree said, not missing a beat. "You know that you're our favorite loose end."

"And you two are like roaches. You turn on the light and there you are."

"Still a smartass, I see," Tyree retorted.

Frazier, ever the silent presence, unfolded his arms and stepped forward. "You've been real slippery, Gray. But we're still tying you to three murders. Dixon, Blackwell, and let's not forget Yvonne Montgomery."

"In fact, the Montgomery County Police would like to have a word or two with you," snickered Tyree.

Monroe exhaled, already feeling the frustration bubbling up. He knew they were like dogs with a bone, unwilling to let go. He raised his hands in mock surrender. "Look, I get it. I'm at the center of a lot of messes, but I'm not your guy. I had nothing to do with those murders. If you'll give me a minute, I can clear this up for you."

"You can clear it up by coming with us," Frazier chimed in, his voice low and threatening. "The good folks at the 17th Precinct offered us some office space so that we could spend a little time with you."

"Still barking up the wrong tree, guys," Monroe shot back, keeping his tone calm even though his pulse had quickened. "But, hey, let's walk over to the phones. I'll make a call, and afterward you can use what little expense money you have to enjoy the rest of the day in New York."

Tyree's eyes narrowed suspiciously. "A phone call? You're not serious."

Monroe nodded. "Dead serious. Trust me, it'll save you some time."

Tyree exchanged a glance with Frazier, plainly irritated. "This better not be a waste of time, Gray."

Monroe pulled out some coins, picked up the receiver, and punched in some numbers. When the line connected, he quickly spoke into the phone, his voice tense. "Malaika? I've got a situation here."

On the other end, Malaika's voice was stern and commanding. "Put them on."

Monroe handed the phone to Tyree, who begrudgingly took it. After a few seconds of listening, his face fell, and he passed the phone to Frazier. A moment later, both detectives looked like they'd swallowed something bitter. Frazier handed the phone back to Monroe without a word.

"You may have been given a pass for now," Tyree muttered, a cloud of displeasure hanging over him. "But don't think we're done with you. We'll be watching."

"You do that," Monroe said with a smirk. "Always a pleasure, gentlemen. Enjoy the Big Apple."

Leaving them standing in the lobby, Monroe made his way out of the hotel and hailed a cab for his trip to Brooklyn.

47

THE CITY THAT NEVER SLEEPS seemed to be in a rare moment of pause this Sunday morning, its restless spirit still there but temporarily softened, waiting to be unleashed. Fortunately, there were plenty of taxis cruising along, and Monroe was able to flag one down almost immediately. Malaika's parents lived on Bergen Street in Brooklyn Heights, not far from Vanderbilt Avenue. Monroe found it odd that the FBI had chosen the house for their planning,

The sun was bright but gentle, casting a golden glow across the city as the cabbie drove across the Brooklyn Bridge. Traffic was lighter than it would be on a weekday, though the occasional honk or distant siren reminded him that the city was never truly quiet. Pedestrians, clutching their morning coffees and newspapers, moved at a more relaxed pace than Monroe was used to seeing. The Yellow Taxi sailed down Atlantic Avenue, and as it neared Brooklyn Heights, Monroe found himself thinking about his past encounters with Malaika and the abrupt change that had recently occurred. While he understood the new dynamics of their relationship, he was still shadowed by disappointment over what could have been.

The taxi pulled in front of a rowhouse of modest appearance on the outside. Monroe paid the driver and proceeded toward the door. It only took one ring of the doorbell for her to answer.

"Thanks for coming here," she said, her voice lower than usual. "It's not our standard planning area, but there were too many distractions at the office. Besides, the field headquarters is just across the bridge."

Walking into the living room. Malaika explained that this had been her childhood home, but it bore little resemblance to the house she had cherished growing up. The renovation that the home had undergone was recent and extensive. The interior of her parents' home was especially well-appointed. The furniture was surprisingly modern, the hardwood floors that spanned the entire first floor were immaculately polished, and the artwork that adorned the walls appeared to rival some of the museum pieces he had eyed on various museum visits. The lofty, well-formed ceilings made the space seem larger than it was. It was impressive.

"By the way, thanks for handling those two pricks from DC," Monroe said, breaking the brief silence.

"Just doing what I had to do to keep this operation on track," Malaika replied. "I've got a lot of eyes on me."

After their short trek through the dining area, Malaika approached a door on the right and opened it. It led to the basement. Carefully descending the stairs that were designed to look like they floated in mid-air without any structural support, they entered an area of the house that was an unusual but functional setting for an FBI briefing. Malaika briefly explained that in normal times, the room would be immaculate, neatly arranged with family memorabilia on the shelves and framed photos lining the walls.

The room's centerpiece was a vintage billiard table, the kind that spoke of friendly family games and leisurely gatherings. But today, the table was covered with a large board, transforming it into an impromptu planning station. Maps, surveillance photos, and notes were carefully pinned in place, forming a mosaic of information that stretched from one side of the table to the other. Notes scribbled with a black magic marker and images of persons of interest were displayed on a large whiteboard that stood nearby.

Once Monroe's feet hit the basement floor, he was immediately greeted by an atmosphere that was tense but focused. Despite the circumstances, the room still retained a sense of order—a testament to the orderly nature of Malaika's parents. The soft lighting from the recessed ceiling lamps illuminated the space with a warm glow, contrasting sharply with the cool, professional demeanor of the FBI agents gathered around the table.

They were a mix of seasoned professionals and younger agents, all dressed casually to avoid drawing attention. A few wore dark slacks and button-down shirts, while others were in jeans and jackets. Each one was locked in on their respective tasks, their faces etched with concentration as they reviewed the latest intelligence on the upcoming sting operation. Monroe couldn't help but be impressed.

Two agents caught his attention, Mitchell and Carter. First names weren't part of the introductions. Mitchell was a stocky White man in his mid-forties. His close-cropped hair was flecked with gray, and a permanent scowl seemed etched into his weathered face. He wore a charcoal-gray suit that looked like it had seen better days, his white shirt open at the collar. His jacket strained slightly across his broad shoulders, and his tie had been hastily loosened as though it had spent hours knotted tight around his neck. He looked like the kind of man who had been through a few too many long days and even longer nights.

The other agent, Carter, a tall Black man with a lean, athletic build, moved efficiently around the room. He was dressed in a navy polo shirt tucked into jeans and wore a baseball cap pulled low over his eyes. His expression was stoic, but his sharp gaze took in everything. Monroe could tell Carter was the kind of agent who didn't say much but missed even less. Monroe would later learn that Carter was Malaika's partner and knew more about him than he could have guessed.

It was apparent that Malaika's presence commanded attention, and even in the midst of controlled chaos, there was no doubt that she was in charge. She gave Monroe a quick, assessing glance as he positioned himself on one side of the room.

"You're late," Agent Carter said sharply, his voice cutting through the low murmur of conversation.

"Ran into some old friends," Monroe said dryly, walking toward the table. "She saved my ass," he added, pointing toward Malaika.

"Okay, folks, We don't have time for pleasantries," Malaika firmly stated. "We need to go over the plan."

Monroe nodded and sat down as Agent Mitchell spread out documents on the table, including building blueprints and surveillance maps. His thick fingers traced the routes with methodical precision.

"Here's the deal," Malaika began, her gaze locking on to Monroe. "The meeting is set for ten tonight on the 9th floor of a building just up the street from the Milano Royale, where most of our persons of interest are staying. The building is mostly vacant because of the economic downturn, and with it being a Sunday, there won't be much foot traffic. Our team will be stationed on the 10th floor, monitoring everything with hidden mics we'll plant earlier. We'll also have a couple of agents working undercover as building staff and some posing as workers on the street. One caveat: One of the men who normally works security will be at his usual post at the front desk."

Mitchell cleared his throat, his voice gravelly. "We've got all the exits covered, including the service corridors. No one's getting out without us knowing. But this is a delicate operation—we need them to think everything's normal until we're ready to move in."

Agent Carter, still standing to the side, chimed in, his deep voice calm and steady. "It's about keeping the situation contained. Once you're in there, Monroe, stick to the plan. If anything changes, we'll adapt, but we need you to stay cool."

Monroe leaned in, a shadow of concern spread across his face. "So, what's my part in all this?"

"You're going to walk into that meeting like everything's business as usual," Malaika explained, her tone serious. "Ambrose expects you to be there. Your job is to keep the conversation flowing and, more importantly, steer it. We need these guys to confirm the identity of both 'The Investor' and 'The Broker.' And we need them to connect the dots—Africa, St. Louis, Hancock's role. Once we have that on tape, we'll be able to bring them down."

Monroe's mind raced as he thought about the complexity of his role. "And if it goes sideways?" he asked, his voice steady despite the nerves creeping in.

"If things go south, you get out of there," Malaika said, looking directly at Monroe. "Our team will move the second we have what we need, but until then, you're on your own. Don't be a hero."

Monroe leaned back in his chair, absorbing her words. "That's the least of your worries," Monroe replied with a subtle grin.

Malaika, ever the strategist, took a step closer to Monroe. "I know this isn't going to be easy, but we need this to go smoothly. These people are dangerous. If they even suspect you're working with us, they'll kill you without hesitation. So, stick to the plan."

"So I should leave my piece at the hotel, I guess," he responded.

"You guess?" Malaika snapped. "They're probably going to search you, which is why you won't be wired."

"Okay, okay," Monroe said, ceding the fact that getting caught with a gun wouldn't end with a good outcome. "And after the meeting?"

Carter, arms crossed again, responded before Malaika could. "We'll take them down, one by one. But for now, your job is to keep things cool and get them to talk. Got it?"

Monroe stood up, exhaling slowly as he weighed everything in his mind. "Yeah, I've got it. Just make sure your guys are ready. I don't plan on dying tonight."

Malaika, her voice softer now, added, "We'll be ready. Why don't you go back to your hotel and try to get some rest. You'll need it."

As the briefing wrapped up, Monroe reached under his jacket and pulled out a slightly worn manilla folder that had been tucked into the back of his pants. He held it out to Malaika, his face serious.

"I've been holding onto this," Monroe said, his voice low. "It's copies of everything Yvonne left for me. But I need you to promise me something."

Malaika raised an eyebrow as she took the folder from him. "What's that?"

"Don't open it until after the meeting tonight. Whatever's in there, it could change things, and I need to see how this all plays out first. You'll understand why soon enough."

She studied him for a moment before nodding, her fingers tightening around the folder. "Alright, Monroe. I'll wait."

With one last glance around the room, Monroe climbed the basement stairs and headed for the front door. The cool air greeted him, but as he moved through the quiet Brooklyn streets, a sense of unease tugged at him. The short distance to Atlantic Avenue felt like the first step toward an inevitable conclusion, his fate hidden just beyond the horizon, unknown but approaching.

48

THE RETURN TRIP TO MIDTOWN felt surprisingly short compared to the ride to Brooklyn. Maybe it was the deluge of thoughts that dashed through Monroe's mind that made time pass so quickly. With his head full of what lay ahead, Monroe headed straight for the Sheraton to meet up with Nitro. He knew he had to find a way to keep Nitro involved—he was the one who could be counted on in a drama where trust was a rare commodity.

Stepping into the Sheraton's bustling lobby, alive with guests scurrying to check out, gathering their luggage, and flagging down taxis, Monroe moved with purpose, wasting no time heading toward one of the available house phones. He could have gone straight up, but the last thing he wanted was to stumble into an awkward moment if Esterka was still on the scene.

Picking up the receiver, he dialed Nitro's room. The eager voice on the other end ensured him that the coast was clear. Satisfied, Monroe crossed the gleaming marble floor, his shoes echoing faintly as he approached the elevator. He pressed the button for the 5th floor, leaning back against the cool metal wall as the lift whirred to life, swiftly carrying him upward with the low hum of its gears serving as background sound.

Anticipating Monroe's arrival, Nitro had left the door ajar. Monroe stepped in, closing the door behind him with a quiet click.

The room was dimly lit, the heavy curtains drawn to keep any prying eyes at bay while Nitro was entertaining. It had been a long morning after his tense encounter with Tyree and Frazier and the trip to Brooklyn. Now, he was back with Nitro to go over what the FBI had laid out for him. Before getting down to business, though, Monroe couldn't resist poking fun.

"C'mon, man, give it up. How was it?" Monroe teased, leaning back against the door and crossing his arms. A sly grin was displayed on his lips as he took in Nitro, who was lounging on the bed with an amused look of his own.

"Jealous?" Nitro shot back, unfazed. "Just 'cause you're too busy dodging cops and federal agents doesn't mean the rest of us can't have a little fun."

Monroe chuckled. "I'm not the jealous type. Just surprised that you closed on that so quickly."

Nitro rolled his eyes and sat up, swinging his legs off the bed. "Sometimes a man has to answer that call to glory."

"Well, now that you've done your version of *Pretty Woman*, can we get down to business?" Monroe said, moving over to the table and tossing his jacket on the back of a chair, "Let's talk about what's next."

Nitro retrieved a cigarette from the pack on the nightstand and ambled over to the table, taking the chair opposite Monroe.

"Yeah, yeah. Back to work," Nitro muttered, lighting the cigarette with a quick flick of the lighter. He blew out a puff of smoke, then eyed Monroe. "What's the FBI want from you?"

"First off, can you put that damn thing out?" Monroe demanded. "You know I can't stand the smell of smoke. I'm surprised you haven't been able to quit yet," he added.

Nitro got up and walked to the bathroom, taking several extra puffs before dousing it. "Satisfied?"

Monroe paused, gathering his thoughts before diving in. "The reason they want me in that big meeting tonight is to get those greedy assholes to give the identities of 'The Investor' and 'The Broker' on tape. They think once those names come out, they'll have all we need to take them down."

"Sounds simple," Nitro said, sarcasm dripping from his voice. He leaned back, his arms stretching across the back of the chair. "And I assume they've got you wired up for this?"

Monroe shook his head. "As I thought, they don't think it would be wise since I might get searched before going in. Can't risk blowing the whole thing because someone found a mic tucked in my shirt."

"That's probably a smart move," Nitro said, nodding approvingly. "So, what's my role in all this?"

"That's what we're going to come up with right now," Monroe replied. "While I'm in the meeting, the FBI will be one floor above, recording everything. But we need more eyes on the ground, keeping tabs on the key players. Ambrose, Nimbus, especially Hancock. We both know that this "Broker" character is in town, and it would be advantageous to know who he is before the meeting. If you see anything, leave a note for me downstairs at the front desk. I'll swing by before I make my way over there."

Nitro looked out toward the window as he considered Monroe's words. "So I'm tailing these guys, huh? Seeing if anyone's acting sketchy or if 'The Broker' pops up."

"Exactly," Monroe said, leaning forward. "You're better at staying under the radar than most, and neither he nor the feds know your face. You can blend in and monitor the building where the meeting's going down. Look for anything suspicious—anyone hanging around who doesn't fit. The FBI will have undercover agents on the ground, but I need someone I know who will have my back."

Nitro's gaze returned to meet Monroe's. "Alright, sounds like a plan. But I'm telling you now, if things start going off track, I'm not sticking around to see the fireworks."

"Fair enough," Monroe said with a wry smile. "But seriously, if you can identify 'The Broker,' this whole thing will fall into place. I'll keep the conversation flowing inside, but I need you to gather intel out there so that after the meeting, we can take action if needed."

Nitro's eyes narrowed in focus, his usual laid-back demeanor replaced by the sharp instincts of a man who'd seen too much in his lifetime. "I'll stick close to Ambrose, Nimbus, and Hancock and I'll keep watch on the building—see if any unusual characters are milling around. If our mystery man is on the scene, I'll find him."

"Good," Monroe said. "We'll meet back up here afterward. If we can pull this off, it's game over for all of them."

Nitro stood up and grabbed his jacket from the bed. "You know, M.G., you're lucky to have me on your side. These guys won't see me coming."

Monroe chuckled. "Yeah, I'm counting on it."

As they prepared to leave, Monroe's tone grew more serious. "Just be careful out there, Nitro. This is bigger than both of us, and these people won't hesitate to take us out if they feel threatened."

"M.G., you forget who you're talking to. This ain't my first rodeo. Dodging bullets is second nature to me—it's like breathing. Trust me, I'll be fine." Just make sure you don't get yourself killed in that meeting."

"Not planning on it," Monroe said confidently, though the unease in his stomach lingered. The countdown had begun, and it wouldn't be long before both men found themselves in a game where the rules no longer mattered and determination was their only currency. But for now, there was a mission to complete, and failure wasn't an option.

49

ONROE SHIFTED UNCOMFORTABLY IN HIS CHAIR as the tension in the room reached a boiling point. Nimbus was practically shouting across the table at Ambrose, who fired back with equal venom, the air thick with accusations and the greed that had been simmering for months. Prior to the start of the meeting, Monroe had retrieved a note from the front desk at his hotel from Nitro. It read: *The Broker's in town, but I don't have a description or name. Will continue to work on it. Nitro.* Malaika's source was also right. Neither Hancock, Darnell, nor Tammy were on site, which was a red flag for Monroe. But since things were underway, he'd have to improvise.

"You and your partner were never in the mix to obtain a license in St. Louis!" Nimbus barked, slamming his fist down on the table. "Hancock already promised us control over St. Louis. Now you think you're gonna muscle in?"

Ambrose offered a mocking grin, his confidence unshaken. "Funny how promises work. Especially when Hancock isn't here to back you up."

The argument quickly spiraled, with Prigmore and Steptoe jumping in, their voices rising in anger. Monroe felt more than a sense of unease. Things were unraveling fast, and he couldn't afford to be caught in the crossfire—literally or figuratively.

"I'm gonna use the restroom," he muttered, sliding his chair back. No one paid him any attention as he moved toward the door, the shouting continuing unabated.

It was just after 10:15 p.m., and outside the meeting room, the dim hallway in the largely vacant building felt eerily still. Monroe splashed cold water on his face in the adjacent bathroom, hoping to clear his head for whatever would come next. He listened to the muffled shouts from the conference area through the door—until, suddenly, they stopped.

An unsettling silence followed. Monroe tensed. Something was wrong. He waited several minutes before stepping cautiously out of the bathroom, he slowly opened the door. His breath caught in his throat as his eyes scanned the scene. Nimbus, Ambrose, Prigmore, Garland, and Steptoe—every one of them—were slumped in their chairs, blood pooling beneath them. The metallic stench of gunfire lingered in the room, but there had been no sound. No shots. Nothing.

"Jesus Christ," Monroe whispered, staggering backward.

Adrenaline surged through his veins. "Malaika! Get down here, now!" he shouted, knowing the FBI team was listening in.

Within seconds, the door burst open as Malaika and her agents stormed in, guns drawn, their expressions shifting from confusion to shock as they took in the massacre. Malaika crouched by Nimbus' lifeless form, her voice barely a whisper. "How the hell did this happen? We didn't hear a thing!"

"No one came in or out that I heard," Monroe muttered, his voice strained with disbelief. "It was pure luck that I was just in the bathroom. It's like a ghost did this."

Her team rushed to check the exits. The doors were all still locked, and the agents stationed outside reported no one had entered or exited the building. Yet, the assassin had struck, leaving no trace.

"Based on the precision and quickness of the hits, I'd guess a Heckler & Koch MP5 with a silencer," Monroe surmised, utilizing his military background. "Someone planned this down to the second."

"Good call," Malaika said before spinning toward her team. "Sweep the service corridors! Check the stairwells and the roof! Someone's still in this building." Her voice carried a mix of urgency and frustration as agents rushed to follow her orders.

As the team scurried in all directions, their flashlights bouncing off the walls and casting long, erratic shadows, Monroe stood frozen in the center of the room. His heart pounded in his chest, but his mind was operating even faster. The pieces of the puzzle were there—right in front of him—but they had refused to fall into place.

Whoever had done this had been efficient. More than that, they knew exactly how to get in and out without leaving a trace. It was no amateur. This was the work of a professional—a master manipulator who could slip through cracks even when no one believed there were any.

He guessed that the assassin was also former military. His eyes darted to the blood-spattered bodies around the table, all silenced in an instant.

Just then, he caught sight of Malaika huddled with a couple of agents, directing them with the intensity of someone determined to take down the entire operation. He moved toward her, his pulse still pounding in his ears.

"Malaika," Monroe called out, grabbing her attention. She turned quickly, her eyes sharp but questioning. "You need to find Hancock, Darnell, and Tammy," Monroe said, his voice low but urgent. "The package I gave you earlier—Yvonne's notes and the recordings—that has more than enough to put all three of them away for a very long time."

Malaika's expression shifted, a flicker of something unreadable crossing her face before she quickly masked it. She sighed as if wrestling with a burden she had kept hidden.

Monroe frowned, sensing something was off. "What is it?" he asked.

Malaika hesitated for a beat, then finally locked eyes with him. "You mean two of them," she said softly.

A perplexed look crept across Monroe's face. "What do you mean, two?"

Malaika glanced around quickly as if ensuring no one else was listening. Then she leaned in closer. "Tammy Treadwell is a criminal informant, Monroe. She's been working with us for months. The FBI struck a deal with her—immunity and placement in the Witness Protection Program in exchange for her testimony against Hancock and Darnell."

Monroe stared at her, dumbfounded. "Tammy? A CI? I thought she was neck-deep in this mess."

Malaika nodded grimly. "She was. But the bureau made a calculated decision—Tammy had access to a lot of inside information on Hancock's operations, not just in St. Louis, but with his overseas deals too. She handed over everything. She knows where the bodies are buried, and in return, she'll testify against Hancock and Darnell in exchange for immunity. Plus, she never forgave Hancock for setting up her father."

Monroe's mind reeled. He had been ready to lump Tammy in with the rest of them, but this? She was flipping on them? "So, Tammy walks away from all of this, and Hancock and Darnell take the fall?"

Malaika's eyes were steely. "That's right. With Tammy's testimony and the evidence Yvonne left behind, we'll have more than enough to put those two away. They're looking at a long time in the federal prison system."

Monroe rubbed his chin, processing this bombshell. It felt like a gut punch. He had seen Tammy as a key player in the conspiracy, not someone who would turn state's evidence. He swallowed the bitterness rising in his throat.

"And all this time, she was playing both sides?" Monroe muttered, shaking his head.

"Look," Malaika said, her voice softening, "I know it's not the resolution you wanted. But it's what's going to bring those two down. Tammy's too smart—she knew when it was time to get out and save her own skin."

Monroe let out a long breath, still reeling from the revelation. "I can't believe I didn't see it," he muttered. "It all makes sense now. The way she maneuvered through everything... So clean... Too clean."

"That's the game, Monroe," Malaika said, her tone heavy with resignation. She gestured toward the blood-soaked corpses that would soon occupy body bags for their trip to the morgue. "Whoever pulled this off just saved the government a small fortune—and five more messy prosecutions."

Monroe let the words settle, his mind still catching up to the fact that Tammy Treadwell, the same woman who had played such a key role in Darnell's rise, was now the person who would dismantle his budding empire.

"Alright," Monroe said finally, his voice low but resolved. "Let's finish this."

Malaika gave him a tight nod before turning back to her agents, barking out more orders as they scrambled to track down the person responsible for the earlier carnage.

Monroe became oblivious to the activity surrounding him. He was lost in thought. But all of a sudden, it hit him like a punch to the gut. "Oswald," Monroe whispered to himself, barely audible over the commotion around him. His hands instinctively clenched into fists, the name sending chills down his spine.

Malaika, who had been barking orders to her team, noticed Monroe's change in demeanor. "Monroe? What is it?" she asked, stepping toward him.

But Monroe wasn't listening. His mind flashed back to the meeting in St. Louis when he first met Oswald Dixon, the nephew—Carlton Dixon's supposed black sheep, the outsider who didn't seem to fit into any of his family's enterprises. But in that brief encounter, Oswald knew too much.

The memories flooded back. Oswald had revealed just enough about the conspiracy to gain Monroe's trust and just enough to make it seem like he was some marginal player with insider knowledge. But there had been a flicker of something else in his demeanor, something Monroe hadn't seen until now—control. In that moment, Monroe realized the truth. Oswald wasn't a bit player or some sidelined family member. He was "The Broker." He had been orchestrating everything from the shadows, and Monroe had been played like a fiddle.

"Oswald Dixon...he's 'The Broker,'" Monroe said aloud, his voice steady but filled with dread. He turned to face Malaika, who was staring at him, eyes widening in disbelief.

"Oswald? Carlton Dixon's nephew?" she echoed, trying to process the information.

"It all makes sense," Monroe muttered, pacing as the pieces began to connect. "He was at the funeral, mingling with the crowd, and he knew way more than anyone on the outside should've known. That was no coincidence, Malaika," Monroe said with certainty.

"Make a call to somebody, anybody who can get you some background on him."

"Are you sure?" Malaika asked, her tone urgent but calm, knowing this was the breakthrough they needed.

Monroe nodded, the grim realization settling in. "He's been playing all sides. He fed me information, just enough to keep me in the dark, while he maneuvered everything behind the scenes. He's been pulling strings from the start. Not to mention tonight. He was tying up loose ends. This whole thing was to get rid of the dead weight, just as "The Investor" had wanted. Ambrose, Garland, Nimbus, and the rest were expendable, which is why Hancock, Darnell, and Tammy were kept away."

Malaika's eyes flickered with recognition. She quickly turned to one of her agents. "Get every available man out there looking for Oswald Dixon. Now! And see what you can find out about him."

The room was a flurry of movement, but Monroe stood still, anger bubbling just beneath the surface. He had once been steps away from Oswald, never realizing the danger he posed. And now, the blood of everyone in that room stained Monroe's hands, too, not that he was concerned about their fate. But Oswald wasn't going to get away—not if he could help it. With clenched jaw, Monroe muttered under his breath, "You slippery son of a bitch. I should've seen it sooner," livid that he hadn't done his due diligence on Oswald.

Just then, one of the FBI agents shouted from across the room, "We've got nothing! No sign of him!" Monroe shot a glance at Malaika, the gravity of the situation sinking in. They had all been played. And now Oswald Dixon—"The Broker"—was out there, disappearing into the night.

***

Down in a service corridor, a heavyset janitor casually pushed a cleaning cart through the dimly lit hallway. His large belly stretched his uniform, and the hat pulled low over his face, shielding his eyes from view. No one gave him a second look. The janitor reached a service exit, nodding at a security guard on his way out. His face was hidden beneath a thick mustache and wig, his belly nothing more than a padded disguise.

Once outside, in the cool night air, he turned into an alley, quickening his pace. Rounding a corner, he shed the janitor's uniform and padding, revealing his slim figure. He pulled off the mustache and wig, stuffing them into a duffel bag as he approached a waiting car. Inside the car, he sat behind the wheel, glanced in the rearview mirror, and gave a gloating look.

It was just before 11 p.m. in New York City, and the streets were quiet for a Sunday evening. By the time anyone figured out what had happened, "The Broker" would be long gone. He started the car and drove away, blending into the still night, leaving behind nothing but the carnage in that crimson-splattered room.

EPILOGUE

Two Continents–Two Cafés–Two Months Later

Café de France, Marrakesh, Morocco

THE DESERT EVENING HAD BEGUN ITS gentle descent upon Marrakesh, soft shadows creeping over the bustling Jemaa el-Fnaa square below. Jean-Marc Baptiste, a French African casino magnate with vast business interests in West Africa and Europe, sat with Oswald Dixon at a table on the rooftop terrace of the Café de France, watching the frenzied scene unfold—a symphony of street performers, vendors, and curious tourists moving to the rhythm of the ancient city. Despite the liveliness below, a comfortable silence hung between the two men.

Jean-Marc Baptiste, with his striking, dark skin and sharp features, exuded a quiet charisma. His full lips barely moved as he spoke, his soft, French-African accent rolling easily with each word. His attire was an impeccable blend of luxury and practicality—an olive-green shirt unbuttoned just enough to reveal a glimpse of gold, tailored pants that draped perfectly over his polished shoes, and a light, tailored jacket that seemed to float over his frame as though it belonged to a man accustomed to wealth and power. His dark, closely cropped hair and well-groomed beard framed his face, adding a certain mystique to his piercing gaze.

Oswald Dixon sat back in his chair, his posture relaxed but alert, as he cradled a glass of deep amber whiskey in one hand. The rich, smoky scent rose from the glass, its color catching the dim light of the café. He took a slow sip, savoring the burn that slid down his throat, the drink grounding him in the present moment. His eyes, dark and sharp, scanned the surroundings with quiet intensity, as though every movement, every shift in the room, was part of the calculation running in his mind. His suit jacket rested lightly across his shoulders, the dark fabric contrasting against the bright white of his shirt, the top button casually undone.

He leaned forward slightly, setting the glass down with a soft clink, his gaze returning to Jean-Marc across the table. His fingers lingered on the glass, tapping lightly against the base, as he considered his next words carefully. The movement was subtle, yet telling—Oswald never rushed, not in conversation, not in action. Everything was measured, every gesture a part of his calculated, calm exterior.

"You really believe we're any different from the people we've been playing against?"

Jean-Marc swirled his mint tea, his eyes half-closed as he took in the scene, but his mind was far from the square. "Different? No. Just better at hiding it and I'd like to think better at it" he murmured, his voice barely audible over the hum of the crowd below.

Jean-Marc had been the money behind Oswald and Hancock's efforts in St. Louis. Baptiste had been looking for a way to break into the US market while expanding his empire in Africa and Europe. He saw Oswald as a sharp and ambitious figure who could not only deliver on his initiatives in North America but also contribute to his other enterprises.

Oswald gave a slight nod, his gaze fixed somewhere in the distance. He wasn't bitter—not exactly. After all, they had nearly pulled it off. If it hadn't been for those women—Tammy, Yvonne, and that FBI agent Malaika—they'd be celebrating in St. Louis right now. He let out a quiet laugh, more at himself than anyone else. "Three women and an ambulance chaser," Oswald said, shaking his head. "Hell of a combination. Back in the day, in the Army, they taught you to watch your back in the field, but I think in this instance, we let our guard down."

Jean-Marc raised an eyebrow. "Feeling outsmarted, are we?"

Oswald shrugged, faintly smiling. "Maybe. Doesn't happen often." His tone was casual, but underneath it was the sharp edge of a man who wasn't used to losing. "I'll give them credit—the women played their parts well. And then there's Monroe Gray. Luck was on his side. He was perfectly set up to take the fall for my uncle's murder, but the police were slow getting to the hotel. As if that weren't enough, after I masterfully finished off Blackwell on the train, those two incompetent thugs of Prigmore—who were supposed to ice Gray after I dealt with Yvonne Montgomery—let him get away. He survived it all, but surviving isn't the same as winning."

Jean-Marc listened, his fingers tracing the rim of his cup. "Well, we're not exactly out in the cold, are we?" he said, gesturing to the bustling city around them. "You've still got enough stashed away in Switzerland and a few other places to live comfortably. And Europe... Africa...they offer new opportunities. So what's the rush to get back to the States?"

Oswald leaned back, looking out at the darkening sky. "True. With Swiss banks and their privacy laws and a few other discreet spots, I'm not hurting for cash. I could live like a king in Europe or Africa for years if I wanted to." But his eyes held something more—a flicker of the unrelenting drive that had fueled him his whole life. "That's not the point, though. I've always excelled. I didn't get through Ranger School and every other challenge I've taken on just to sit back and be content. I'm used to winning, Jean-Marc." He paused, his fingers drumming lightly on the table. "And those women—along with Monroe—might think they've taken us down. But this isn't over."

Jean Luc smiled slightly. "Revenge doesn't come cheap, my friend."

"It never does," Oswald said, his voice low but firm. "Monroe Gray may think he's won the war, but that was just the first battle. He hasn't seen the last of me."

The two men fell silent again, the measured confidence in Oswald's voice hanging in the air like a promise. While the world below them hummed with life, Oswald's gaze remained fixed on a distant horizon, already plotting his next move. Marrakesh was now his laboratory, and Europe and Africa were ripe with opportunities, but success in the US was still the ultimate goal. And Oswald Dixon wasn't one to leave unfinished business behind. Quietly stoking the fires of vengeance, he was determined that his next encounter with Monroe Gray wouldn't be left to chance. Dixon had learned from his mistakes, and when that time came, the stakes would be deadlier than ever.

Manoir LeMoyne Hotel,
Montreal, Quebec, Canada

On a beautiful June morning, with noon rapidly approaching, Monroe Gray relaxed at a small table located on the outdoor terrace of Le Jardin du Palais that looked out onto De Maisonneuve West, a bustling Montreal boulevard. The patio area at the bistro-styled restaurant was adorned with lush greenery, twinkling string lights, and wrought-iron tables. It provided a pleasant dining experience with a touch of European flair. He sat under the shade of a wide umbrella, a half-empty glass of champagne beside him. The French-accented hotel, though understated in appearance, still held the elegance of an era past—its whitewashed walls and iron balconies, whispered of secrets shared over decades, now long gone.

Montreal's skyline rose in the distance to his east, with the forestry leading to the peak of Mount Royal standing before him. Monroe watched the pedestrians passed by, lost in thought as the sun bathed the street in a golden hue.

It had been two months since the events in New York, but the fallout was still unfolding. Hancock and Darnell were in custody and awaiting their trials, their web of corruption laid bare for all to see. Both had been removed from office, with the former congressman's son, along with Arthur Trimble, caught in the sweep. Even Chauncy Prigmore's once-impenetrable organization had crumbled under the weight of its own rot. Tammy was relocated somewhere by the feds as part of her deal.

And then there was Cleo Hancock. The frame job meant to tie her to Dixon's murder had fallen apart under scrutiny, and she'd been vindicated. In a twist of irony, she had been appointed to her father's seat in Congress. *Guess she got the last laugh.* With the dust settling, St. Louis had a new mayor—an outspoken anti-corruption alderman who had reissued the casino bid. The prize had gone to the last player standing: Shantelle Dixon. Now, she was at the helm of the largest development project in the city's history.

As for him and Malaika, well, their paths had diverged. They had shared something—something real, even—but Malaika was married to her job, and Monroe needed to rebuild his life. She did admit to him that she was the one who took down the amoral mayor she was with when she and Monroe first met, a fact that he had come to suspect. They remain friends, though, and who knew? Maybe their paths would cross again in some other city for some other purpose.

Monroe owed a deep debt of gratitude to Nitro, the unsung hero who had proven to be more than just a streetwise ally. He was a lifeline, keeping Monroe one step ahead when the stakes were life or death. This whirlwind of danger had shown Monroe that there was no going back to defending low-level crooks for chump change—clients whose guilt was often as predictable as their lack of funds. The adrenaline, the puzzle-solving, the high-wire tension of survival had awakened something in him, something more than mere curiosity. He had found his purpose, a new path—and Nitro would be at his side for whatever came next.

"Here's your champagne, Sugar." Monroe turned at the sound of the voice, a slow smile spreading across his face. "Thank you, baby," he said, looking up at Shantelle Dixon. She was radiant, wearing a sleeveless, form-fitting black sundress that fell just above her knees, paired with comfortable yet stylish strappy sandals. Her natural makeup and tousled hair gave her an effortlessly sexy, laid-back vibe.

She leaned down, planting a soft kiss on his cheek before standing tall. "I'll be right back," she said, smiling. "Just need to run up to our suite for a moment."

Monroe watched her walk away, his eyes following her until she disappeared into the hotel. He turned back to his view of Mount Royal, raising the glass of champagne to his lips. As he took a sip, he could feel the burdens—the choices, the risks, the disorder that had brought him to this moment. Slowly, he lowered the glass, gaze lingering on the distant peak of Mount Royal as if he were having a conversation with the mountain itself.

I know what you're thinking. I could tell you it's not about the money, and maybe you'd believe me. Or maybe it's just my curiosity—unfinished business if you like. Whatever you decide, that's on you. But from where I sit, some doors are just too tempting to leave unopened. And besides, Eola Gray didn't raise no fools.

Monroe leaned back in his chair, finally allowing himself to relax, As he savored this rare moment of calm, His thoughts drifted to Gordon and their early conversations. One remark stood out, laced with irony in hindsight: the casino deal, Gordon had said, would be their ticket to 'financial paradise.' But in light of all that had transpired, it was painfully clear—there was no room in paradise for either of them.

www.ingramcontent.com/pod-product-compliance
Lightning Source LLC
Chambersburg PA
CBHW070111120726